ALPHA
6

ALPHA
6

Edited by

ROBERT
SILVERBERG

A BERKLEY MEDALLION BOOK
published by
BERKLEY PUBLISHING CORPORATION

Scott Meredith Literary Agency, Inc.
580 Fifth Avenue
New York, New York 10036

SBN 425-03048-2

BERKLEY MEDALLION BOOKS *are published by*
Berkley Publishing Corporation
200 Madison Avenue
New York, N.Y. 10016

BERKLEY MEDALLION BOOK ® TM 757,375

Printed in the United States of America

Berkley Medallion Edition, APRIL, 1976

ACKNOWLEDGMENTS

CONTENTS

INTRODUCTION

More of the same, the mixture as before—so I am tempted to describe this sixth annual *Alpha* collection. Not unfair phrases, either, for, like its five predecessors, *Alpha Six* is a volume of science-fiction stories that have no thematic links, that are held together only by their general literary excellence and stimulating science-fictional content. As before, *Alpha* owes no allegiance to any single literary ''school'' within the faction-ridden science-fiction cosmos: it hews to a solidly middle-of-the-road line, seeking strong narrative drive and avoiding the excesses of the zap-zap ray-gun school on the one hand and the evanescently precious avant-garde on the other. And, as before, *Alpha's* stories represent a four-dimensional slice across the past few decades of science-fiction publishing—four of them more than twenty years old, most of the others dating from the fertile 1960s, two more recent than that.

More of the same, yes, but the reservoir from which these stories come seems all but inexhaustible and is constantly being replenished. Science fiction has become one of the last refuges of real inventiveness for the short story—which, while veering into extinction in the world of mainstream publishing, has since about 1950 become ever more vital, ever more ingenious, when the subject matter is the unique thematic content of science fiction. The literary renaissance within science fiction has now amply been recognized on the campus, where courses in s-f as literature are now routinely offered; and the six volumes of the *Alpha* series to date are, I think, fair representatives of the sort of work that has been done in science fiction; work that is at last being seen as the remarkable achievement it is. *Alpha* will go on offering the mixture as before—and a rich and heady brew it will be.

—Robert Silverberg

THE LOST CONTINENT

Norman Spinard

Norman Spinrad ("Carcinoma Angels," *Alpha Four*) returns to this series with a long, vigorous story of a dismal, ruined United States in which all the nightmares of the 1960s have manifested their ultimate ferocity at once. Spinrad, a Los Angeles-based ex-New Yorker well known for such novels as *Bug Jack Barron* and *The Iron Dream,* is probably science-fiction's most politically oriented writer—by which I mean not that his work consists of clarion calls for reform and reconstruction, but that as an artist his main concern is the *polis,* the commonwealth, the relationships of human beings within the civic framework. "The Lost Continent" is one of his most searching explorations of his chosen theme.

I felt a peculiar mixture of excitement and depression as my Pan African jet from Accra came down through the interlocking fringes of the East Coastal and Central American smog banks above Milford International Airport, made a slightly bumpy landing on the east-west runway, and taxied through the thin blue haze toward a low, tarnished-looking aluminum dome that appeared to be the main international arrivals terminal.

Although American history *is* my field, there was some-

thing about actually being in the United States for the first
time that filled me with sadness, awe, and perhaps a little
dread. Ironically, I believe that what saddened me about
being in America was the same thing that makes that country
so popular with tourists, like the people who filled most of the
seats around me. There is nothing that tourists like better than
truly servile natives, and there are no natives quite so servile
as those living off the ruins of a civilization built by ancestors
they can never hope to surpass.

For my part—perhaps because I am a professor of history
and can appreciate the parallels and ironies—I not only feel
personally diminished at the thought of lording it over the
remnants of a once-great people, it reminds me of our own
civilization's inevitable mortality. Was not Africa a continent
of so-called Underdeveloped Nations not two centuries ago
when Americans were striding to the Moon like gods?

Have we in Africa *really* preserved the technical and
scientific heritage of Space Age America intact, as we like to
pretend? We may claim that we have not repeated the American feat of going to the Moon because it was part of the
overdevelopment that destroyed Space Age civilization, but
few reputable scientists would seriously contend that we
could go to the Moon if we so chose. Even the jet in which I
had crossed the Atlantic was not quite up to the airliners the
Americans had flown two centuries ago.

Of course, the modern Americans are still less capable
than we of re-creating twentieth-century American technology. As our plane reached the terminal, an atmosphere-
sealed extensible ramp reached out creakily from the building
for its airlock. Milford International was the port of entry for
the entire northeastern United States; yet the best it had was
recently obsolescent African equipment. Milford itself, one
of the largest modern American towns, would be lost next to
even a city like Brazzaville. Yes, African science and
technolgy are certainly now the most advanced on the planet,
and some day perhaps we will build a civilization that can
truly claim to be the highest the world has yet seen, but we
only delude ourselves when we imagine that we have such a

civilization now. As of the middle of the twenty-second century, Space Age America still stands as the pinnacle of man's fight to master his environment. Twentieth-century American man had a level of scientific knowledge and technological sophistication that we may not fully attain for another century. What a pity he had so little deep understanding of his relationship to his environment, or of himself.

The ramp linked up with the plane's airlock, and after a minimal amount of confusion we debarked directly into a customs control office, which consisted of a drab dun-colored, medium-sized room divided by a line of twelve booths across its width. The customs officers in the booths were very polite, hardly glanced at our passports, and managed to process nearly a hundred passengers in less than ten minutes. The American government was apparently justly famous for doing all it could to smooth the way for African tourists.

Beyond the customs control office was a small auditorium in which we were speedily seated by courteous uniformed customs agents. A pale, sallow, well-built young lady in a trim blue customs uniform entered the room after us and walked rapidly through the center aisle and up onto the little low stage. She was wearing face-fitting atmosphere goggles, even though the terminal had a full seal.

She began to recite a little speech; I believe its actual wording is written into the American tourist-control laws.

"Good afternoon, ladies and gentlemen, and welcome to the United States of America. We hope you'll enjoy your stay in our country, and we'd like to take just a few moments of your time to give you some reminders that will help make your visit a safe and pleasurable one."

She put her hand to her nose and extracted two small transparent cylinders filled with gray gossamer. "These are government-approved atmosphere-filters," she said, displaying them for us. "You will be given complimentary sets as you leave this room. You are advised to buy only filters with the official United States Government Seal of Approval. Change your filters regularly each morning, and your stay here should in no way impair your health. However, it is understood that all visitors to the United States travel at their own risk. You are advised not to remove your filters except inside buildings or conveyances displaying a green circle containing the words 'Full Atmosphere Seal.' ''

She took off her goggles, revealing a light red mask of welted skin that their seal had made around her eyes. ''These are self-sealing atmospheric goggles,'' she said. ''If you have not yet purchased a pair, you may do so in the main lobby. You are advised to secure goggles before leaving this terminal and to wear them whenever you venture out into the open atmosphere. Purchase only goggles bearing the Government Seal of Approval, and always take care that the seal is airtight.

''If you use your filters and goggles properly, your stay in the United States should be a safe and pleasant one. The government and people of the United States wish you good day, and welcome you to our country.''

We were then handed our filters and guided to the baggage area, where our luggage was already unloaded and waiting for us. A sealed bus from the Milford International Inn was already waiting for those of us who had booked rooms there, and porters loaded the luggage on the bus while a representative from the hotel handed out complimentary atmosphere goggles. The Americans were most efficient and most courteous; there was something almost unpleasant about the way we moved so smoothly from the plane to seats on a bus headed through the almost empty streets of Milford toward the faded white plastic block that was the Milford International Inn, by far the largest building in a town that seemed to be mostly small houses, much like an African residential village. Perhaps what disturbed me was the knowledge that Americans were so good at this sort of thing strictly out of necessity. Thirty percent of the total American Gross National Product comes from the tourist industry.

I keep telling my wife I gotta get out of this tourist business. In the Good Old Days, our ancestors would've given these African brothers nothing but about eight feet of rope. They'd've shot off a nuclear missile and blasted all those black brothers to atoms! If the damn brothers didn't have so much loose money, I'd be for riding every one of them back to Africa on a rail, just like the Space Agers did with their black brothers before the Panic.

And I bet we could do it, too. I hear there's all kind of Space Age weapons sitting around in the ruins out west. If we could only get ourselves together and dig them out, we'd show those Africans whose ancestors went to the Moon while they were still eating each other.

But, instead, I found myself waiting with my copter bright and early at the International Inn for the next load of customers of Little Old New York Tours, as usual. And I've got to admit that I'm doing pretty well off of it. Ten years ago, I just barely had the dollars to make a down payment on a used ten-place helicopter, and now the thing is all paid off, and I'm shoveling dollars into my stash on every day tour. If the copter holds up another ten years—and this is a genuine Space Age American Air Force helicopter restored and converted to energy cells in Aspen, not a cheap piece of African junk—I'll be able to take my bundle and split to South America, just like a tycoon out of the Good Old Days. They say they've got places in South America where there's nothing but wild country as far as you can see. Imagine that! And you can buy this land. You can buy jungle filled with animals and birds. You can buy rivers full of fish. You can buy air that doesn't choke your lungs and give you cancer and taste like fried turds even through a brand-new set of filters.

Yeah, that's why I suck up to Africans! That's worth spending four or five hours a day in that New York hole, even worth looking at Subway Dwellers. Every full day tour I take in there is maybe $20,000 net toward South America. You can buy ten acres of prime Amazon swampland for only $56 million. I'll still be young ten years from now. I'll only be forty. I take good care of myself, I change my filters every day just like they tell you to, and I don't use nothing but Key West Supremes, no matter how much the damn things cost. I'll have at least ten good years left, why I could even live to be fifty-five! And I'm gonna spend at least ten of those fifty-five years someplace where I can walk around without filters shoved up my nose, where I don't need goggles to keep my eyes from rotting, where I can finally die from something better than lung cancer.

I picture South America every time I feel the urge to tell off those brothers and get out of this business. For ten years with Karen in that Amazon swampland, I can take their superior civilization crap and eat it and smile back at 'em afterward.

With filters wadded up my nose and goggle seals bruising the tender skin under my eyes, I found myself walking through the blue haze of the open American atmosphere, away from the second-class twenty-second-century comforts of the International Inn, and toward the large and apparently ancient tour helicopter. As I walked along with the other tourists, I wondered just what it was that had drawn me here.

Of course Space Age America is my specialty, and I had reached the point where my academic career virtually required a visit to America, but aside from that, I felt a personal motivation that I could not quite grasp. No doubt I know more about Space Age America than all but a handful of modern Americans, but the reality of Space Age civilization seems elusive to me. I am an enlightened modern African, five generations removed from the bush; yet I have seen films—the obscure ghost-town of Las Vegas sitting in the middle of a terrible desert clogged with vast mechanized temples to the God of Chance, Mount Rushmore where the Americans carved an entire landscape into the likenesses of their national heroes, the Cape Kennedy National Shrine where rockets of incredible size are preserved almost intact— which have made me feel like an ignorant primitive trying to understand the minds of gods. One cannot contemplate the Space Age without concluding that the Space Agers possessed a kind of sophistication which we modern men have lost. Yet they destroyed themselves.

Yes, perhaps the resolution of this paradox was what I hoped to find here, aside from academic merit. Certainly, true understanding of the Space Age mind cannot be gained from study of artifacts and records—if it could, I would have it. A true scholar, it has always seemed to me, must seek to understand, not merely to accumulate knowledge. No doubt it was understanding that I sought here. . . .

Up close, the Little Old New York Tours helicopter was truly impressive—an antique ten-seater built during the Space Age for the military by the look of it, and lovingly restored. But the American atmosphere had still been breathable even in the cities when it was built, so I was certain that this copter's filter system would be of questionable quality, no doubt installed by the contemporary natives, in modern times. I did not want anything as flimsy as that between my eyes and lungs and the American atmosphere, so I ignored the ''Full Atmosphere Seal'' sign and kept my filters in and my goggles on as I boarded. I noticed that the other tourists were doing the same.

Mike Ryan, the native guide and pilot, had been recommended to me by a colleague from the University of Nairobi. A professor's funds are quite limited of course—especially one who has not attained significant academic stature as yet—and the air fares ate into my already meager budget to the point where all I could afford was three days in Milford, four in Aspen, three in Needles, five in Eureka, and a final three at Cape Kennedy on the way home. Aside from the Cape Kennedy National Shrine, none of these modern American towns actually contained Space Age ruins of significance. Since it is virtually impossible and at any rate prohibitively dangerous to visit major Space Age ruins without a helicopter and a native guide, and since a private copter and guide would be far beyond my means, my only alternative was to take a day tour like everyone else.

My Kenyan friend had told me that Ryan was the best guide to Old New York that he had in his three visits. Unlike

most of the other guides, he actually took his tours into a
Subway station to see live Subway Dwellers; there are repor-
tedly only a thousand or two Subway Dwellers left, they are
nearing extinction. It seemed like an opportunity I should not
miss. At any rate, Ryan's charge was only about $500 above
the average guide's.

Ryan stood outside the helicopter in goggles helping us
aboard. His appearance gave me something of a surprise. My
Kenyan informant had told me that Ryan had been in the tour
business for ten years; most guides who had been around that
long were in terrible shape. No filters could entirely protect a
man from that kind of prolonged exposure to saturation
smog; by the time they're thirty, most guides already have
chronic emphysema, and their lung-cancer rate at age thirty-
five is over fifty percent. But Ryan, who could not be under
thirty, had the general appearance of a forty-year old Boer;
physiologically, he should have looked a good deal older.
Instead he was short, squat, had only slightly-graying black
hair, and looked quite alert, even powerful. But of course he
had the typical American grayish-white pimply pallor.

There were eight other people taking the tour, a full copter.
A prosperous-looking Kenyan who quickly introduced himself as Roger Koyinka, traveling with his wife; a rather
strange-looking Ghanaian in very rich-looking old-fashioned
robes and his similarly clad wife and young son; two rather
willowy and modishly dressed young men who appeared to
be Luthuliville dandies; and the only other person in the tour
who was traveling alone, an intense young man whose great
bush of hair, stylized dashiki, and gold earring proclaimed
that he was an Amero-African.

I drew a seat next to the Amero-African, who identified
himself as Michael Lumumba rather diffidently when I
introduced myself. Ryan gave us a few moments to get
acquainted—I learned that the Ghanaian was named
Kulongo, that Koyinka was a department store executive
from Nairobi—that the two young men were named Ojubu
and Ruala—while he checked out the helicopter, and then
seated himself in the pilot's seat, back toward us, goggles still

in place, and addressed us without looking back through an internal public address system.

"Hello ladies and gentlemen, and welcome to your Little Old New York Tour. I'm Mike Ryan, your guide to the wonders of Old New York, Space Age America's greatest city. Today you're going to see such sights as the Fuller Dome, the Empire State Building, Rockefeller Plaza, and even, as a grand finale, a Subway station still inhabited by the direct descendants of the Space Age inhabitants of the city. So don't just think of this as a guided tour, ladies and gentlemen, you are about to take part in the experience of a lifetime—an exploration of the ruins of the greatest city built by the greatest civilization ever to stand on the face of the earth."

"Stupid arrogant honkie!" the young man beside me snarled aloud. There was a terrible moment of shocked, shamed embarrassment in the cabin, as all of us squirmed in our seats. Of course the Amero-Africans are famous for this sort of tastelessness, but to be actually confronted with this sort of blatant racism made one for a moment ashamed to be black.

Ryan swiveled very slowly in his seat. His face displayed the characteristic red flush of the angered Caucasian, but his voice was strangely cold, almost polite: "You're in the *United States* now, *Mr.* Lumumba, not in Africa. I'd watch what I said if I were you. If you don't like me or my country, you can have your lousy money back. There's a plane leaving for Conakry in the morning."

"You're not getting off that easy, honkie," Lumumba said. "I paid my money, and you're not getting me off this helicopter. You try, and I go straight to the tourist board, and there goes your license."

Ryan stared at Lumumba for a long moment. Then the flush began to fade from his face, and he turned his back on us again, muttering "Suit yourself, pal. I promise you an interesting ride."

A muscle twitched in Lumumba's temple; he seemed about to speak again. "Look here, Mr. Lumumba," I whispered at him sharply, "we're guests in this country and you're making us look like boorish louts in front of the natives. If you have no respect for your own dignity, have some respect for ours."

"You stick to your pleasures, and I'll stick to mine," he told me, speaking more calmly, but obviously savoring his own bitterness. "I'm here for the pleasure of seeing the descendants of the stinking honkies who kicked my ancestors out to grovel in the putrid mess they made for themselves. And I intend to get my money's worth."

I started to reply, but then restrained myself. I would have to remain on civil terms with this horrid young man for hours. I don't think I'll ever understand these Amero-Africans and their pointless blood-feud. I doubt if I want to.

I started the engines, lifted her off the pad, and headed east into the smog bank trying hard not to think of that black brother Lumumba. No wonder so many of his ancestors were lynched by the Space Agers! Sometime during the next few hours, that crut was going to get his. . . .

Through my cabin monitor (this Air Force Iron was just loaded with real Space Age stuff), I watched the stupid looks on their flat faces as we headed for what looked like a solid wall of smoke at about 100 miles per hour. From the fringes, a major smog bank looks like that—solid as a steel slab—but once you're inside there's nothing but a blue haze that anyone with a halfway-decent set of goggles can see right through.

"We are now entering the East Coastal smog bank, ladies and gentlemen," I told them. "This smog bank extends roughly from Bangor, Maine in the north to Jacksonville, Florida in the south, and from the Atlantic coastline in the east to the slopes of the Alleghenies in the west. It is the third largest smog bank in the United States."

Getting used to the way things look inside the smog always holds 'em for a while. Inside a smog bank, the color of everything is kind of washed-out, grayed and blued. The air is something you can see, a mist that doesn't move; it almost sparkles at you. For some reason, these Africans always seem to be knocked out by it. Imagine thinking stuff like that is beautiful, crap that would kill you horribly and slowly in a couple of days if you were stupid or unlucky enough to breathe it without filters.

Yeah, they sure were a bunch of brothers! Some executive from Nairobi who acted like just being in the same copter with an American might give him lung cancer and his wife. Two rich young fruits from Luthuliville who seemed to be traveling together so they could congratulate themselves on how smart they both were for picking such rich parents. Some professor named Balewa who had never been to the States before but probably was sure he knew what it was all about. A backwood jungle-bunny named Kulongo who had struck it rich off uranium or something taking his wife and kid on the grand tour. And of course, that creep Lumumba. The usual load of African tourists. Man, in the Good Old Days, these niggers wouldn't have been good enough to shine our shoes!

Now we were flying over the old State of New Jersey. The Space Agers did things in New Jersey that not even the African professors have figured out. It was weird country we were crossing: endless patterns of box-houses, all of them the same, all bleached blue-gray by two centuries of smog; big old freeways jammed with the wreckage of cars from the Panic of the Century; a few twisted gray trees and a patch of dry grass here and there that somehow managed to survive in the smog.

And this was western Jersey; this was nothing. Further east, it was like an alien planet or something. The view from the Jersey Turnpike was a sure tourist-pleaser. It really told them just where they were. It let them know that the Space Agers could do things they couldn't hope to do. Or want to.

Yeah, the Jersey Lowlands are spectacular all right, but why in hell did our ancestors want to do a thing like that? It really makes you think. You look at the Jersey Lowlands and you know that the Space Agers could do about anything they wanted to. . . .

But why in hell did they want to do some of the things they did?

There was something about actually standing in the open American atmosphere that seemed to act directly on the consciousness, like kif. Perhaps it was the visual effect. Ryan had landed the helicopter on a shattered arch of six-lane freeway that soared like the frozen contrail of an ascending jet over a surreal metallic jungle of amorphous Space Age rubble on a giant's scale—all crumbling rusted storage tanks, ruined factories, fantastic mazes of decayed valving and piping—filling the world from horizon to horizon. As we stepped out onto the cracked and pitted concrete, the spectrum of reality changed, as if we were suddenly on the surface of a planet circling a bluer and grayer sun. The entire grotesque panorama appeared as if through a blue-gray filter. But we were inside the filter; the filter was the open American smog and it shone in drab sparkles all around us. Strangest of all, the air seemed to remain completely transparent while possessing tangible visible substance. Yes, the visual effects of the American atmosphere alone are enough to affect you like some hallucinogenic drug: distorting your consciousness by warping your visual perception of your environment.

Of course the exact biochemical effects of breathing saturation smog through filters are still unknown. We know that the American atmosphere is loaded with hydrocarbons and nitrous oxides that would kill a man in a matter of days if he breathed them directly. We know that the atmosphere filters developed toward the end by the Space Agers enable a man to breathe the American atmosphere for up to three months without permanent damage to his health and enable the modern Americans—who have to breathe variations of this filtered poison every moment of their lives—to often live to be fifty. We know how to duplicate the Space Age atmosphere filters, and we more or less know how their complex catalytic fibers work, but the reactions that the filters must put the

American atmosphere through to make it breathable are so complex that the only thing we can say for sure of what comes out the other side is that it usually takes about four decades to kill you.

Perhaps that strange feeling that came over me was a combination of both effects. But for whatever reasons, I saw that weird landscape as if in a dream or a state of intoxication: everything faded and misty and somehow unreal, vaguely supernatural.

Beside me, staring silently and with a strange dignity at the totally artificial vista of monstrous rusted ruins, stood the Ghanaian, Kulongo. When he finally spoke, his wife and son seemed to hang on his words, as if he were one of the old chiefs dispensing tribal wisdom.

"I have never seen such a place as this," Kulongo said. "In this place, there once lived a race of demons or witch-doctors or gods. There are those who would call me an ignorant savage for saying this thing, but only a fool doubts what he sees with his eyes or his heart. The men who made these things were not human beings like us. Their souls were not as our souls."

Although he was putting it in naïve and primitive terms, there was the weight of essential truth in Kulongo's words. The broken arch of freeway on which we stood reared like the head of a snake whose body was a six-lane road clogged with the rusted corpses of what had been a region-wide traffic jam during the Panic of the Century. The freeway led south, off into the fuzzy horizon of the smog bank, through a ruined landscape in which nothing could be seen that was not the decayed work of man; that was not metal or concrete or asphalt or plastic or Space Age synthetic. It was like being perched above some vast ruined machine the size of a city, a city never meant for man. The scale of the machinery and the way it encompassed the visual universe made it very clear to me that the reality of America was something that no one could put into a book or a film.

I was in America with a vengeance. I was overwhelmed by the totality with which the Space Agers had transformed their

environment, and by the essential incomprehensibility—
despite our sophisticated sociological and psychohistorical
explanations—of why they had done such a thing and of how
they themselves had seen it. "Their souls were not as our
souls" was as good a way to put it as any.

"Well, it's certainly spectacular enough," Ruala said to
his friend, the rapt look on his face making a mockery of his
sarcastic tone.

"So it is," Ojubu said softly. Then, more harshly: "It's
probably the largest junk-heap in the world."

The two of them made a halfhearted attempt at laughter,
which withered almost immediately under the contemptuous
look that the Kulongos gave them; the timeless look that the
people of the bush have given the people of the towns for
centuries, the look that said only cowardly fools attempt to
hide their fears behind a false curtain of contempt, that only
those who fear magic need openly to mock it.

And again, in their naïve way, the Kulongos were right.
Ojubu and Ruala were just a shade too shrill, and even while
they played at diffidence their eyes remained fixed on that
totally surreal metal landscape. One would have to be a lot
worse than a mere fool not to feel the essential strangeness of
that place.

Even Lumumba, standing a few yards from the rest of us,
could not tear his eyes away.

Just behind us, Ryan stood leaning against the helicopter.
There was a strange power, perhaps a sarcasm as well, in his
words as he delivered what surely must have been his routine
guide's speech about this place.

"Ladies and gentlemen, we are now standing on the New
Jersey Turnpike, one of the great freeways that linked the
mighty cities of Space Age America. Below you are the
Jersey Lowlands, which served as a great manufacturing,
storage, power-producing and petroleum refining and dis-
tribution center for the greatest and largest of the Space Age
cities, Old New York. As you look across these incredible
ruins larger than most modern African cities—think of this:
all of this was nothing to the Space Age Americans but a

minor industrial area to be driven through at a hundred miles an hour without even noticing. You're not looking at one of the famous wonders of Old New York, but merely at an unimportant fringe of the greatest city ever built by man. Ladies and gentlemen, you're looking at a very minor work of Space Age man!''

''Crazy damn honkies . . .'' Lumumba muttered. But there was little vehemence or real meaning in his voice, and like the rest of us, he could not tear his eyes away. It was not hard to understand what was going through his mind. Here was a man raised in the Amero-African enclaves on an irrational mixture of hate for the fallen Space Agers, contempt for their vanished culture, fear of their former power, and perhaps a kind of twisted blend of envy and identification that only an Amero-African could fully understand. He had come to revel in the sight of the ruins of the civilization that had banished his ancestors, and now he was confronted with the inescapable reality that the ''honkies'' whose memory he both hated and feared had indeed possessed power and knowledge not only beyond his comprehension, but applied to ends which his mind was not equipped to understand.

It must have been a humbling moment for Michael Lumumba. He had come to sneer and had been forced to gape.

I tore my gaze away from that awesome vista to look at Ryan; there was a grim smile on his pale unhealthy face as he drank in our reactions. Clearly, he had meant this sight to humble us, and just as clearly, it had.

Ryan stared back at me through his goggles as he noticed me watching him. I couldn't read the expression in his watery eyes through the distortion of the goggle lenses. All I understood was that somehow some subtle change had occurred in the pattern of the group's interrelationships. No longer was Ryan merely a native guide, a functionary, a man without dignity. He had proven that he could show us sights beyond the limits of the modern world. He had reminded us of just where we were, and who and what his ancestors had been. He had suddenly gained secondhand stature from the incredible

ruins around him, because, in a very real way, they were *his*
ruins. Certainly they were not ours.

"I've got to admit they were great engineers," Koyinka,
the Kenyan executive, said.

"So were the ancient Egyptians," Lumumba said, recov-
ering some of his bitterness. "And what did it get *them?* A
fancy collection of old junk over their graves—exactly what
it got these honkies."

"If you keep it up, pal," Ryan said coldly, "you may get a
chance to see something that'll impress you a bit more than
these ruins."

"Is that a threat or a promise, Ryan?"

"Depends on whether you're a man . . . or a *boy,* Mr.
Lumumba."

Lumumba had nothing to say to that, whatever it all had
meant. Ryan appeared to have won a round in some contest
between them.

And when we followed Ryan back into the helicopter, I
think we were all aware that for the next few hours, this pale,
unhealthy American would be something more than a mere
convenient functionary. We were the tourists; he was the
guide.

But as we looked over our shoulders at the vast and
overwhelming heritage that had been created and then squan-
dered by his ancestors, the relationship that those words
described took on a new meaning. The ancestral ruins off
which he lived were a greater thing in some absolute sense
than the totality of our entire living civilization. He had
convinced us of that, and he knew it.

That view across the Jersey Lowlands always seems to shut
them up for a while. Even that crut Lumumba. God knows
why. Sure it's spectacular, bigger than anything these Africans could ever have seen where they come from, but when
you come right down to it, you gotta admit that Ojubu was
right—the Jersey Lowlands are nothing but a giant pile of
junk. Crap. Space Age garbage. Sometimes looking at a
place like that can piss me off. I mean, we had *some* ances-

tors, they built the greatest civilization the world ever saw, but what did they leave for us? The most spectacular junk-piles in the world, air that does you in sooner or later even through filters, and a continent where seeing something alive that people didn't put there is a big deal. Our ancestors went to the Moon, they were a great people, the greatest in history, but sometimes I get the feeling they were maybe just a little out of their minds. Like that crazy "Merge With the Cosmic All" thing I found that time in Grand Central—still working after two centuries or so; it must do *something* besides kill people, but *what?* I dunno, maybe our ancestors went a little over the edge, sometimes. . . .

Not that I'd ever admit a thing like that to any black brothers! The Space Agers may have been a little bit nuts, but who are these Africans to say so, who are they to decide whether a civilization that had them beat up and down the line was sane or not? Sane according to who? Them, or the Space Agers? For that matter, who am I to think a thing like that? An ant or a rat living off their garbage. Who are nobodies like us and the Africans to judge people who could go to the Moon?

Like I keep telling Karen, this damn tourist business is getting to me. I'm around these Africans too much. Some-times, if I don't watch myself, I catch myself thinking like them. Maybe it's the lousy smog this far into the smog bank—but hell, that's another crazy African idea!

That's what being around these Africans does to me, and looking at Subway Dwellers five times a week sure doesn't help either. Let's face it, stuff like the Subways and the Lowlands is really depressing. It tells a man he's a nothing. Worse, it tells him that people who were better than he is still managed to screw things up. It's just not good for your mind.

But as the copter crested the lip of the Palisades ridge and we looked out across that wide Hudson River at Manhattan, I was reminded again that this crummy job had its compensa-tions. If you haven't seen Manhattan from a copter crossing the Hudson from the Jersey side, you haven't seen nothing, pal. That Fuller Dome socks you right in the eye. It's ten

miles in diameter. It has facets that make it glitter like a giant
blue diamond floating over the middle of the island. Yeah,
that's right, it floats. It's made of some Space Age plastic
that's been turned blue and hazy by a couple centuries of
smog, it's ten miles wide at the base, and the goddamn thing
floats over the middle of Manhattan a few hundred feet off the
ground at its rim like a cloud or a hover or something. No
motors, no nothing. It's just a hemisphere made of plastic
panels and alloy tubing and it floats over the middle of
Manhattan like half a giant diamond all by itself. Now *that's*
what I call a *real* piece of Space Age hardware!

I could hear them suck in their breaths behind me. Yeah, it
really does it to you. I almost forgot to give them the spiel, I
mean who wants to, what can you really say to someone
while he's looking at the Fuller Dome for the first time?

"Ladies and gentlemen, you are now looking at the world-
famous Fuller Dome, the largest architectural structure ever
built by the human race. It is ten miles in diameter. It
enclosed the center of Manhattan Island, the heart of Old
New York. It has no motors, no power source, and no moving
parts. But it floats in the air like a cloud. It is considered the
First Wonder of the World."

What else is there to say?

We came in low across the river toward that incredible
floating blue diamond, the Fuller Dome, parallel to the ruins
of a great suspension bridge which had collapsed, and now
hung in fantastic rusted tatters half in and half out of the
water. Aside from Ryan's short guidebook speech, no one
said a word as we crossed the waters to Manhattan.

Like the Moon Landing, the Fuller Dome was one of the
peak achievements of the Space Age, a feat beyond the power
of modern African civilization. As I understand it, the Dome
held itself aloft by convection currents created by its own
greenhouse effect, though this has always seemed to me the
logical equivalent of a man lifting himself by his own shoulders. No one quite knows exactly how a dome this size was
built, but the records show that it required a fleet of two

hundred helicopters. It took six weeks to complete. It was named after Buckminster Fuller, one of the architectural geniuses of the early Space Age, but it was not built till after his death, though it is considered his monument. But it was more than that; it was staggeringly, overwhelmingly beautiful.

We crossed the river and headed toward the rim of the Fuller Dome at about two hundred feet, over a shoreline of crumbling docks and the half-sunken hulks of rusted-out ships; then over a wide strip of elevated highway filled with the usual wrecked cars; and finally we slipped under the rim of the Dome itself, an incredibly thin metal hoop floating in the air, from which the Dome seemed to blossom like a soap bubble from a child's bubble-pipe.

And we were flying inside the Fuller Dome. It was an incredible sensation—the world inside the Dome existed in blue crystal. Our helicopter seemed like a buzzing fly that had intruded into an enormous room. The room was a mile high and ten miles wide. The facets of the Fuller Dome had been designed to admit natural sunlight and thus preserve the sense of being outdoors, but they had been weathered to a bluish hue by the saturation smog. As a result, the interior of the Dome was a room on a superhuman scale, a room filled with a pale blue light—and a room containing a major portion of a giant city.

Towering before us were the famous skyscrapers of Old New York, a forest of rectangular monoliths hundreds of feet high; in some cases well over a thousand feet tall. Some of them stood almost intact, empty concrete boxes transformed into giant somber tombstones by the eerie blue light that permeated everything. Others had been ripped apart by explosions and were jagged piles of girders and concrete. Some had had walls almost entirely of glass; most of these were now airy mazes of framework and concrete platforms, where the blue light here and there flashed off intact patches of glass. And far above the tops of the tallest buildings was the blue stained-glass faceted sky of the Fuller Dome.

Ryan took the helicopter up to the five hundred foot level and headed for the giant necropolis, a city of monuments built on a scale that would have caused the Pharaohs to whimper, packed casually together like family houses in an African residential village. And all of it bathed in a sparkly blue-gray light which seemed to enclose a universe—here in the very core of the East Coastal smog bank, everything seemed to twinkle and shimmer.

We all gasped as Ryan headed at 100 mph for a thin canyon that was the gap between two rows of buildings which faced each other across a not-very-wide street hundreds of feet below.

For a moment, we seemed to be a stone dropping toward a narrow shaft between two immense cliffs—then suddenly, the copter's engines screamed, and the copter seemed to somehow skid and slide through the air to a dead hover no more than a hundred feet from the sheer face of a huge gray skyscraper.

Ryan's laugh sounded unreal, partially drowned out by the descending whine of the copter's relaxing engines. "Don't worry folks," he said over the public address system, "I'm in control of this aircraft at all times. I just thought I'd give you a little thrill. Kind of wake up those of you who might be sleeping. Because you wouldn't want to miss what comes next: a helicopter tour of what the Space Agers called 'The Sidewalks of New York.' "

And we inched forward at the pace of a running man; we seemed to drift into a canyon between two parallel lines of huge buildings that went on for miles.

Man, no matter how many times I come here, I still feel weird inside the Fuller Dome. It's another world in there. New York seems like it's built for people fifty feet tall, it makes you feel so small, like you're inside a giant's room, but when you look up at the inside of the Dome, the buildings that seemed so big seem so small; you can't get a grasp on the scale of anything. And everything is all blue. And the smog is so heavy you think you could eat it with a fork.

And you know that the whole thing is completely dead. Nothing lives in New York between the Fuller Dome and the Subways where a couple thousand Subway Dwellers stew in their own muck. Nothing can. The air inside the Fuller Dome is some of the worst in the country, almost as bad as that stuff they say you can barely see through that fills the Los Angeles basin. The Space Agers didn't put up the Dome to atmosphere-seal a piece of the city; they did it to make the city warmer and keep the snow off the ground. The smog was still breathable then. So the inside of the Dome is open to the naked atmosphere, and it actually seems to suck in the worst of the smog, maybe because it's about twenty degrees hotter inside the Dome than it is outside, something about convection currents the Africans say. I dunno.

It's creepy, that's what it is. Flying slowly between two lines of skyscrapers, I had the feeling I was tiptoeing very carefully around some giant graveyard in the middle of the night. Not any of that crap about ghosts that I'll bet some of these Africans still believe deep down; this whole city really *was* a graveyard. During the Space Age, millions of people lived in New York; now there was nothing alive here but a couple thousand stinking subhuman Subway Dwellers slowly strangling themselves in their stinking sealed Subways.

So I kind of drifted the copter in among the skyscrapers for a while, at about a hundred feet, real slow, almost on hover, and just let the customers suck in the feel of the place, keeping my mouth shut.

After a while, we came to a really wide street, jammed to overflowing with wrecked and rusted cars that even filled the sidewalks, as if the Space Agers had built one of their crazy car-pyramids right here in the middle of Manhattan, and it had just sort of run like hot wax. I hovered the copter over it for a while.

"Folks," I told the customers, "below you you see some of the wreckage from the Panic of the Century which fills the Sidewalks of New York. The Panic of the Century started right here in New York. Imagine, ladies and gentlemen, at the height of the Space Age, there were more than one hundred million cars, trucks, buses, and other motor vehicles operating on the freeways and streets of the United States. A car for every two adults! Look below you and try to imagine

the magnificence of the sight of all of them on the road at
once!''

Yeah, that would've been something to see all right! From
a helicopter, that is. Man, those Space Agers sure had guts,
driving around down there jammed together on the freeways
at copter speeds with only a few feet between them. They
must've had fantastic reflexes to be able to handle it. Not for
me, pal—I couldn't do it, and I wouldn't want to.

But God, what this place must've been like, all lit up at
night in bright colored lights, millions of people tearing
around in their cars all at once! Hell, what's the population of
the United States today, thirty, forty million, not a city with
500,000 people, and nothing in all the world on the scale of
this. Damn it, those were the days for a man to have lived!

Now look at it! The power all gone except for whatever
keeps the Subway electricity going, so the only light above
ground is that blue stuff that makes everything seem so still
and quiet and weird, like the city's embalmed or something.
The buildings are all empty crumbling wrecks, burnt out,
smashed up by explosions, and the cars are all rusted garbage, and the people are dead, dead, dead.

It's enough to make you cry, if you let it get to you.

We drifted among the ruins of Old New York like some
secretive night insect. By now it was afternoon, and the
canyons formed by the skyscrapers were filled with deep
purple shadows and intermittent avenues of pale blue light.
The world under the Fuller Dome was composed of relative
darknesses of blue, much as the world under the canopy of a
heavy rain forest is a world of varying greens.

We dipped low and drifted for a few moments over a large
square where the top of a low building had been removed by
an explosion to reveal a series of huge cuts and caverns
extending deep into the bowels of the earth, perhaps some
kind of underground railway terminal, perhaps even a ruined
part of the famous New York Subways.

"This is a burial ground of magics," Kulongo said. "The
air is very heavy here."

"They sure knew how to build," Koyinka said.

Beside me, Michael Lumumba seemed subdued, perhaps even nervous. "You know, I never knew it was all so big," he muttered to me. "So big, and so strange, and so . . . so . . ."

"*Space Age,* Mr. Lumumba?" Rayn suggested over the intercom.

Lumumba's jaw twitched. He was obviously furious at having Ryan supply the precise words he was looking for. "Inhuman, honkie, inhuman, was what I was going to say," he lied transparently. "Wasn't there an ancient saying, 'New York is a nice place to visit, but I wouldn't want to live there.' "

"Never heard that one, pal," Ryan said. "But I can see how your ancestors might've felt that way. New York was always too much for anyone but a *real* Space Ager."

There was considerable truth in what they both said, though of course neither was interested in true insight. Here in the blue crystal world under the Fuller Dome, in a helicopter buzzing about noisily in the graveyard silence, reduced by the scale of the buildings to the relative size of an insect, I felt the immensity of what had been Space Age America all around me. I felt as if I were trespassing in the mansions of my betters. I felt like a bug, an insect. I remembered from history, not from instinct, how totally America had dominated the world during the Space Age—not by armed conquest, but by the sheer overwhelming weight of its very existence. I had never before been quite able to grasp that concept.

I understood it perfectly now.

I gave them the standard helicopter tour of the Sidewalks of New York. We floated up Broadway, the street that had been called The Great White Way, at about fifty feet, past crazy rotten networks of light steel girders, crumbled signs and wiring on a monster scale. At a thousand feet, we circled the Empire State Building, one of the oldest of the great skyscrapers, and now one of the best preserved, a thousand-foot slab of solid concrete, probably just the kind of tomb-stone the Space Agers would've put up for themselves if they had thought about it.

Yeah, I gave them all the usual stuff. The ruins of Rockefeller Center. The UN Plaza Crater.

Of course, they were all sucking it up, even Lumumba, though of course the slime wouldn't admit it. After this, they'd be ripe for a nasty peek at the Subway Dwellers, and after they got through gaping at the animals, they'd be ready for dinner back in Milford, feeling they had got their money's worth.

Yeah, I can get the same money for a five-hour tour that most guides get for six because I've got the stomach to take them into a Subway station. As usual, it had just the right effect when I told them we were going to end the tour with a visit on foot to an inhabited Subway station. Instead of bitching and moaning that the tour was too short, that they weren't getting their money's worth, they were all eager and maybe a little scared at actually walking among the *really* primitive natives. Once they'd had their fill of the Subway Dwellers, a ride home across the Hudson into the sunset would be enough to convince them they'd had a great day.

So we *were* going to see the Subway Dwellers! Most of the native guides avoided the Subways and the American government for some reason seemed to discourage research by foreigners. A suble discouragement, perhaps, but discouragment nevertheless. In a paper he published a few years ago, Omgazi had theorized that the modern Americans in the vicinity of New York had a loathing of the Subway Dwellers that amounted to virtually a superstitious dread. According to him, the Subway Dwellers, because they were direct descendants of diehard Space Agers who had atmosphere-sealed the Subways and set up a closed ecology inside rather than abandon New York, were identified with their ancestors in the minds of the modern Americans. Hence, the modern Americans shunned the Subway Dwellers because they considered them shamans on a deep subconscious level.

It had always seemed to me that Omgazi was being rather ethnocentric. He was dealing, after all, with modern Americans, not nineteenth-century Africans. Now I would have a chance to observe some Subway Dwellers myself. The prospect was most exciting. For although the Subway Dwellers were apparently degenerating towards extinction at a rapid rate, in one respect they were unique in all the world: they still lived in an artifical environment that had been constructed during the Space Age. True, it had been a hurried, makeshift environment in the first place, and it and its inhabitants had deteriorated tremendously in two centuries, but whatever else they were or weren't, the Subway Dwellers were the only enclave of Space Age Americans left on the face of the earth.

If it were possible at all for a modern African truly to come to understand the reality of Space Age America, surely confrontation with the lineal descendants of the Space Age would provide the key.

Ryan set the helicopter down in what seemed to be some kind of large open terrace behind a massive, low, concrete building. The terrace was a patchwork of cracked concrete walkways and expanses of bare gray earth. Once, apparently, it had been a small park, before the smog had become lethal to vegetation. As a denuded ruin in the pale blue light, it seemed like some strange cold corpse as the helicopter kicked up dry clouds of dust from the surface of the dead parkland.

As I stepped out with the others into the blue world of the Fuller Dome, I gasped: I had a momentary impression that I had stepped back to Africa, to Accra or Brazzaville. The air was rich and warm and humid on my skin. An instant later, the visual effect—everything a cool pale blue—jarred me with its arctic-vista contrast. Then I noticed the air itself and I shuddered, and was suddenly hyperconscious of the filters up my nostrils and the goggles over my eyes, for here the air was so heavy with smog that it seemed to sparkle electrically in the crazy blue light. What incredible, beautiful, foul poison!

Except for Ryan, all of us were clearly overcome, each in his own way. Kulongo blinked and stared solemnly for a moment like a great bear; his wife and son seemed to lean into the security of his calm aura. Koyinka seemed to fear that he might strangle; his wife twittered about excitedly, tugging at his hand. The two young men from Luthuliville seemed to be self-consciously making an effort to avoid clutching at each other. Michael Lumumba mumbled something unintelligible under his breath.

"What was that you said, *Mr.* Lumumba?" Ryan said a shade gratingly as he led us out of the park down a crumbling set of stone-and-concrete stairs. Something seemed to snap inside Lumumba; he broke stride for a moment, frozen by some inner event while Ryan led the rest of us onto a walkway between a line of huge silent buildings and a street choked with the rusted wreckage of ancient cars, timelessly locked in their death-agony in the sparkly blue light.

"What do you want from me, you damned honkie?" Lumumba shouted shrilly. "Haven't you done enough to us?"

Ryan broke stride for a moment, smiled back at Lumumba rather cruelly, and said: "I don't know what you're talking about, pal. I've got your money already. What the hell else could I want from *you?*"

He began to move off down the walkway again, threading his way past and over bits of wrecked cars, fallen masonry, and amorphous rubble. Over his shoulder, he noticed that Lumumba was following along haltingly, staring up at the buildings, nibbling at his lower lip.

"What's the matter, Lumumba," Ryan shouted back at him, "aren't these ruins good enough for you to gloat over? You wouldn't be just a little bit afraid, would you?"

"*Afraid?* Why should I be afraid?"

Ryan continued on for a few more meters; then he stopped and leaned up against the wall of one of the more badly-damaged skyscrapers, close by a jagged cavelike opening that led into the dark interior. He looked directly at Lumumba. "Don't get me wrong, pal," he said, "I wouldn't blame you if you were a little scared of the Subway Dwellers.

After all, they're the direct descendants of the people that kicked your ancestors out of this country. Maybe you got a right to be nervous.''

"Don't be an idiot, Ryan, why should a civilized African be afraid of a pack of degenerate savages?'' Koyinka said as we all caught up to Ryan.

Ryan shrugged. "How should I know?'' he said. "Maybe you ought to ask Mr. Lumumba.''

And with that, he turned his back on us and stepped through the jagged opening into the ruined skyscraper. Somewhat uneasily, we followed him into what proved to be a large antechamber that seemed to lead back into some even larger cavernous space that could be sensed rather than seen looming in the darkness. But Ryan did not lead us towards this large open space; instead, he stopped before he had gone more than a dozen steps and waited for us near a crumbling metal-pipe fence that guarded two edges of what looked like a deep pit. One long edge of the pit was flush with the right wall of the antechamber; at the far short edge, a flight of stone stairs began which seemed to go all the way to the shadow-obscured bottom.

Ryan led us along the railing to the top of the stairs, and from this angle I could see that the pit had once been the entrance to the mouth of a large tunnel whose floor had been the floor of the pit at the foot of the stairs. Now an immense and ancient solid slab of steel blocked the tunnel-mouth and formed the fourth wall of the pit. But in the center of this rusted steel slab was a relatively new airlock that seemed of modern design.

"Ladies and gentlemen,'' Ryan said, "we're standing by a sealed entrance to the Subways of Old New York. During the Space Age, the Subways were the major transportation system of the city, and there were hundreds of entrances like this one. Below the ground was a giant network of stations and tunnels through which the Space Agers could go from any point in the city to any other point. Many of the stations were huge and contained shops and restaurants. Every station had automatic vending machines which sold food and drinks and a lot of other things too. Even during the Space Age, the Subways were a kind of little world."

He started down the stairs, still talking. "During the Panic of the Century, some of the New Yorkers chose not to leave the city. Instead, they retreated to the Subways, sealed all the entrances, installed Space Station life-support machinery— everything from a fusion reactor to hydroponics—and cut themselves off from the outside world. Today, the Subway Dwellers, direct descendants of those Space Agers, still inhabit several of the Subway stations. And most of the Space Age life-support machinery is still running. There are probably Space Age artifacts down here that no modern man has ever seen."

At the bottom of the pit, Ryan led us to the airlock and opened the outer door. The airlock proved to be surprisingly large. "This airlock was installed by the government about fifty years ago, soon after the Subway Dwellers were discovered," he told us as he jammed us inside and began the cycle. "It was part of the program to recivilize the Subway Dwellers. The idea was to let scientists get inside without contaminating the Subway atmosphere with smog. Of course, the whole program was a flop. Nobody's ever going to get through to the Subway Dwellers, and there are less of 'em every year; they don't breed much, and in a generation or so they'll be extinct. So you're all in for a really unique experience. Not everyone will be able to tell their grandchildren that they actually saw a live Subway Dweller!"

The inner airlock door opened into an ancient square cross-sectioned tunnel made of rotting gray concrete. The air, even through filters, tasted horrible: very thin, somehow crisp without being at all bracing, with a chemical undertone, yet reeking with organic decay odors. Breathing was very difficult; it felt like we were at the fifteen-thousand-foot level.

"I'm not telling you all this for my health," Ryan said as he moved us out of the airlock. "I'm telling it to you for *your* health: don't mess with these people. Look and don't touch.

Listen, but keep your mouths shut. They may seem harmless, they may be harmless, but no one can be sure. That's why not many guides will take people down here. I hope you *all* have that straight.''

The last remark had obviously been meant for Lumumba, but he didn't seem to react to it; he seemed subdued, drawn up inside himself. Perhaps Ryan was right—perhaps in some unguessable way, Lumumba *was* afraid. It's impossible to really understand these Amero-Africans.

We moved off down the corridor. The overhead lights—at least in this area—were clearly modern, probably installed when the airlock had been installed, centuries ago by the Space Agers themselves. The air we were breathing was produced by a Space Age atmosphere plant that had been designed for actual Space Stations! It was a frightening and at the same time thrilling feeling: our lives were dependent on actual functioning Space Age equipment. It was almost like stepping back in time.

The corridor made a right-angle turn and became a downward-sloping ramp. The ramp leveled off after a few dozen feet, passed some crumbling ruins inset into one of the walls—apparently a ruined shop of some strange sort with massive chairs bolted to the floor and pieces of mirror still clinging to patches of its walls—and suddenly opened out into a wide, low, cavelike space lit dimly and erratically by ancient Space Age permabulbs which still functioned in many places along the grime-encrusted ceiling.

It was the strangest room—if you could call it that—that I had ever been in. The ceiling seemed horribly low, lower even than it actually was, because the room seemed to go on under it indefinitely, in all sorts of seemingly random directions. Its boundaries faded off into shadows and dim lights and gloom; I couldn't see any of the far walls. It was impossible to feel exactly claustrophobic in a place like that, but it gave me an analogous sensation without a name, as if the ceiling and floor might somehow come together and squash me flat.

Strange figures shuffled around in the gloom, moving

about slowly and aimlessly. Other figures sat singly or in small groups on the bare filthy floor. Most of the Subway Dwellers were well under five feet tall. Their shoulders were deeply stooped making them seem even shorter, and their bodies were thick, rickety, and emaciated under the tattered and filthy scraps of multicolored rags which they wore. I was deeply shocked. I don't really know what I had expected, but I certainly had not been prepared for the unmistakable aura of diminished humanity which these pitiful creatures exuded even at a distant first glance.

Immediately before us was a kind of concrete hut. It was pitted with what looked like bullet scars and parts of it were burned black. It had tiny windows, one of which still held some rotten metal grillwork. Apparently it had been a kind of sentry-box, perhaps during the Panic of the Century itself. A complex barrier cut off the section where we stood from the main area of the Subway station. It consisted of a ceiling-to-floor metal grillwork fence on either side of a line of turnstiles. On either side of the line of turnstiles, gates in the fence clearly marked "Exit" in peeling white and black enamel had been crudely welded shut, by the look of the weld, perhaps more than a century ago.

On the other side of the barrier stood a male Subway Dweller wearing a kind of long shirt patched together out of every conceivable type and color of cloth and rotting away at the edges and in random patches. He stood staring at us, or at least with his deeply squinted expressionless eyes turned in our direction, rocking back and forth slightly from the waist, but otherwise not moving. His face was unusually pallid even for an American, and every inch of his skin and clothing was caked with an incredible layer of filth.

Ignoring the Subway Dweller as thoroughly as that stooped figure was ignoring us, Ryan led us to the line of turnstiles and extracted a handful of small greenish-yellow coins from a pocket.

"These are Subway Tokens," he told us, dropping ten of the coins into a small slot atop one of the turnstiles. "Space Age money that was only used down here. It's good in all the vending machines, and in these turnstiles. The Subway Dwellers still use the Tokens to get food and water from the machines. When I want more of these things, all I have to do is break open a vending machine, so don't worry, admission isn't costing us anything. Just push your way through the turnstile like this. . . ."

He demonstrated by walking straight through the turnstile. The turnstile barrier rotated a notch to let him through when he applied his body against it.

One by one we passed through the turnstile. Michael Lumumba passed through immediately ahead of me, then paused at the other side to study the Subway Dweller, who had drifted up to the barrier. Lumumba looked down at the Subway Dweller's face for a long moment; then a sardonic smile grew slowly on his face, and he said: "Hello, honkie, how are things in the Subway?"

The subway Dweller turned his own eyes in Lumumba's direction. He did nothing else.

"Hey, just what *are* you, some kind of cretin?" Lumumba said as Ryan, his face flushed red behind his pallor, turned in his tracks and started back towards Lumumba. The Subway Dweller's face did not change expression; in fact it could hardly have been said to have had an expression in the first place. "I think you're a brain-damage case, honkie."

"I told you not to talk to the Subway Dwellers!" Ryan said, shoving his way between Lumumba and the Subway Dweller.

"So you did," Lumumba said coolly. "And I'm beginning to wonder why."

"They can be dangerous."

"*Dangerous?* These little moronic slugs? The only thing these brainless white worms can be dangerous to is your pride. Isn't that it, Ryan? Behold the remnants of the great Space Age honkies! See how they haven't the brains left to wipe the drool off their chins—"

"Be silent!" Kulongo suddenly bellowed with the authority of a chief in his voice. Lumumba was indeed silenced, and even Ryan backed off as Kulongo moved near them. But the

self-satisfied look that Lumumba continued to give Ryan was
a weapon that he was wielding, a weapon that the American
obviously felt keenly.

Through it all, the Subway Dweller continued to rock back
and forth, gently and silently, without a sign of human
sentience.

Goddamn that black brother Lumumba and goddamn the
stinking Subway Dwellers! Oh how I hate taking these Africans down there, sometimes I wonder why the hell I do it.
Sometimes I feel there's something unclean about it all,
something rotten. Not just the Subway Dwellers, though
those horrible animals are rotten enough, but taking a bunch
of stinking African tourists in there to look at them, and me
making money off of it. It's a great selling-point for the
day-tour—those black brothers eat it up, especially the cruts
like Lumumba—but if I didn't need the money so bad, I
wouldn't do it. Call it patriotism, maybe. I'm not patriotic
enough not to take my tours to see the Subway Dwellers, but
I'm patriotic enough not to feel too happy about it.

Of course I know what it is that gets to me. The Subway
Dwellers are the last direct descendants of the Space Agers,
in a way the only piece of the Space Age still alive, and what
they are is what Lumumba said they are: slugs, morons, and
cretins. And physical wrecks on top of it. Lousy eyesight,
rubbery bones, rotten teeth, and if you find one more than
five feet tall, it's a giant. They're lucky to live to thirty.
There's no smog in the recirculated chemical crap they
breathe, but there's not enough oxygen in the long run either,
and after two centuries of sucking in its own gunk, God only
knows exactly what's missing and what there's too much of
in the air that the Subway life-support system puts out. The
Subway Dwellers have just about enough brains left to keep
the air plant and the hydroponics and stuff going without
really knowing what the hell they're doing. Every one of
them is a born brain-damage case, and year by year the air
keeps getting crummier and crummier and the crap they eat
gets lousier and lousier and there are fewer and fewer Subway

Dwellers and they're getting stupider and stupider. They say in another fifty years, they'll be extinct. They're all that's left of the Space Agers, and they're slowly strangling their brains in their own crap.

Like I keep telling Karen, the tourist business is a rotten way to earn a living. Every time I come down into this stinking hole in the ground, I have to keep reminding myself that I'm a day closer to owning a piece of that Amazon swampland. It helps settle my stomach.

I led my collection of Africans further out into the upper level of the station. It's hard to figure out just what this level was during the Space Age—there's nothing up here but a lot of old vending machines and ruined stalls and garbage. This level goes on and on in all directions; there are more old Subway entrances leading into it than I've counted. I've been told that during the Space Age thousands of people crowded in here just on their way to the trains below, but that doesn't make sense. Why would they want to hang around in a hole in the ground any longer than they had to?

The Subway Dwellers, of course, just mostly hung around doing what Subway Dwellers do—stand and stare into space, or sit on their butts and chew their algacake, or maybe even stand and stare and chew at the same time, if they're real enterprising. Beats me why the Africans are so fascinated by them. . . .

Then, a few yards ahead of us, I saw a vending machine servicer approaching a water machine. Now there was a piece of luck! I sure didn't get to show every tour what passed for a "Genuine Subway Dweller Ceremony." I decided to really play it up. I held the tourists off about ten feet from the water machine so they wouldn't mess things up, and started to give them a fancy pitch.

"You're about to witness an authentic water machine servicing by a Subway Dweller Vending Machine Servicer," I told them, as a crummy Subway Dweller slowly inched up to a peeling red and white water machine dragging a small cart which held four metal kegs and a bunch of other old crap. "During the Space Age, this machine dispensed the traditional Space Age beverage, Coca-Cola—still enjoyed in some parts of the world—as you can see from some of the lettering still on the machine. Of course the Subway Dwellers have no Coca-Cola to fill it with now.''

The Subway Dweller took a ring of keys out of the cart, fumbled one of them into a keyhole on the face of the machine after a few tries, and opened a plate on the front of the machine. Tokens came tumbling out onto the floor. The Subway Dweller got down on its hands and knees, picked up the Tokens one by one, and dropped them into a moldy-looking rubber sack from the cart.

''The Servicer has now removed the Tokens from the water machine. In order to get a drink of water, a Subway Dweller drops a Token into the slot in the face of the machine, pulls the lever, and cups his hands inside the little opening.''

The Subway Dweller opened the back of the water machine with another key, struggled with one of the metal kegs, then finally lifted it and poured some pretty green-looking water into the machine's tank.

''The Servicers buy the water from the Reclamation Tenders with the Tokens they get from the machines. They also Service the food machines with algacake they get from the Hydroponic Tenders the same way.''

The Vending Machine Servicer replaced the back-plate of the water machine and dragged its cart slowly off further on into the shadows of the station towards the next water machine.

''How do they make the Tokens?'' Koyinka asked.

''Nobody makes Tokens,'' I told him. ''They're all left over from the Space Age.''

''That doesn't make sense. How can they run an economy without a supply of new money? Profits always bring new money into circulation. Even a socialist economy has to print new money each year.''

Huh? What the hell was he talking about? These damn Africans!

''I think I can explain,'' the college professor said. ''According to Kusongeri, the Subway Dwellers do not have a real money economy. The same Tokens get passed around continually. For instance, the Servicers probably take exactly as many Tokens out of the water machine as they have to give to the Reclamation Tenders for the water in the first place. No concept of profit exists here."

"But then why do they bother with Tokens in the first place"?

The professor shrugged. "Ritual, perhaps, or—"

"Why does a bee build honeycombs?" Lumumba sneered. "Why does a magpie steal bright objects? Because they think about it—or because it's just the nature of the animal? Don't you see, Koyinka, these white slugs aren't people, they're animals! They don't *think*. They don't have *reasons* for doing anything. Animals! Stupid pale white animals! The last descendants of the Space Age honkies end up like when they don't have black men to think for them, how—"

Red sparks went off in my head. "They were good enough to ride your crummy ancestors back to Africa on a rail, you black brother!"

"You watch your mouth when you're talking to your betters, honkie!"

"Mr. Lumumba!" the professor shouted. Koyinka looked ready to take a swing at me. Kulongo had moved towards Lumumba and looked disgusted. The Luthuliville fruits were wrinkling their dainty noses. Christ, we were all a hair from a brawl. A thing like that could kill business for a month, or even cost me my license. I thought of that Amazon swampland, blue skies and green trees and brown earth as far as the eye could see . . .

I kept thinking of the Amazon as I unballed my fists and swallowed my pride, and turned my back on Lumumba and led the whole lousy lot of them deeper into the upper level of the station.

Man, I just better give them about another twenty minutes down here and get the hell out before I tear that Lumumba to pieces. I had half a mind to take him back in there to that electric people-trap and jam one of those helmets on his head and leave him there. Then we'd see how much laughing he'd do at the Space Agers!

The tension kept building between Ryan and Lumumba as we continued to move among the Subway Dwellers; it was so painfully obvious that it was only a matter of time before the next outburst that one might have almost expected the wretched creatures who inhabited the Subways to notice it.

But it was also rather obvious that the Subway Dwellers had only a limited perception of their environment and an even more limited conceptualization of interpersonal relationships. It would be difficult to say whether or not they were capable of comprehending anything so complex as human emotion. It would be almost as difficult to say whether or not they were human.

The Vending Machine Servicer had performed a complicated task, a task somewhat too complex for even an intelligent chimpanzee, though conceivably a dolphin might have the mental capacity to master it if it had the physical equipment. But no one has been able to say clearly whether or not a dolphin should be considered sapient; it seems to be a borderline situation.

Lumumba had obviously made up his mind that the Subway Dwellers were truly subhuman animals. As Ryan led us past a motley group of Subway Dwellers who squatted on the bare floor mechanically eating small slabs of some green substance, Lumumba kept up a loud babble, ostensibly to me, but actually for Ryan's benefit.

"Look at the dirty animals chewing their cud like cows! Look what's left of the great Space Agers who went to the Moon—a few thousand brainless white slugs rotting in a sealed coffin!"

"Even the greatest civilization falls sometime," I mumbled somewhat inanely, trying to soften the situation, for Ryan was clearly engaged in a fierce struggle for control of his temper. I could understand why Ryan and Lumumba hated each other, but why did Lumumba's remarks about the Subway Dwellers hurt Ryan so deeply?

As we walked further on in among the rusting steel pillars and scattered groups of ruminating Subway Dwellers, I happened to pass close by a female Subway Dweller, perhaps four and a half feet tall, stooped and leathery with stringy gray hair, and dressed in the usual filthy rags. She was inserting a Token into the slot of a vending machine. She dropped the coin, and pulled a lever under one of the small broken windows that formed a row above the trough of the machine. A green slab dropped down into the trough. The female Subway Dweller picked it up and began chewing on it.

A sense of excitement came over me. I was determined to actually speak with a Subway Dweller. "What is your name?" I said slowly and distinctly.

The female Subway Dweller turned her pale expressionless little eyes in my direction. A bit of green drool escaped her lips. Other than that, she made no discernible response.

I tried again. "What is your name?"

The creature stared at me blankly. "Whu . . ee . . . na . ." she finally managed to stammer in a flat, dull monotone.

"I told you people not to talk to the damn Subway Dwellers!"

Ryan had apparently noticed what I was doing; he was rushing towards me past Michael Lumumba. Lumumba grabbed him by the elbow. "What's the matter, Ryan?" he said. "Do the animals bite?"

"Get your slimy hand off me, you black brother!" Ryan roared, ripping his arm out of Lumumba's grasp.

"I'll bet you bite too, honkie," Lumumba said. "After all, you're the same breed of animal they are."

Ryan lunged at Lumumba, but Kulongo was on him in three huge strides, and hugged him from behind with a powerful grip. "Please do not be as foolish as that man, Mr. Ryan," he said softly. "He dishonors us all. You have been a good guide. Do not let that man goad you into doing something that will allow him to disgrace your name with the authorities."

Kulongo held on to Ryan as the redness in his face slowly

faded. The female Subway Dweller began to wander away. Lumumba backed off a few paces, then turned his back, walked a bit further away and pretended to study a group of seated Subway Dwellers.

Finally, Kulongo released his grip on Ryan. "Yeah, you're right pal," Ryan said. "That crut would like nothing better than to be able to report that I bashed his face in. I guess I should apologize to the rest of you folks. . . ."

"I think Mr. Lumumba should apologize as well," I said.

"I don't apologize to animals," Lumumba muttered. Really, the man was disgusting!

God, what I really wanted to do was bury that Lumumba right there, knock him senseless and let him try to get back to Milford by himself, or better yet take him back to that crazy "Cosmic All" thing, jam a helmet on his head, and find out how the thing kills in the pleasantest way possible.

But of course I couldn't kill him or maroon him in front of eight witnesses. So instead of giving that black brother what he deserved, I decided to just let them all walk around for about another ten minutes, gawking at the animals, and then call it a day. Seemed to me that all of them but Lumumba and maybe the professor had had their fill of the Subway Dwellers anyway. Mostly, the Subway Dwellers just sit around chewing algacake. Some of them just stare at nothing for hours. Let's face it, the Subway Dwellers *are* animals. They've degenerated all the way. I figured just about now the Africans would've had their nasty thrill. . . .

But I figured without that stinking Lumumba. Just when the whole bunch of them were standing around in a mob looking thoroughly bored and disgusted, he started another "conversation" with the professor, real loud. Real subtle, that black brother.

"You're a professor of American history, aren't you, Dr. Balewa?"

Got to give Balewa credit. He didn't seem to want any part of Lumumba's little game. "Uh . . . Space Age history is my major field," he muttered, and then tried to turn away.

But Lumumba would just as soon have run his mouth at a Subway Dweller; he didn't care if Balewa was really listening to him as long as I was.

"Well then maybe you can tell me whether or not the honkies could really have built all that Space Age technology on their own. After all, look at these brainless animals, the direct descendants of the Space Age honkies. Sure, they've degenerated since the first of them locked themselves up down here, but degenerated from *what*? Didn't they have to be pretty stupid to seal themselves up in a tomb like this in the first place? And they did have twenty or thirty million black men to do their thinking for them before the Panic. Take a look around you, professor—did these slugs *really* have ancestors capable of creating the Space Age on their own?"

He stared dead at me, and I saw his slimy game. If I didn't cream him, I'd be a coward, and if I did, I'd lose my license. "Take a look at the modern example of the race, professor," he said. "Could a nation of *Ryans* have built anything more than a few junk heaps on their own? With captive blacks to do the thinking for them, they went to the Moon, and then they choked themselves in their own waste. Hardly the mark of a great civilized race."

"Your kind quaked in their boots every time one of my ancestors walked by them, and you know it," I told the crut.

Lumumba would've gone white if he could have. In more ways than one, I'll bet. "You calling me a coward, honkie?"

"I'm calling you a yellow coward, *boy.*"

"No honkie calls me a coward."

"This honkie does . . . *nigger.*"

Ah, that got him! There's one or two words these Amero-Africans just can't take, brings up frightening memories. Lumumba went for me, the professor tried to grab him and missed, and then that big ape Kulongo had him in one of those bear-hugs of his. And suddenly I had an idea how to fix Mr. Michael Lumumba real good, without laying a finger on him, without giving him anything he could complain to the government about.

"You ever hear about a machine that's supposed to 'Merge you with the Cosmic All', professor?" I said.

"Why . . . that would be the ECA, the electronic consciousness augmenter. It was never clear whether more than a few prototypes were built or not, the device was developed shortly before the Panic. Some sort of scientific religion built the ECA, the Brotherhood of the Cosmic All, or some such group. The claim was that the machine produced a transcendental experience of some sort electronically. No one has ever proved whether or not there was any truth to it, since none of the devices have ever been found. . . ."

Kulongo relaxed his grip on Lumumba. I had them now. I had Mr. Michael Lumumba real good. "Well I think I found one of them, right here in this station, a couple of years ago. It's still working. Maybe the Subway Dwellers keep it going —probably it was built to keep itself going; it looks like real late Space Age stuff. I could take you all to it."

I gave Lumumba a nice smile. "How about it, pal?" I said. "Let's see if you're a coward or not. Let's see you walk in there and put a working Space Age gizmo on your head and Merge With the Cosmic All."

"Have you ever done it, Ryan"? Lumumba sneered.

"Sure pal," I lied. "I do it all the time. It's fun."

"I think you're a liar."

"I *know* you're a coward."

Lumumba gave me a look like a snake. "All right, honkie," he said. "I'll try it if you try it with me."

Christ, what was I getting myself into? That thing killed people, all those bones. . . . Yeah, but I knew that and Lumumba didn't. When he saw the bones, he wouldn't dare put a helmet on his head. Yeah, I knew that he wouldn't, and he didn't, so that still put me one up on him.

"You're afraid, aren't you Ryan? You've never really done it yourself. You're afraid to do it, and I'm not. Who does that make the coward?"

Oh you crut, I got you right where I want you! "Okay boy," I said, "you're on. You do it and I'll do it. We'll see who's the coward. The rest of you folks can come along for the ride. A free extra added attraction, courtesy of Little Old New York Tours."

Ryan led us deeper into a more shadowed part of the station, where the still-functioning bulbs in the ceiling were farther and farther apart, and where, perhaps because of the darkness, the Subway Dwellers were fewer and fewer. As we went further and further into the deepening darkness, the floor of the Subway station was filled with small bits of rubble, then larger and larger pieces, till finally, dimly outlined by a single bulb a few yards ahead of us, we could see a place where the ceiling had fallen in. A huge dam of rubble which filled the station from floor to ceiling cut off a corner much like the one into which we had originally come from the rest of the station.

Ryan led us out of the pool of light and into the blackness. "In here," he called back. "Everyone touch the one ahead of you."

I touched Michael Lumumba's back with some distaste, but also with a kind of gratitude. Because of him, I was getting to see a working wonder of the Space Age, a device whose very existence was a matter of academic dispute. My reputation would be made!

I felt Kulongo's somehow-reassuring hand on my shoulder as we groped our way through the darkness. Then I felt Lumumba stoop, and I was passing through a narrow opening in the pile of rubble, where two broken girders wedged against each other held up the crumbled fragments of ceiling.

Beyond, I could see by a strange flickering light just around a bend that we had emerged in a place very much like the Subway entrance. The ceiling had fallen on a set of turnstiles and grillwork barriers, crushing them, but clearing a way for us. We picked our way past the ruined barriers and entered a side-tunnel, which was filled with the strange flickering light, a light which seemed to cut each moment off from the next, like a faulty piece of antique motion picture film, such as the specimens of Chaplin I've seen in Nairobi. It made me feel as if I were moving inside such a film. Time seemed to be composed of separate discrete bursts of duration.

Ryan led us up the tunnel, both sides of which were composed of the ruins of recessed shops, like some underground market arcade. Then I saw that one shop in the arcade was not ruined. It stood out from the rubble, a gleaming anachronism. Even a layman would've recognized it as a specimen of very late Space Age technology. And it was a working specimen.

It had that classic late Space Age style. The entire front of the shop was made of some plastic substance that flickered luminescently, that was the source of the strange pale light. There has been some literature on this material, but a specimen had never been examined as far as I knew. The substance itself is woven of fibers called light-guides—modern science has been able to produce such fibers, but to weave a kind of cloth of them by known methods would be hideously expensive. But Space Age light-guide cloth, however it was made, enabled a single light-source to cast its illumination evenly over a very wide area. So the flickering was probably produced simply by using a stroboscope as a light-source for the wall. Very minor Space Age wizardry, but very effective: it made the entire shopfront a psychologically powerful attention-getting device, such as the Space Agers commonly employed in their incredibly sophisticated science of advertising.

A small doorless portal big enough for one man at a time was all that marred the flickering luminescence of the wall of shopfront. Above the shop a smaller strobe-panel—but this one composed of blue and red fibers which flashed independently—proclaimed "Merge With The Cosmic All" red on blue for half of every second, a powerful hypnotic that drew me towards the shop despite my abstract knowledge of its workings.

That the device was working at all in this area of the station where all other power seemed cut off was proof enough of its very late Space Age dating: only in the decade before the Panic had the Space Agers developed a miniaturized isotopic power-source cheap enough to warrant installation of self-contained five-hundred-year generators in something like this.

The very fact that we were staring into the flickering light of a Space Age device whose self-contained power-source had kept it going totally untended for centuries was enough to overwhelm us. I'm sure the rest of them felt what I felt; even Lumumba just stood there and gaped. On Ryan's face, even beneath the tight lines of his anger, was something akin to awe. Or was it some kind of superstitious dread?

"Well here it is, Lumumba," Ryan said softly, the strobe-wall making the movements of his mouth appear to be mechanical. "Shall we step inside?"

"After you, Ryan. You're the . . . native guide." Fear flickered in the strobe flashes off Lumumba's eyes, but like all of us, he found it impossible to look away from the entrance for long. There seemed to be subtle and complex waves in the strobe flashes drawing us to the doorway; perhaps there were several stroboscopes activating the wall in a psychologically-calculated sequence. In this area, the Space Age Americans had been capable of any subtlety a modern mind could imagine, and infinitely more.

"And you're the . . . *tourist,*" Ryan said softly. "A tourist who thinks he knows what the Space Agers were all about. Step inside, sucker!"

And with a grim, knowing grin, Ryan stepped through the doorway. Without hesitation, Lumumba followed after him. And without hesitation, drawn by the flickering light and so much more, I entered the chamber behind them.

The inside of the chamber was a cube of some incredible hyper-real desert night as seen through the eyes of a prophet or a madman. The walls and ceiling of the room were light: mosaics of millions of tiny deep-blue twinkling pinpoints of brilliance, here and there leavened with intermittent prickles of red and green and yellow, all flashing in seemingly-random sequences of a tenth of a second or so each. Beneath this preternatural electronic sky, we stood transfixed. The dazzling universe of winking light filled our brains; before it we were as Subway Dwellers chewing their cud.

Behind me, I dimly heard Kulongo's deep voice saying:

"There are demons in there that would drink a man's soul. We will not go in there." How foolish those far-away words sounded. . . .

"There's nothing to be afraid of . . ." I heard my own voice saying. The sound of my own voice broke my light trance almost as I realized that I had been in a trance. Then I saw the bones.

The chamber was filled with six rows of strange chairs, six of them to a row. They were like giant red eggs standing on end, hollowed out, and fitted inside with reclining padded seats. Inside the red eggs, metal helmets designed to fit over the entire head dangled from cables at head-level. Most of the eggs contained human skeletons. The floor was littered with bones.

Ryan and Lumumba seemed to have been somewhat deeper in trance; it took them a few seconds longer to come out of it. Lumumba's eyes flashed sudden fear as he saw the bones. But Ryan grinned knowingly as he saw the fear on Lumumba's face.

"Scares you a bit, doesn't it, boy?" Ryan said. "Still game to put on one of these helmets?" The wall seemed to pick up the sparkle of his laugh.

"What killed them?" was all Lumumba said.

"How should I know?"

"But you said you'd tried it!"

"So I'm a liar. And you're a coward."

I walked forward as they argued, and read a small metal plaque that was affixed to the outer shell of each red egg:

"2 Tokens—MERGE WITH THE COSMIC ALL—2 Tokens Drop Tokens in slot. Place helmet over head. Pull lever and experience MERGER WITH THE COSMIC ALL. Automatic timer will limit all MERGERS to 2 minutes duration, in compliance with Federal Law."

"I'm no more a coward than you are, Ryan. You had no intention of putting on one of those things."

"I'd do it if you'd do it," Ryan insisted.

"No, you wouldn't! You're not that crazy and neither am I. Why would you risk your life for something as stupid as that?"

"Because I'd be willing to bet my life any day that a black brother like you would never have the guts to put on a helmet."

"You stinking honkie!"

"Why don't we end this crap, Lumumba? You're not going to put on one of these helmets, and neither am I. The big difference between us is that I won't have to because you can't."

Lumumba seemed like a carven idol of rage in that fantastic cube of light. "Just a minute, honkie," he said. "Professor, you have any idea why they died when they put the helmets on?"

It was starting to make sense to me. What if the claims made for the device were true? What if 2 Tokens could buy a man total transcendental bliss? "I don't think they died when they put the helmets on," I said. "I think they starved to death days later. According to this plaque, whatever happens is supposed to last no longer than two minutes before an automatic circuit shuts it off. What if this device involves electronic stimulation of the pleasure center? No one has yet unearthed such a device, but the Space Age literature was full of it. Pleasure center stimulation was supposed to be harmless in itself, but what if the timer circuit went out? A man could be paralyzed in total bliss while he starved to death. I think that's what happened here."

"Let me get this straight," Lumumba said, his rage seeming to collapse in upon itself, becoming a manic shrewdness. "The helmets themselves are harmless? Even if we couldn't take them off ourselves, one of the others could take them off. . . . We wouldn't be in any real danger?"

"I don't think so," I told him. "According to the inscription, one paid 2 Tokens for the experience. I doubt that even the Space Agers would've been willing to pay money for something that would harm them, certainly not en masse.

And the Space Agers were very conscious of profit.''

"Would you be willing to stake your life on it, Dr. Balewa? Would you be willing to try it too?"

Try it? Actually put on a helmet, give myself over to a piece of Space Age wizardry, an electronic device that was supposed to produce a mystical experience at the flick of a switch? A less stable man might say that if it really worked, there was a god inside the helmets, a god that the Space Agers had created out of electronic components. If this were actually true, it surely must represent the very pinnacle of Space Age civilization—who but the Space Agers would even contemplate the fabrication of an actual god?

Yes, of course I would try it! I had to try it; what kind of scholar would I be if I passed by an opportunity to understand the Space Agers as no modern man has understood them before? Neither Ryan nor Lumumba had the background to make the most of such an experience. It was my duty to put on a helmet as well as my pleasure.

"Yes, Mr. Lumumba," I said. "I intend to try it too."

"Then we'll all try it," Lumumba said. "Or will we, Mr. Ryan? I'm ready to put on a helmet and so is the professor; are you?"

They were both nuts, Lumumba and the professor! Those helmets had killed people. How the hell could Balewa know what had happened from reading some silly plaque? These goddamn Africans always think they can understand the Space Agers from crap other Africans have put in books. What the hell do they know? What do they really know?

"Well, Ryan, what about it? Are you going to admit you don't have the guts to do it, so we can all forget it and go home?"

"All right, pal, you're on!" I heard myself telling him. Damn, what was I getting myself into? But I couldn't let that slime Lumumba call my bluff; no African's gonna bluff down an *American!* Besides, Balewa was probably right; what he said made sense. Sure, it had to make sense. That stinking black brother!

"Mr. Kulongo, would you come in here and take the helmets off our heads in two minutes?" I asked. I'd trust that Kulongo further than the rest of the creeps.

"I will not go in there," Kulongo said. "There is juju in there, powerful and evil. I am ashamed before you because I say these words, but my fear of what is in this place is greater than my shame."

"This is ridiculous!" Koyinka said, pushing past Kulongo. "Evil spirits! Come on, will you, this is the twenty-third century! I'll do it, if you want to go through with this nonsense."

"All right, pal, let's get on with it."

I handed out the Tokens and the three of us went to the nearest three stalls. I cleared a skeleton out of mine, sent it clattering to the floor, and so what, what's to be scared of in a pile of old dead bones? But I noticed that Lumumba seemed a little green as he cleared the bones out for himself.

I pulled myself up into the hollowed-out egg and sat down on the padded couch inside. Some kind of plastic covering made the thing still clean and comfortable, not even dusty, after hundreds of years. Those Space Agers were really something. I dropped the Tokens into a little slot in the arm of the couch. Next to the slot was a lever. The room sparkled blue all around me; somehow that made me feel real good. The couch was comfortable. Koyinka was standing by. I was actually beginning to enjoy it. What was there to be afraid of? Jeez, the professor thought this thing gave you pure pleasure or something. If he was right, this was really going to be something. If I lived through it.

I put my right hand on the lever. I saw that the professor and Lumumba were already under their helmets. I fitted the helmet down over my head. Some kind of pad inside it fitted down on my skull all around my head, down to the eyebrows; it seemed almost alive, molding itself to my head like a second skin. It was very dark inside the helmet. Couldn't see a thing.

I took a deep breath and pulled the lever.

The tips of my fingers began to tingle, throbbing with

pleasure, not pain. My feet started to tingle too, and shapes
that had no shape, that were more black inside the black,
seemed to be floating around inside my head. The tingling
moved up my fingers to my hands, up my feet to my knees.
Now my arms were tingling. Oh man, it felt so good! No
woman ever felt this good! This felt better than kicking in
Lumumba's face!

The whirling things in my head weren't really in my head,
my head was in them, or they were my head, all whirling
around some deep dark hole that wasn't a hole but was
something to whirl off into, fall off into, sucking me in and
up. My whole body was tingling now. Man I *was* the tingling
now, my body was nothing but the tingling now.

And it was getting stronger, getting better all the time, I
wasn't a tingle, I was a glow, a warmth, a throbbing, a fire of
pure pleasure, a roaring burning whirling fire sucking spinning up towards a deep black hole inside me blowing up in a
blast of pure FEELING SO GOOD SO GOOD SO GOOD—

Oh, forever, whirling, whirling, a fire SO GOOD SO
GOOD SO GOOD, and on THROUGH! into the black hole
fire I was BURNING UP IN MY OWN ORGASM, I was my
own orgasm of body mind sex taste smell touch feel, I went
on FOREVER FOREVER FOREVER FOREVER in pure
blinding burning SO GOOD SO GOOD SO GOOD nothing-
ness blackness dying orgasm FOREVER FOREVER
FOREVER spurting out of myself in sweet moment of total
pain-pleasure SO GOOD SO GOOD SO GOOD moment of
dying pain burning sex FOREVER FOREVER FOREVER
SO GOOD SO GOOD FOREVER SO GOOD FOREVER
SO GOOD FOREVER—

I pulled the lever and waited in my private darkness. The
first thing I felt was a tingling of my fingertips, as if with
some mild electric charge; not at all an unpleasant feeling. A
similar pleasurable tingle began in my feet. Strange vague
patterns seemed to swirl around inside my eyes.

My hands began to feel the pleasant sensation now, and the
lower portions of my legs. The feeling was getting stronger

and stronger as it moved up my limbs. I felt physically pleasurable in a peculiarly abstract way, but there was something frightening about it, something vaguely unclean.

The swirling patterns seemed to be spinning around a bottomless vortex now; they weren't exactly inside my eyes or my head, my head was inside of them, or they *were* me. The experience was somehow visual-yet-non-visual, my being spinning downward and inward in a vertiginous spiral towards a black, black hole that seemed tingling now; I felt nothing *but* the strange, forcefully pleasureable sensation. It filled my entire sensorium, became *me*.

And it kept getting stronger and stronger, no longer a tingle, but a pulsing of cold electric pleasure, stronger and stronger, wilder and wilder, the voltage increasing, the amperage increasing, whirling me down and around and down and around towards that terrible deep black hole inside me burning with hunger to swallow myself up becoming a pure black fire vortex pain of pleasure down and down and around and around. . . .

Sucking myself up through the terrible black vortex of my own pure pleasure-pain, compressed against the interface of my own being, squeezed against the instant of my own DEATH Oh! Oh! DEATH DEATH DEATH No No pleasure pain death sex orgasm everything that was me popping No! No! ON THROUGH! becoming moment of death senses flashing pure pleasure pain terror black hole FOREVER FOREVER in this terrible universe was timeless moment of orgasm death total electric pleasure NO! NO! delicious horrible moment of pure DEATH PAIN ORGASM BLACK HOLE VORTEX NO! NO! NO! NO—

Suddenly I was seated on a couch inside a red egg in a room filled with blue sparkles, and I was looking up at Koyinka's silly face.

"You all right?" he said. Now *there* was a question!

"Yeah, yeah," I mumbled. Man, those Space Agers! I wanted to puke. I wanted to jam that helmet back on my head. I wanted to get the hell out of there! I wanted to live forever in that fantastic perfect feeling until I rotted into the bonepile.

I was scared out of my head.

I mean, what happened inside that helmet was the best and the worst thing in the world. You could stay there with that thing on your head and die in pure pleasure thinking you were living forever. Man, you talk about *temptation!* Those Space Agers had put a god or a devil in there, and who could tell which? Did they even know which? Man, that crazy jungle-bunny Kulongo was right after all: there *were* demons in here that would drink your soul. But maybe the demons were *you.* Sucking up your own soul in pure pleasure till it choked you to death. But wasn't it maybe worth it?

As soon as he saw I was okay, Koyinka ran over to the professor, who was still sitting there with the helmet over his head. That crut Lumumba was out of it already. He was staring at me; he wasn't mad, he wasn't exactly afraid, he was just trying to look into my eyes. I guess because I felt what he felt too.

I stared back into Lumumba's big eyes as Koyinka took the helmet off the professor's head. I couldn't help myself. I didn't like the black brother one bit more, but there was something between us now, god knows what. The professor looked real green. He didn't seem to notice us much. Lumumba and I just kept staring at each other, nodding a little bit. Yeah, we had both been someplace no living man should go. The Space Agers had been gods or demons or maybe something that would drive both gods and demons screaming straight up the wall. When we call them men, we don't mean the same thing we do when we call us men. When they died off, something we'll never understand went out of the world. I don't know whether to thank God or to cry.

It seemed to me that I could read exactly what was going on inside Lumumba's head; his thoughts were my thoughts.

"They were a great and terrible people," Lumumba finally said. "And they were out of their minds."

"Pal, they were something we can never be. Or want to."

"You know honkie, I think for once you've got a point."

There was a strange feeling hovering in the air between Ryan and Lumumba as we made our way back through the Subway station and up into the sparkly blue unreal world of the Fuller Dome. Not comradeship, not even grudging respect, but some subtle change I could not fathom. Their eyes keep meeting, almost furtively. I couldn't understand it. I couldn't understand it at all.

Had they experienced what I had? Coldly, I could now say that it had been nothing but electronic stimulation of some cerebral centers; but the horror of it, the horror of being forced to experience a moment of death and pain and total pleasure all bound up together and extended towards infinity, had been realer than real. It had indeed been a genuine mystical experience, created electronically.

But why would people do a thing like that to themselves? Why would they willingly plunge themselves into a moment of pure horror that went on and on and on?

Yet as we finally boarded the helicopter, I somehow sensed that what Lumumba and Ryan had shared was not what I felt at all.

As I flew the copter through the dead tombstone skyscrapers towards the outer edge of the Fuller Dome, I knew that I had to get out of this damn tourist business, and fast. Now I knew what was really buried here, under the crazy spooky blue light, under all the concrete, under the stinking saturation smog, under a hole inside a hole in the ground; the bones of a people that men like us had better let lie.

Our ancestors were gods or demons or both. If we get too close to the places where what they *really* were is buried, they'll drink our souls yet.

No more tours to the Subways anyway; what good is the Amazon if I don't live to get there? If I had me an atom bomb, I'd drop it right smack on top of this place. To make sure I never go back.

As we headed into a fantastic blazing orange and purple

sunset, towards Milford and modern America—a pallid replica of African civilization huddling in the interstices of a continent of incredible ruins—I looked back across the wide river, a flaming sea below and behind us ignited by the setting sun. The Fuller Dome flashed in the sunlight, a giant diamond set in the tombstone of a race that had soared to the Moon, that had turned the atmosphere to a beautiful and terrible poison, that had covered a continent with ruins that overawed the modern world, that had conjured up a demon out of electronic circuitry, that had torn themselves to pieces in the end.

A terrible pang of sadness went through me as the rest of my trip turned to ashes in my mouth, as my future career became a cadaver covered with dust. I could crawl over these ruins and exhaust the literature for the rest of my life, and I would never understand what the Space Age Americans had been. Not a man alive ever would. Whatever they had been, such things lived on the face of the earth no more.

In his simple way, Kulongo had said all that could be said: "Their souls were not as ours."

LIGHT OF OTHER DAYS

Bob Shaw

First published in 1966, "Light of Other Days" is a firmly established classic of science fiction by now, one of those basic stories that must be reprinted every few years for the benefit of latecomers. Its central idea is one so obvious, so beautiful, so elegant, that it draws an immediate "of course" from every reader—but, in fact, had not Bob Shaw troubled to invent slow glass for us, our imaginations would be poorer for one extraordinary concept, the most delightful new idea in science fiction in years. Obviously "Light of Other Days" must have made a clean sweep of the trophies in its year— yet, through some vagary of the electoral process, the Hugo and Nebula went elsewhere then, which is hard to believe in retrospect. No matter. Trophies come and go; winners often are forgotten; here is a story that will last. Bob Shaw is a native of Northern Ireland, now living in England. He is the author of many short stories and several novels, including one dealing at length with slow glass *(Other Days, Other Eyes)*.

Leaving the village behind, we followed the heady sweeps of the road up into a land of slow glass.

I had never seen one of the farms before and at first found them slightly eerie—an effect heightened by imagination and circumstance. The car's turbine was pulling smoothly and quietly in the damp air so that we seemed to be carried over the convolutions of the road in a kind of supernatural silence. On our right the mountain sifted down into an incredibly perfect valley of timeless pine, and everywhere stood the great frames of slow glass, drinking light. An occasional flash of afternoon sunlight on their wind bracing created an illusion of movement, but in fact the frames were deserted. The rows of windows had been standing on the hillside for years, staring into the valley, and men only cleaned them in the middle of the night when their human presence would not matter to the thirsty glass.

They were fascinating, but Selina and I didn't mention the windows. I think we hated each other so much we both were reluctant to sully anything new by drawing it into the nexus of our emotions. The holiday, I had begun to realize, was a stupid idea in the first place. I had thought it would cure everything, but, of course, it didn't stop Selina being pregnant and, worse still, it didn't even stop her being angry about being pregnant.

Rationalizing our dismay over her condition, we had circulated the usual statements to the effect that we would have *liked* having children—but later on, at the proper time. Selina's pregnancy had cost us her well-paid job and with it the new house we had been negotiating and which was far beyond the reach of my income from poetry. But the real source of our annoyance was that we were face to face with the realization that people who say they want children later always mean they want children never. Our nerves were thrumming with the knowledge that we, who had thought ourselves so unique, had fallen into the same biological trap as every mindless rutting creature which ever existed.

The road took us along the southern slopes of Ben Cruachan until we began to catch glimpses of the gray Atlantic far ahead. I had just cut our speed to absorb the view better when I noticed the sign spiked to a gatepost. It said: "SLOW GLASS—Quality High, Prices Low—J. R. Hagan." On an impulse I stopped the car on the verge, wincing slightly as tough grasses whipped noisily at the bodywork.

"Why have we stopped?" Selina's neat, smoke-silver head turned in surprise.

"Look at that sign. Let's go up and see what there is. The stuff might be reasonably priced out here."

Selina's voice was pitched high with scorn as she refused, but I was too taken with my idea to listen. I had an illogical conviction that doing something extravagant and crazy would set us right again.

"Come on," I said, "the exercise might do us some good. We've been driving too long anyway."

She shrugged in a way that hurt me and got out of the car. We walked up a path made of irregular, packed clay steps nosed with short lengths of sapling. The path curved through trees which clothed the edge of the hill and at its end we found a low farmhouse. Beyond the little stone building tall frames of slow glass gazed out towards the voice-stilling sight of Cruachan's ponderous descent towards the waters of Loch Linnhe. Most of the panes were perfectly transparent but a few were dark, like panels of polished ebony.

As we approached the house through a neat cobbled yard, a tall middle-aged man in ash-colored tweeds arose and waved to us. He had been sitting on the low rubble wall which bounded the yard, smoking a pipe and staring towards the house. At the front window of the cottage a young woman in a tangerine dress stood with a small boy in her arms, but she turned disinterestedly and moved out of sight as we drew near.

"Mr. Hagan?" I guessed.

"Correct. Come to see some glass, have you? Well, you've come to the right place." Hagan spoke crisply, with traces of the pure Highland which sounds so much like Irish to the unaccustomed ear. He had one of those calmly dismayed faces one finds on elderly road-menders and philosophers.

"Yes," I said. "We're on holiday. We saw your sign."

Selina, who usually has a natural fluency with strangers, said nothing. She was looking towards the now empty window with what I thought was a slightly puzzled expression.

"Up from London, are you? Well, as I said, you've come to the right place—and at the right time, too. My wife and I don't see many people this early in the season."

I laughed. "Does that mean we might be able to buy a little glass without mortgaging our home?"

"Look at that now," Hagan said, smiling helplessly. "I've thrown away any advantage I might have had in the transaction. Rose, that's my wife, says I never learn. Still, let's sit down and talk it over." He pointed at the rubble wall then glanced doubtfully at Selina's immaculate blue skirt. "Wait till I fetch a rug from the house." Hagan limped quickly into the cottage, closing the door behind him.

"Perhaps it wasn't such a marvelous idea to come up here," I whispered to Selina, "but you might at least be pleasant to the man. I think I can smell a bargain."

"Some hope," she said with deliberate coarseness. "Surely even you must have noticed that ancient dress his wife is wearing? He won't give much away to strangers."

"Was that his wife?"

"Of course that was his wife."

"Well, well," I said, surprised. "Anyway, try to be civil with him. I don't want to be embarrassed."

Selina snorted, but she smiled whitely when Hagan reappeared and I relaxed a little. Strange how a man can love a woman and yet at the same time pray for her to fall under a train.

Hagan spread a tartan blanket on the wall and we sat down, feeling slightly self-conscious at having been translated from our city-oriented lives into a rural tableau. On the distant slate of the Loch, beyond the watchful frames of slow glass, a slow-moving steamer drew a white line towards the south. The boisterous mountain air seemed almost to invade our lungs, giving us more oxygen than we required.

"Some of the glass farmers around here," Hagan began, "give strangers, such as yourselves, a sales talk about how beautiful the autumn is in this part of Argyll. Or it might be the spring, or the winter. I don't do that—any fool knows that a place which doesn't look right in summer never looks right. What do you say?"

I nodded compliantly.

"I want you just to take a good look out towards Mull, Mr. . . ."

"Garland."

". . . Garland. That's what you're buying if you buy my glass, and it never looks better than it does at this minute. The glass is in perfect phase, none of it is less than ten years thick—and a four-foot window will cost you two hundred pounds."

"*Two hundred!*" Selina was shocked. "That's as much as they charge at the Scenedow shop in Bond Street."

Hagan smiled patiently, then looked closely at me to see if I knew enough about slow glass to appreciate what he had been saying. His price had been much higher than I had hoped—but *ten years thick!* The cheap glass one found in places like the Vistaplex and Pane-o-rama stores usually consisted of a quarter of an inch of ordinary glass faced with a veneer of slow glass perhaps only ten or twelve months thick.

"You don't understand, darling," I said, already determined to buy. "This glass will last ten years, and it's in phase."

"Doesn't that only mean it keeps time?"

Hagan smiled at her again, realizing he had no further necessity to bother with me. "Only, you say! Pardon me, Mrs. Garland, but you don't seem to appreciate the miracle, the genuine honest-to-goodness miracle, of engineering precision needed to produce a piece of glass in phase. When I say the glass is ten years thick, it means it takes light ten years to pass through it. In effect, each one of those panes is ten light-years thick—more than twice the distance to the nearest star—so a variation in actual thickness of only a millionth of an inch would . . ."

He stopped talking for a moment and sat quietly looking towards the house. I turned my head from the view of the Loch and saw the young woman standing at the window again. Hagan's eyes were filled with a kind of greedy reverence which made me feel uncomfortable and at the same time convinced me Selina had been wrong. In my experience husbands never looked at wives that way—at least, not at their own.

The girl remained in view for a few seconds, dress glowing warmly, then moved back into the room. Suddenly I received a distinct, though inexplicable, impression she was blind. My feeling was that Selina and I were perhaps blundering through an emotional interplay as violent as our own.

"I'm sorry," Hagan continued, "I thought Rose was going to call me for something. Now, where was I, Mrs. Garland? Ten light-years compressed into a quarter of an inch means . . ."

I ceased to listen, partly because I was already sold, partly because I had heard the story of slow glass many times before and had never yet understood the principles involved. An acquaintance with scientific training had once tried to be helpful by telling me to visualize a pane of slow glass as a hologram which did not need coherent light from a laser for the reconstitution of its visual information, and in which every photon of ordinary light passed through a spiral tunnel coiled outside the radius of capture of each atom in the glass. This gem of, to me, incomprehensibility not only told me nothing, it convinced me once again that a mind as nontechnical as mine should concern itself less with causes than effects.

The most important effect, in the eyes of the average individual, was that light took a long time to pass through a sheet of slow glass. A new piece was always jet black because nothing had yet come through, but one could stand the glass beside, say, a woodland lake until the scene emerged, perhaps a year later. If the glass was then removed and installed in a dismal city flat, the flat would—for that year—appear to overlook the woodland lake. During the year it wouldn't be merely a very realistic but still picture—the water would ripple in sunlight, silent animals would come to drink, birds would cross the sky, night would follow day, season would follow season. Until one day, a year later, the beauty held in the subatomic pipelines would be exhausted and the familiar gray cityscape would reappear.

Apart from its stupendous novelty value, the commercial success of slow glass was founded on the fact that having a scenedow was the exact emotional equivalent of owning land. The meanest cave dweller could look out on misty parks—and who was to say they weren't his? A man who really owns tailored gardens and estates doesn't spend his time proving his ownership by crawling on his ground, feeling, smelling, tasting it. All he receives from the land are light patterns, and with scenedows those patterns could be taken into coal mines, submarines, prison cells.

On several occasions I have tried to write short pieces about the enchanted crystal but, to me, the theme is so ineffably poetic as to be, paradoxically, beyond the reach of poetry—mine at any rate. Besides, the best songs and verse had already been written, with prescient inspiration, by men who had died long before slow glass was discovered. I had no hope of equaling, for example, Moore with his:

> *Oft in the stilly night,*
> *Ere slumber's chain has bound me,*
> *Fond Memory brings the light,*
> *Of other days around me . . .*

It took only a few years for slow glass to develop from a scientific curiosity to a sizable industry. And much to the astonishment of we poets—those of us who remain convinced that beauty lives though lilies die—the trappings of that industry were no different from those of any other. There

were good scenedows which cost a lot of money, and there
were inferior scenedows which cost rather less. The thickness, measured in years, was an important factor in the cost
but there was also the question of *actual* thickness, or phase.

Even with the most sophisticated engineering techniques
available thickness control was something of a hit-and-miss
affair. A coarse discrepancy could mean that a pane intended
to be five years thick might be five and a half, so that light
which entered in summer emerged in winter; a fine discrepancy could mean that noon sunshine emerged at midnight. These incompatibilities had their peculiar charm—
many night workers, for example, liked having their own
private time zones—but, in general, it cost more to buy
scenedows which kept closely in step with real time.

Selina still looked unconvinced when Hagan had finished
speaking. She shook her head almost imperceptibly and I
knew he had been using the wrong approach. Quite suddenly
the pewter helmet of her hair was disturbed by a cool gust of
wind, and huge clean tumbling drops of rain began to spang
round us from an almost cloudless sky.

"I'll give you a check now," I said abruptly, and saw
Selina's green eyes triangulate angrily on my face. "You can
arrange delivery?"

"Aye, delivery's no problem," Hagan said, getting to his
feet. "But wouldn't you rather take the glass with you?"

"Well, yes—if you don't mind." I was shamed by his
readiness to trust my scrip.

"I'll unclip a pane for you. Wait here. It won't take long to
slip it into a carrying frame." Hagan limped down the slope
towards the seriate windows, through some of which the view
towards Linnhe was sunny, while others were cloudy and a
few pure black.

Selina drew the collar of her blouse closed at her throat.
"The least he could have done was invite us inside. There
can't be so many fools passing through that he can afford to
neglect them."

I tried to ignore the insult and concentrated on writing the check. One of the outsize drops broke across my knuckles, splattering the pink paper.

"All right," I said, "let's move in under the eaves till he gets back." You worm, I thought as I felt the whole thing go completely wrong. I just had to be a fool to marry you. A prize fool, a fool's fool—and now that you've trapped part of me inside you I'll never ever, never ever, *never ever* get away.

Feeling my stomach clench itself painfully, I ran behind Selina to the side of the cottage. Beyond the window the neat living room, with its coal fire, was empty but the child's toys were scattered on the floor. Alphabet blocks and a wheelbarrow the exact color of freshly pared carrots. As I stared in, the boy came running from the other room and began kicking the blocks. He didn't notice me. A few moments later the young woman entered the room and lifted him, laughing easily and wholeheartedly as she swung the boy under her arm. She came to the window as she had done earlier. I smiled self-consciously, but neither she nor the child responded.

My forehead prickled icily. *Could they both be blind?* I sidled away.

Selina gave a little scream and I spun towards her.

"The rug!" she said. "It's getting soaked."

She ran across the yard in the rain, snatched the reddish square from the dappling wall and ran back, towards the cottage door. Something heaved convulsively in my subconscious.

"Selina," I shouted. "Don't open it!"

But I was too late. She had pushed open the latched wooden door and was standing, hand over mouth, looking into the cottage. I moved close to her and took the rug from her unresisting fingers.

As I was closing the door I let my eyes traverse the cottage's interior. The neat living room in which I had just seen the woman and child was, in reality, a sickening clutter of shabby furniture, old newspapers, cast-off clothing and smeared dishes. It was damp, stinking and utterly deserted. The only object I recognized from my view through the window was the little wheelbarrow, paintless and broken.

I latched the door firmly and ordered myself to forget what I had seen. Some men who live alone are good housekeepers; others just don't know how.

Selina's face was white. "I don't understand. I don't understand it."

"Slow glass works both ways," I said gently. "Light passes out of a house, as well as in."

"You mean . . .?"

"I don't know. It isn't our business. Now steady up— Hagan's coming back with our glass." The churning in my stomach was beginning to subside.

Hagan came into the yard carrying an oblong plastic-covered frame. I held the check out to him, but he was staring at Selina's face. He seemed to know immediately that our uncomprehending fingers had rummaged through his soul. Selina avoided his gaze. She was old and ill-looking, and her eyes stared determinedly towards the nearing horizon.

"I'll take the rug from you, Mr. Garland," Hagan finally said. "You shouldn't have troubled yourself over it."

"No trouble. Here's the check."

"Thank you." He was still looking at Selina with a strange kind of supplication. "It's been a pleasure to do business with you."

"The pleasure was mine," I said with equal senseless formality. I picked up the heavy frame and guided Selina towards the path which led to the road. Just as we reached the head of the now slippery steps Hagan spoke again.

"Mr. Garland!"

I turned unwillingly.

"It wasn't my fault," he said steadily. "A hit-and-run driver got them both, down on the Oban road six years ago. My boy was only seven when it happened. I'm entitled to keep something."

I nodded wordlessly and moved down the path, holding my wife close to me, treasuring the feel of her arms locked around me. At the bend I looked back through the rain and saw Hagan sitting with squared shoulders on the wall where we had first seen him.

He was looking at the house, but I was unable to tell if there was anyone at the window.

THE SECRET OF THE OLD CUSTARD

John Sladek

John Sladek, an American who has lived in Great Britain since the mid-1960s, is a charter member of that crew of irreverent, mordantly brilliant young writers whom Michael Moorcock gathered around himself when he assumed the editorship of *New Worlds*. Much of Sladek's most successful work appeared in that iconoclastic and unpredictable magazine, although many of his stories have appeared in more conventional science-fiction publications—among them this one, a corrosive little item that somehow made its way into the pages of that usually unadventurous journal, *If*. Sladek's two comic novels, *The Reproductive System* and *The Müller-Fokker Effect*, have won him a passionate underground following in the United States and Great Britain; with Thomas M. Disch he collaborated on a third novel, *Black Alice*, which has been purchased for motion-picture adaptation.

Agnes had been wishing for a baby all day, so it was no surprise to her when she peeked through the glass door of the oven and found one.

Bundled in clean flannel, it slept on the wire rack while she scrubbed out dusty bottles, fixed formula and dragged down the crib from the attic. By the time Glen came home from work, she was giving the baby its first bottle.

"Look!" she exclaimed. "A baby!"

"Oh, my God, where did you get that?" he said, his healthy pink face going white. "You know it's illegal to have babies."

"I found it. Why illegal?"

"Everything is illegal," he whispered, parting the curtains cautiously to peer out. "Damn near." The face upon Glen's big pink cubical head looked somewhat drawn.

"What's the matter?"

"Oh, nothing," she said testily. "We're going to have a gas war, that's all."

Glen was a pathetic figure as he moved so as not to cast a shadow on the curtains. His bright, skintight plastic suit was far from skintight, and even his cape looked baggy.

"Is it? Is that all?"

"No. Say, that neighbor of ours has been raking leaves an awfully long time."

"Answer me. What's wrong? Something at the office?"

"Everything. The carbon paper and stamps and paper clips have begun to disappear. I'm afraid they'll blame me. The boss is going to buy a computer to keep track of the loss. Someone stole my ration book on the train, and I found I had last week's newspaper. IBM stock is falling, faintly falling. I have a cold, or something. And—and they're doing away with the Dewey Decimal System."

"You're just overwrought. Why don't you just sit down and dandle our new baby on your knee, while I rustle up some supper."

"Stealing food! It's indecent!"

"Everyone does it, dear. Did you know I found the baby in the oven?"

"No!"

"Yes, the queerest thing. I had just been wishing I'd find a baby somewhere."

"How are the other appliances doing?"

"The automatic washer tried to devour me. The

dishwasher is fading away; we must have missed a payment.''

"Yes, and we're overdrawn," he said, sighing.

"The garbage disposal is hulking."

"Hulking?"

"Over there."

He did not look where she was pointing. He continued to peer out the window, where the weather situation was building up. A Welcome Wagon moved slowly down the street. He could not read the sign, but he recognized the armor plating and the blue snouts of machine guns.

"Yes, it just sits there hulking in the sink, and it won't eat anything. It ate its guarantee, though."

The neighbor, a "Mr. Green," paused in his raking to note down the Welcome Wagon's license number.

"Not hulking, darling. *Sulking,*" Glen said.

"You have such a big vocabulary. And you don't even read *How to Build Big Words.*"

"I read *Existential Digest,* when I find the time," he confessed. "But last week I took their test and learned that I'm not alienated enough. That's why I'm so damned proud of our kids."

"Jenny and Peter?"

"The same."

Agnes sighed. "I'd like to read a copy of the *Irish Mail* sometime. By the way, the potatoes had poison again. Every eye." She went into the bedroom and laid the baby in its crib.

"I'm going down and turn something on the lathe," Glen announced. "Something good."

"Take off your cape first. You remember the safety laws we learned at PTA."

"Lord, how could I forget? Snuff out all candles. Never stand in a canoe or bathtub. Give name, rank and serial number only. Accept checks only if endorsed in your presence. Do not allow rats to chew on matches, should they so desire."

He disappeared, and, at the same time, Jenny and Peter came home from school, demanding a "snack." All the kids on television had "snacks," they explained. Agnes gave them Hungarian goulash, bread and butter, coffee and apple pie. They paid 95¢ each, and each tipped her 15¢. They were gruff, dour eight-year-olds, who talked little while they ate. Agnes was a little afraid of them. After their snack, they belted on guns and went out to hunt other children, before it grew too dark to see them.

Agnes sighed and sat down to her secret transmitter.

"AUNT ROSE EXPECTED BY NOON TRAIN," she sent. "HAVE MADE ARRGTS FOR HER GLADIOLI. SEE THAT FUDGE MEETS 0400 PARIS PLANE WITH CANDLES, THE GARDENER NEEDS TROWEL XPRESS."

In a moment, the reply came. "TROWEL ARRGD. FUDGE HAS NO REPEAT NO CANDLES. WILL USE DDT. HOLD ROSE TILL VIOLET HEARD FROM."

Always the same tired meaningless messages.

Agnes sighed again and hid her transmitter in the cookie jar as Glen came up the stairs. He had, she knew, his own transmitter in the basement. For all she could tell, it was him she was calling each evening.

"Look at this!" he said proudly and displayed a newel post.

Outside, a plane dropped leaflets. The neighbor rushed about, raking them up and burning them.

"Every night, the same damned thing," said Glen, gnashing his teeth. "Every night they drop leaflets telling us to give up, and every night that jerk burns them all. At this rate, we'll never even learn who 'they' are."

"Is it really so important?" she asked. He would not answer. "Come on, quit hulking. I'll tell you what I want to do. I want to ride on a realway train."

"*Railway,*" he corrected. "You can't. The Public Health Department says that going more than thirty miles an hour contributes significantly to cancer."

"A lot you care what happens to me!"

Glen bowed his great cube of a head resignedly over the

television set. "You'll notice," he said, "that it looks like an innocent Army-Navy football game. And so it may be. Perhaps the ball won't blow up when he kicks it. Perhaps that series of plays is only a coincidence."

"No. 27 fades back to pass," she murmured. "What would that mean, I wonder?"

Glen felt her hand reach out to touch his. He held hands with his wife in the darkened living room, after making sure she was not wearing her poison ring.

"The common cold," he muttered. "*They* call it the 'common cold.' By the way, have I told you we're over-drawn?"

"Yes. It's that damned car. You would have to order all those special features."

"The bazooka in the trunk? The direction-finder radio? The gun turret? Everyone else has had them for years, Agnes. What am I supposed to do if the police start chasing me? Try to outrun them, me with all that armor plate?"

"I just don't see what we're going to live on," she said.

"We can eat green stamps, until—"

"No. They confiscated them this morning, I forgot to tell you."

The children trooped in, smelling of mud and cordite. Jenny had scratched her knee on a barbed wire barrier. Agnes applied a bandaid to it, gave them coffee and donuts, 15¢, and sent them upstairs to brush their teeth.

"And don't, for God's sake, use the tapwater," Glen shouted. "There's something in it."

He walked into the room where the baby slept and returned in a moment, shaking his head. "Could have sworn I heard him ticking."

"Oh Glen, let's get away for a few days. Let's go to the country."

"Oh sure. Travel twenty miles over mined roads to look at a couple of cowpies. You wouldn't dare get out of the car, for the deadly snakes. They've sowed the ground with poison ivy and giant viruses."

"I wouldn't care! Just a breath of fresh air—"

"Sure. Nerve gas. Mustard gas. Tear gas. *Pollen*. Even if we survived, we'd be arrested. No one ever goes into the country any more but dope peddlers, looking for wild tobacco."

Agnes began to cry. Everyone was someone else. No one was who they were. The garbageman scrutinized her messages to the milkman. In the park, the pigeons all wore metal capsules taped to their legs. There were cowpies in the country, but no cows. Even at the supermarket you had to be careful. If you picked out items that seemed to form any sort of pattern—

"Are there any popsicles left?" Glen asked.

"No. There's nothing in the icebox but a leftover custard. We can't eat that; it has a map in it. Glen, what *are* we going to eat?"

"I don't know. How about . . . the baby? Well, don't look at me like that! You found him in the oven, didn't you? Suppose you had just lit the oven without looking in?"

"No! I will not give up my baby for a—a casserole!"

"All right! I was merely making a suggestion, that's all."

It was dark, now, throughout the lead-walled house, except in the kitchen. Out the quartz picture window, dusk was falling on the lawn, on the lifeless body of "Mr. Green." The television showed a panel discussion of eminent doctors, who wondered if eating were not the major cause of insanity.

Agnes went to answer the front door, while Glen went back to the kitchen.

"Excuse me," the priest said to Agnes. "I'm on a sick call. Someone was good enough to loan me his Diaper Service truck, and I'm afraid it has broken down. I wonder if I might use your phone?"

"Certainly, father. It's bugged, of course."

"Of course."

She stood aside to let him pass, and just then Glen shouted, "The baby! He's at the custard!"

Agnes and the priest dashed out to see. In the clean well-lighted kitchen, Glen stood gaping at the open refrigerator.

Somehow the baby had gotten into it, for now Agnes could see his diapered bottom and pink toes sticking out from a lower shelf.

"He's hungry," she said.

"Take another look," Glen grated.

Leaning closer, she saw the child had pulled the map from the custard. He was taking photos of it with a tiny baby-sized camera.

"Microfilm!" she gasped.

"Who are you?" Glen asked the priest.

"I'm—"

"Wait a minute. You don't look like a man of the cloth to me."

It was true, Agnes saw in the light. The breeze rustled the carbon-paper cassock, and she saw it was held together with paper clips. His stole was, on closer examination, a strip of purple stamps.

"If you're a priest," Glen continued, "why do I see on your Roman collar *the letterhead of my office?*"

"Very clever of you," said the man, drawing a pistol from his sleeve. "I'm sorry you saw through our little ruse. Sorry for you, that is."

"Our?" said Glen. He looked at the baby. "Hold on. Agnes, what kind of vehicle did he drive up in?"

"A diaper truck."

"Aha! I've been waiting a long time to catch up with you—Diaper Man! Your checkered career has gone on far too long."

"Ah, so you've recognized me and my dimple-kneed assistant, have you? But I'm afraid it won't do you much good. You see, we already have the photos, and there is a bullet here for each of you. Don't try to stop me!"

Watching them, the false priest scooped up the baby. "I think I had better kill the two of you in any case," he said. "You already know too much about my *modus operandi.*" The baby in his arms waved the camera gleefully and gooed its derision.

"All right," said Diaper Man. "Face the wall, please."

"Now!" Glen said. He leaped for the gun, while Agnes deftly kicked the camera from the baby's chubby fist.

The infant spy looked startled, but he acted fast, a tiny blur of motion. Scooping up two fistfuls of custard, he flung them in Glen's eyes. Gasping, Glen dropped the gun, as the infamous pair made their dash for freedom.

"You'll never take me alive!" snarled the false priest, vaulting into his truck.

"Let them go," said Glen. He tasted the custard. "I should have realized earlier the baby wasn't ticking, he was clicking. Let them go. They won't get far, and we've saved the map—for whatever it's worth."

"Are you all right, darling?"

"Fine. Mmm. This is pretty good, Agnes."

She blushed at the compliment. There was a muffled explosion, and in the distance, they could see flames shooting high in the air.

"Esso bombing the Shell station," said Glen.

The gas war had begun.

DOWN AMONG THE DEAD MEN

William Tenn

The estimable William Tenn, one of science fiction's brightest stars since his "Child's Play" and "Brooklyn Project" nearly thirty years ago, makes his second appearance in *Alpha* with a somber and potent account of a vast human recycling project. Though it has a grimly contemporary ring, "Down among the Dead Men," was actually written in the long-ago days of the Eisenhower presidency, before Vietnam, before "ecology" and "recycling" had become universal catchwords, before war had reached its present high level of sociotechnological ingenuity. It was a story well ahead of its time, which may explain the inexplicable neglect it has suffered until now.

I stood in front of the junkyard's outer gate and felt my stomach turn over slowly, grindingly, the way it had when I saw a whole terrestrial subfleet—close to 20,000 men—blown to bits in the Second Battle of Saturn more than eleven years ago. But then there had been shattered fragments of ships in my visiplate and imagined screams of men in my mind; there had been the expanding images of the Eoti's boxlike craft surging through the awful, drifting wreckage they had created, to account for the icy sweat that wound itself like a flat serpent around my forehead and my neck.

Now there was nothing but a large plain building, much like the hundreds of other factories in the busy suburbs of Old Chicago, a manufacturing establishment surrrounded by a locked gate and spacious proving grounds—the Junkyard. Yet the sweat on my skin was colder and the heave of my bowels more spastic than it had ever been in any of those countless, ruinous battles that had created this place.

All of which was very understandable, I told myself. What I was feeling was the great-grandmother hag of all fears, the most basic rejection and reluctance of which my flesh was capable. It was understandable, but that didn't help any. I still couldn't walk up to the sentry at the gate.

I'd been almost all right until I'd seen the huge square can against the fence, the can with the slight stink coming out of it and the big colorful sign on top:

> DON'T *WASTE* WASTE
> PLACE *ALL* WASTE HERE
> remember—
> WHATEVER IS WORN CAN BE SHORN
> WHATEVER IS MAIMED CAN BE RECLAIMED
> WHATEVER IS USED CAN BE RE-USED
> PLACE *ALL* WASTE HERE
> —*Conservation Police*

I'd seen those square, compartmented cans and those signs in every barracks, every hospital, every recreation center, between here and the asteroids. But seeing them, now, in this place, gave them a different meaning. I wondered if they had those other posters inside, the shorter ones. You know: "We need all our resources to defeat the enemy—and GARBAGE IS OUR BIGGEST NATURAL RESOURCE." Decorating the walls of this particular building with those posters would be downright ingenious.

Whatever is maimed can be reclaimed. . . . I flexed my

right arm inside my blue jumper sleeve. It felt like a part of me, always would feel like a part of me. And in a couple of years, assuming that I lived that long, the thin white scar that circled the elbow joint would be completely invisible. Sure. Whatever is maimed can be reclaimed. All except one thing. The most important thing.

And I felt less like going in than ever.

And then I saw this kid. The one from Arizona Base.

He was standing right in front of the sentry box, paralyzed just like me. In the center of his uniform cap was a brand-new, gold-shiny Y with a dot in the center: the insignia of a sling-shot commander. He hadn't been wearing it the day before at the briefing; that could only mean the commission had just come through. He looked real young and real scared.

I remembered him from the briefing session. He was the one whose hand had gone up timidly during the question period, the one who, when he was recognized, had half-risen, worked his mouth a couple of times and finally blurted out: "Excuse me, sir, but they don't—they don't smell at all bad, do they?"

There had been a cyclone of laughter, the yelping laughter of men who've felt themselves close to the torn edge of hysteria all afternoon and who are damn glad that someone has at last said something that they can make believe is funny.

And the white-haired briefing officer, who hadn't so much as smiled, waited for the hysteria to work itself out, before saying gravely: "No, they don't smell bad at all. Unless, that is, they don't bathe. The same as you gentlemen."

That shut us up. Even the kid, blushing his way back into his seat, set his jaw stiffly at the reminder. And it wasn't until twenty minutes later, when we'd been dismissed, that I began to feel the ache in my own face from the unrelaxed muscles there.

The same as you gentlemen. . . .

I shook myself hard and walked over to the kid. "Hello, Commander," I said. "Been here long?"

He managed a grin. "Over an hour, Commander. I caught the eight-fifteen out of Arizona Base. Most of the other fellows were still sleeping off last night's party. I'd gone to bed early: I wanted to give myself as much time to get the feel of this thing as I could. Only it doesn't seem to do much good."

"I know. Some things you can't get used to. Some things you're not *supposed* to get used to."

He looked at my chest. "I guess this isn't your first slingshot command?"

My first? More like my twenty-first, son! But then I remembered that everyone tells me I look young for my medals, and what the hell, the kid looked so pale under the chin— "No, not exactly my first. But I've never had a blob crew before. This is exactly as new to me as it is to you. Hey, listen, Commander: I'm having a hard time, too. What say we bust through that gate together? Then the worst'll be over."

The kid nodded violently. We linked arms and marched up to the sentry. We showed him our orders. He opened the gate and said: "Straight ahead. Any elevator on your left to the fifteenth floor."

So, still arm in arm, we walked into the main entrance of the large building, up a long flight of steps and under the sign that said in red and black:

HUMAN PROTOPLASM RECLAMATION CENTER
THIRD DISTRICT FINISHING PLANT

There were some old-looking but very erect men walking along the main lobby and a lot of uniformed, fairly pretty girls. I was pleased to note that most of the girls were pregnant. The first pleasing sight I had seen in almost a week.

We turned into an elevator and told the girl, "Fifteen." She punched a button and waited for it to fill up. She didn't seem to be pregnant. I wondered what was the matter with her.

I'd managed to get a good grip on my heaving imagination, when I got a look at the shoulder patches the other passengers were wearing. That almost did for me right there. It was a circular red patch, with the black letters TAF superimposed on a white *G*-4. TAF for Terrestrial Armed Forces, of course: the letters were the basic insignia of all rear-echelon outfits. But why didn't they use *G*-1, which represented Personnel? *G*-4 stood for the Supply Division. *Supply!*

You can always trust the TAF. Thousands of morale specialists in all kinds of ranks, working their educated heads off to keep up the spirits of the men in the fighting perimeters —but every damn time, when it comes down to scratch, the good old dependable TAF will pick the ugliest name, the one in the worst possible taste.

Oh, sure, I told myself, you can't fight a shattering, no-quarter interstellar war for twenty-five years and keep every pretty thought dewy-damp and intact. But not *Supply*, gentlemen. Not this place—not the Junkyard. Let's at least try to keep up appearances.

Then we began going up and the elevator girl began announcing floors and I had lots of other things to think about.

"Third floor—Corpse Reception and Classification," the operator sang out.

"Fifth floor—Preliminary Organ Processing."

"Seventh floor—Brain Reconstitution and Neural Alignment."

"Ninth floor—Cosmetics, Elementary Reflexes, and Muscular Control."

At this point, I forced myself to stop listening, the way you do when you're on a heavy cruiser, say, and the rear engine room gets flicked by a bolt from an Eoti scrambler. After you've been around a couple of times when it's happened, you learn to sort of close your ears and say to yourself, "I don't know anybody in that damned engine room, not anybody, and in a few minutes everything will be nice and quiet again." And in a few minutes it is. Only trouble is that then,

like as not, you'll be part of the detail that's ordered into the
steaming place to scrape the guck off the walls and get the jets
firing again.

Same way now. Just as soon as I had that girl's voice
blocked out, there we were on the fifteenth floor ("Final
Interviews and Shipping") and the kid and I had to get out.

He was real green. A definite sag around the knees, shoulders sloping forward like his clavicle had curled. Again I was
grateful to him. Nothing like having somebody to take care
of.

"Come on, Commander," I whispered. "Up and at 'em.
Look at it this way: for characters like us, this is practically a
family reunion."

It was the wrong thing to say. He looked at me as if I'd
punched his face. "No thanks to you for the reminder,
Mister," he said, "Even if we are in the same boat." Then he
walked stiffly up to the receptionist.

I could have bitten my tongue off. I hurried after him.
"I'm sorry, kid," I told him earnestly. "The words just slid
out of my big mouth. But don't get sore at me; hell, I had to
listen to myself say it too."

He stopped, thought about it, and nodded. Then he gave
me a smile. "O.K. No hard feelings. It's a rough war, isn't
it?"

I smiled back. "Rough? Why, if you're not careful, they
tell me, you can get killed in it."

The receptionist was a soft little blonde with two wedding
rings on one hand, and one wedding ring on the other. From
what I knew of current planetside customs, that meant she'd
been widowed twice.

She took our orders and read jauntily into her desk mike:
"Attention Final Conditioning. Attention Final Conditioning. Alert for immediate shipment the following serial numbers: 70623152, 70623109, 70623166, and 70623123. Also
70538966, 70538923, 70538980, and 70538937. Please
route through the correct numbered sections and check all
data on TAF AGO forms 362 as per TAF Regulation 7896, of

15 June, 2145. Advise when available for Final Interviews.''

I was impressed. Almost exactly the same procedure as when you go to Ordnance for a replacement set of stern exhaust tubes.

She looked up and favored us with a lovely smile. ''Your crews will be ready in a moment. Would you have a seat, gentlemen?''

We had a seat gentlemen.

After a while, she got up to take something out of a file cabinet set in the wall. As she came back to her desk, I noticed she was pregnant—only about the third or fourth month—and, naturally, I gave a little, satisfied nod. Out of the corner of my eye, I saw the kid make the same kind of nod. We looked at each other and chuckled. ''It's a rough, rough war,'' he said.

''Where are you from anyway?'' I asked. ''That doesn't sound like a Third District accent to me.''

''It isn't. I was born in Scandinavia—Eleventh Military District. My home town is Goteborg, Sweden. But after I got my—my promotion, naturally I didn't care to see the folks any more. So I requested a transfer to the Third, and from now on, until I hit a scrambler, this is where I'll be spending my furloughs and Earthside hospitalizations.''

I'd heard that a lot of the younger slingshotters felt that way. Personally, I never had a chance to find out how I'd feel about visiting the old folks at home. My father was knocked off in the suicidal attempt to retake Neptune 'way back when I was still in high school learning elementary combat, and my mother was Admiral Raguzzi's staff secretary when the flagship *Thermopylae* took a direct hit two years later in the famous desense of Ganymede. That was before the Breeding Regulations, of course, and women were still serving in administrative positions on the fighting perimeters.

On the other hand, I realized, at least two of my brothers might still be alive. But I'd made no attempt to contact them since getting my dotted Y. So I guessed I felt the same way as the kid—which was hardly surprising.

''Are you from Swdden?'' the blonde girl was asking.

"My second husband was born in Sweden. Maybe you knew him—Sven Nossen? I understand he had a lot of relatives in Oslo."

The kid screwed up his eyes as if he was thinking real hard. You know, running down a list of all the Swedes in Oslo. Finally, he shook his head. "No, can't say that I do. But I wasn't out of Goteborg very much before I was called up."

She clucked sympathetically at his provincialism. The baby-faced blonde of classic anecdote. A real dumb kid. And yet—there were lots of very clever, high-pressure cuties around the inner planets these days who had to content themselves with a one-fifth interest in some abysmal slob who boasted the barest modicum of maleness. Or a certificate from the local sperm bank. Blondie here was on her third full husband.

Maybe, I thought, if I were looking for a wife myself, this is what I'd pick to take the stink of scrambler rays out of my nose and the yammer-yammer-yammer of Irvingles out of my ears. Maybe I'd want somebody nice and simple to come home to from one of those complicated skirmishes with the Eoti where you spend most of your conscious thoughts trying to figure out just what battle rhythm the filthy insects are using this time. Maybe, if I were going to get married, I'd find a pretty fluffhead like this more generally desirable than—oh, well. Maybe. Considered as a problem in psychology it was interesting.

I noticed she was talking to me. "You've never had a crew of this type before either, have you, Commander?"

"Zombies, you mean? No, not yet, I'm happy to say."

She made a disapproving pout with her mouth. It was fully as cute as her approving pouts. "We do not like that word."

"All right, blobs then."

"We don't like bl—that word either. You are talking about human beings like yourself, Commander. Very much like yourself."

I began to get sore feet, just the way the kid had out in the hall. Then I realized she didn't mean anything by it. She didn't know. What the hell—it wasn't on our orders. I relaxed. "You tell me. What do you call them here?"

The blonde sat up stiffly. "*We* refer to them as soldier surrogates. The epithet 'zombie' was used to describe the obsolete Model 21 which went out of production over five years ago. You will be supplied with individuals based on Models 705 and 706 which are practically perfect. In fact, in some respects——"

"No bluish skin? No slow-motion sleepwalking?"

She shook her head violently. Her eyes were lit up. Evidently she'd digested all the promotional literature. Not such a fluffhead, after all; no great mind, but her husbands had evidently had someone to talk to in between times. She rattled on enthusiastically: "The cyanosis was the result of bad blood oxygenation; blood was our second most difficult tissue reconstruction problem. The nervous system was the hardest. Even though the blood cells are usually in the poorest shape of all by the time the bodies arrive, we can now turn out a very serviceable rebuilt heart. But, let there be the teensiest battle damage to the brain or spine, and you have to start right from scratch. And then the troubles in reconstitution! My cousin Lorna works in Neural Alignment, and she tells me all you need to make is just one wrong connection—you know how it is, Commander, at the end of the day your eyes are tired and you're kind of watching the clock—just one wrong connection, and the reflexes in the finished individual turn out to be so bad that they just have to send him down to the third floor and begin all over again. But you don't have to worry about that. Since Model 663, we've been using the two-team inspection system in Neural Alignment. And the 700 series—oh, they've just been *wonderful.*"

"That good, eh? Better than the old-fashioned mother's son type?"

"Well-l-l," she considered. "You'd really be amazed, Commander, if you could see the very latest performance charts. Of course, there is always that big deficiency, the one activity we've never been able to——"

"One thing *I* can't understand," the kid broke in, "why do they have to use corpses! A body's lived its life, fought its war—why not leave it alone? I know the Eoti can outbreed us merely by increasing the number of queens in their flagships; I know that manpower is the biggest single TAF problem— but we've been synthesizing protoplasm for a long, long time now. Why not synthesize the whole damn body, from toenails to frontal lobe, and turn out real honest-to-God androids that don't wallop you with the stink of death when you meet them?''

The little blonde got mad. ''Our product *does not stink!* Cosmetics can now guarantee that the new models have even less of a body odor than you, young man! And we do not reactivate or revitalize corpses, I'll have you know; what we do is *reclaim* human protoplasm, we re-use wornout and damaged human cellular material in the area where the greatest shortages currently occur, military personnel. You wouldn't talk about corpses, I assure you, if you saw the condition that some of those bodies are in when they arrive. Why, sometimes in a whole baling package—a baling package contains twenty casualties—we don't find enough to make one good whole kidney. Then we have to take a little intestinal tissue here and a bit of spleen there, alter them, unite them carefully, activa——''

''That's what I mean. If you go to all that trouble, why not start with real raw material?''

''Like what, for example?''

The kid gestured with his black-gloved hands. ''Basic elements like carbon, hydrogen, oxygen, and so on. It would make the whole process a lot cleaner.''

''Basic elements have to come from somewhere,'' I pointed out gently. ''You might take your hydrogen and oxygen from air and water. But where would you get your carbon from?''

''From the same place where the other synthetics manufacturers get it—coal, oil, cellulose.''

The receptionist sat back and relaxed. ''Those are organic substances,'' she reminded him. ''If you're going to use raw material that was once alive, why not use the kind that comes as close as possible to the end-product you have in mind? It's simple industrial economics, Commander, believe me. The best and cheapest raw material for the manufacture of soldier surrogates is soldier bodies.''

"Sure," the kid said. "Makes sense. There's no other use for dead, old, beaten-up soldier bodies. Better'n shoving them in the ground where they'd be just waste, pure waste.''

Our little blonde chum started to smile in agreement, then shot him an intense look and changed her mind. She looked very uncertain all of a sudden. When the communicator on her desk buzzed, she bent over it eagerly.

I watched her with approval. Definitely no fluffhead. Just feminine. I sighed. You see, I figure out lots of civilian things the wrong way, but only with women is my wrongness an all-the-time proposition. Proving again that a hell of a lot of peculiar things turn out to have happened for the best.

"Commander," she was saying to the kid. "Would you go to Room 1591? Your crew will be there in a moment.'' She turned to me. "And Room 1524 for you, Commander, if you please.''

The kid nodded and walked off, very stiff and erect. I waited until the door had closed behind him, then I leaned over the receptionist. "Wish they'd change the Breeding Regulations again," I told her. "You'd make a damn fine rear-echelon orientation officer. Got more of the feel of the Junkyard from you than in ten briefing sessions.''

She examined my face anxiously. "I hope you mean that, Commander. You see, we're all very deeply involved in this project. We're extremely proud of the progress the Third District Finishing Plant has made. We talk about the new developments all the time, everywhere—even in the cafeteria. It didn't occur to me until too late that you gentlemen might——" she blushed deep, rich red, the way only a blonde can blush "—might take what I said personally. I'm sorry if I——''

"Nothing to be sorry about," I assured her. "All you did was talk what they call shop. Like when I was in the hospital last month and heard two surgeons discussing how to repair a man's arm and making it sound as if they were going to nail a new arm on an expensive chair. Real interesting, and I learned a lot.''

I left her looking grateful, which is absolutely the only way to leave a woman, and barged on to Room 1524.

It was evidently used as a classroom when reconverted human junk wasn't being picked up. A bunch of chairs, a long blackboard, a couple of charts. One of the charts was on the Eoti, the basic information list, that contains all the limited information we have been able to assemble on the bugs in the bloody quarter-century since they came busting in past Pluto to take over the solar system. It hadn't been changed much since the one I had to memorize in high school: the only difference was a slightly longer section on intelligence and motivation. Just theory, of course, but more carefully thought-out theory than the stuff I'd learned. The big brains had now concluded that the reason all attempts at communicating with them had failed was not because they were a conquest-crazy species, but because they suffered from the same extreme xenophobia as their smaller, less intelligent communal insect cousins here on Earth. That is, an ant wanders up to a strange anthill—*zok!* No discussion, he's chopped down at the entrance. And the sentry ants react even faster if it's a creature of another genus. So despite the Eoti science, which in too many respects was more advanced than ours, they were psychologically incapable of the kind of mental projection, or empathy, necessary if one is to realize that a completely alien-looking individual has intelligence, feelings—and rights!—to substantially the same extent as oneself.

Well, it might be so. Meanwhile, we were locked in a murderous stalemate with them on a perimeter of never-ending battle that sometimes expanded as far as Saturn and occasionally contracted as close as Jupiter. Barring the invention of a new weapon of such unimaginable power that we could wreck their fleet before they could duplicate the weapon, as they'd been managing to up to now, our only hope was to discover somehow the stellar system from which they came, somehow build ourselves not one starship but a fleet of them—and somehow wreck their home base or throw enough of a scare into it so that they'd pull back their expedition for defensive purposes. A lot of somehows.

But if we wanted to maintain our present position until the *somehows* started to roll, our birth announcements had to take longer to read than the casualty lists. For the last decade, this hadn't been so, despite the more and more stringent Breeding Regulations which were steadily pulverizing every one of our moral codes and sociological advances. Then there was the day that someone in the Conservation Police noticed that almost half our ships of the line had been fabricated from the metallic junk of previous battles. Where was the personnel that had manned those salvage derelicts, he wondered. . . .

And thus what Blondie outside and her co-workers were pleased to call soldier surrogates.

I'd been a computer's mate, second class, on the old *Jenghiz Khan* when the first batch had come aboard as battle replacements. Let me tell you, friends, we had real good reason for calling them zombies! Most of them were as blue as the uniforms they wore, their breathing was so noisy it made you think of asthmatics with built-in public address systems, their eyes shone with all the intelligence of petroleum jelly—*and the way they walked!*

My friend, Johnny Cruro, the first man to get knocked off in the Great Breakthrough of 2143, used to say that they were trying to pick their way down a steep hill at the bottom of which was a large open family-size grave. Body held strained and tense. Legs and arms moving slow, slow, until suddenly they'd finish with a jerk. Creepy as hell.

They weren't good for anything but the drabbest fatigue detail. And even then—if you told them to polish a gun mounting, you had to remember to come back in an hour and turn them off or they might scrub their way clear through into empty space. Of course, they weren't all that bad. Johnny Cruro used to say that he'd met one or two who could achieve imbecility when they were feeling right.

Combat was what finished them as far as the TAF was concerned. Not that they broke under battle conditions—just the reverse. The old ship would be rocking and screaming as it changed course every few seconds; every Irvingle, scrambler, and nucleonic howitzer along the firing corridor turning bright golden yellow from the heat it was generating; a hoarse yelping voice from the bulkhead loudspeakers pouring out orders faster than human muscles could move, the shock troops—their faces ugly with urgency—running crazily from one emergency station to another; everyone around you working like a blur and cursing and wondering out loud why the Eoti were taking so long to tag a target as big and as slow as the *Khan* . . . and suddenly you'd see a zombie clutching a broom in his rubbery hands and sweeping the deck in the slack-jawed, moronic, and horribly earnest way they had. . . .

I remember whole gun crews going amuck and slamming into the zombies with long crowbars and metal-gloved fists; once, even an officer, sprinting back to the control room, stopped, flipped out his sidearm and pumped bolt after bolt of jagged thunder at a blue-skin who'd been peacefully wiping a porthole while the bow of the ship was being burned away. And as the zombie sagged uncomprehendingly and uncomplainingly to the floor plates, the young officer stood over him and chanted soothingly, the way you do to a boisterous dog: "Down, boy, down, *down, down, damn you, down!*"

That was the reason the zombies were eventually pulled back, not their own efficiency: the incidence of battle psycho around them just shot up too high. Maybe if it hadn't been for that, we'd have got used to everything else in combat. But the zombies belonged to something beyond mere war.

They were so terribly, terribly unstirred by the prospect of dying again!

Well, everyone said the new-model zombies were a big improvement. They'd better be. A slingshot might be one thin notch below an outright suicide patrol, but you need peak performance from every man aboard if it's going to complete its crazy mission, let alone get back. And it's an awful small ship and the men have to kind of get along with each other in very close quarters. . . .

I heard feet, several pairs of them, rapping along the corridor. They stopped outside the door.

They waited. I waited. My skin began to prickle. And then I heard that uncertain shuffling sound. They were nervous about meeting me!

I walked over to the window and stared down at the drill field where old veterans whose minds and bodies were too worn out to be repaired taught fatigue-uniformed zombies how to use their newly conditioned reflexes in close-order drill. It made me remember a high-school athletic field years and years ago. The ancient barking commands drifted tinily up to me: *"Hup* two, three, four." Only they weren't using *hup!*, but a newer, different word I couldn't quite catch.

And then, when the hands I'd clasped behind me had almost squeezed their blood back into my wrists, I heard the door open and four pairs of feet clatter into the room. The door closed and the four pairs of feet clicked to attention.

I turned around.

They were saluting me. Well, what the hell, I told myself, they were supposed to be saluting me, I was their commanding officer. I returned the salute, and four arms whipped down smartly.

I said, "At ease." They snapped their legs apart, arms behind them. I thought about it. I said, "Rest." They relaxed their bodies slightly. I thought about it again. I said, "Hell, men, sit down and let's meet each other."

They sprawled into chairs and I hitched myself up on the instructor's desk. We stared back and forth. Their faces were rigid, watchful: they weren't giving anything away.

I wondered what my face looked like. In spite of all the orientation lectures, in spite of all the preparation, I must admit that my first glimpse of them had hit me hard. They were glowing with health, normality, and hard purpose. But that wasn't it.

That wasn't it at all.

What was making me want to run out of the door, out of the building, was something I'd been schooling myself to expect since that last briefing session in Arizona Base. Four dead men were staring at me. Four very famous dead men.

The big man, lounging all over his chair, was Roger Grey, who had been killed over a year ago when he rammed his tiny scout ship up the forward jets of an Eoti flagship. The flagship had been split neatly in two. Almost every medal imaginable and the Solar Corona. Grey was to be my copilot.

The thin alert man with the tight shock of black hair was Wang Hsi. He had been killed covering the retreat to the asteroids after the Great Breakthrough of 2143. According to the fantastic story the observers told, his ship had still been firing after it had been scrambled fully three times. Almost every medal imaginable and the Solar Corona. Wang was to be my engineer.

The darkish little fellow was Yussuf Lamehd. He'd been killed in a very minor skirmish off Titan, but when he died he was the most decorated man in the entire TAF. A *double* Solar Corona. Lamehd was to be my gunner.

The heavy one was Stanley Weinstein, the only prisoner of war ever to escape from the Eoti. There wasn't much left of him by the time he arrived on Mars, but the ship he came in was the first enemy craft that humanity could study intact. There was no Solar Corona in his day for him to receive even posthumously, but they're still naming military academies after that man. Weinstein was to be my astrogator.

Then I shook myself back to reality. These weren't the original heroes, probably didn't have even a particle of Roger Grey's blood or Wang Hsi's flesh upon their reconstructed bones. They were just excellent and very faithful copies, made to minute physical specifications that had been in the TAF medical files since Wang had been a cadet and Grey a mere recruit.

There were anywhere from a hundred to a thousand Yussuf Lamehds and Stanley Weinsteins, I had to remind myself—and they had all come off an assembly line a few floors down. "Only the brave deserve the future," was the Junkyard's motto, and it was currently trying to assure that future for them by duplicating in quantity any TAF man who went out with especial heroism. As I happened to know, there were one or two other categories who could expect similar honors, but the basic reasons behind the hero-models had little to do with morale.

First, there was that little gimmick of industrial efficiency again. If you're using mass-production methods, and the Junkyard was doing just that, it's plain common sense to turn out a few standardized models, rather than have everyone different—like the stuff an individual creative craftsman might come up with. Well, if you're using standardized models, why not use those that have positive and relatively pleasant associations bound up with their appearance rather than anonymous characters from the designers' drawing boards?

The second reason was almost more important and harder to define. According to the briefing officer, yesterday, there was a peculiar feeling—a superstitious feeling, you might almost say—that if you copied a hero's features, musculature, metabolism, and even his cortex wrinkles carefully enough, well, you might build yourself another hero. Of course, the original personality would never reappear—that had been produced by long years of a specific environment and dozens of other very slippery factors—but it was distinctly possible, the biotechs felt, that a modicum of clever courage resided in the body structure alone. . . .

Well, at least these zombies didn't *look* like zombies!

On an impulse, I plucked the rolled sheaf of papers containing our travel orders out of my pocket, pretended to study it and let it slip suddenly through my fingers. As the outspread sheaf spiraled to the floor in front of me, Roger Grey reached out and caught it. He handed it back to me with the same kind of easy yet snappy grace. I took it, feeling good. It was the way he moved. I like to see a copilot move that way.

"Thanks," I said.

He just nodded.

I studied Yussuf Lamehd next. Yes, he had it too. Whatever it is that makes a first-class gunner, he had it. It's almost impossible to describe, but you walk into a bar in some rest area on Eros, say, and out of the five slingshotters hunched over the blow-top table, you know right off which is the gunner. It's a sort of carefully bottled nervousness or a dead calm with a hair-trigger attachment. Whatever it is, it's what you need sitting over a firing button when you've completed the dodge, curve, and twist that's a slingshot's attacking dash and you're barely within range of the target, already beginning your dodge, curve, and twist back to safety. Lamehd had it so strong that I'd have put money on him against any other gunner in the TAF I'd ever seen in action.

Astrogators and engineers are different. You've just got to see them work under pressure before you can rate them. But, even so, I liked the calm and confident manner with which Wang Hsi and Weinstein sat under my examination. And I liked them.

Right there I felt a hundred pounds slide off my chest. I felt relaxed for the first time in days. I really liked my crew, zombies or no. We'd make it.

I decided to tell them. "Men," I said, "I think we'll really get along. I think we've got the makings of a sweet, smooth slingshot. You'll find me——"

And I stopped. That cold, slightly mocking look in their eyes. The way they had glanced at each other when I told them I thought we'd get along, glanced at each other and blown slightly through distended nostrils. I realized that none of them had said anything since they'd come in: they'd just been watching me, and their eyes weren't exactly warm.

I stopped and let myself take a long, deep breath. For the first time, it was occurring to me that I'd been worrying about just one end of the problem, and maybe the least important end. I'd been worrying about how I'd react to them and how much I'd be able to accept them as shipmates. They were zombies, after all. It had never occurred to me to wonder how they'd feel about me.

And there was evidently something very wrong in how they felt about me.

"What is it, men?" I asked. They all looked at me inquiringly. "What's on your minds?"

They kept looking at me. Weinstein pursed his lips and tilted his chair back and forth. It creaked. Nobody said anything.

I got off the desk and walked up and down in front of the classroom. They kept following me with their eyes.

"Grey," I said. "You look as if you've got a great big knot inside you. Want to tell me about it?"

"No, Commander," he said deliberately. "I don't want to tell you about it."

I grimaced. "If anyone wants to say anything—anything at all—it'll be off the record and completely off the record. Also for the moment we'll forget about such matters as rank and TAF regulations." I waited. "Wang? Lamehd? How about you, Weinstein?" They stared at me quietly. Weinstein's chair creaked back and forth.

It had me baffled. What kind of gripe could they have against me? They'd never met me before. But I knew one thing: I wasn't going to haul a crew nursing a subsurface grudge as unanimous as this aboard a slingshot. I wasn't going to chop space with those eyes at my back. It would be more efficient for me to shove my head against an Irvingle lens and push the button.

"Listen," I told them. "I meant what I said about forgetting rank and TAF regulations. I want to run a happy ship, and I have to know what's up. We'll be living, the five of us, in the tightest, most cramped conditions the mind of man has yet been able to devise; we'll be operating a tiny ship whose only purpose is to dodge at tremendous speed through the fire-power and screening devices of the larger enemy craft and deliver a single crippling blast from a single oversize Irvingle. We've got to get along whether we like each other or not. If we don't get along, if there's any unspoken hostility getting in our way, the ship won't operate at maximum efficiency. And that way, we're through before we____"

"Commander," Weinstein said suddenly, his chair coming down upon the floor with a solid whack, "I'd like to ask you a question."

"Sure," I said and let out a gust of relief that was the size of a small hurricane. "Ask me anything."

"When you think about us, Commander, or when you talk about us, which word do you use?"

I looked at him and shook my head. "Eh?"

"When you talk about us, Commander, or when you think about us, do you call us zombies? Or do you call us blobs? That's what I'd like to know, Commander."

He'd spoken in such a polite even tone that I was a long time in getting the full significance of it.

"Personally," said Roger Grey in a voice that was just a little less polite, a little less even, "personally, I think the Commander is the kind who refers to us as canned meat. Right, Commander?"

Yussuf Lamehd folded his arms across his chest and seemed to consider the issue very thoughtfully. "I think you're right, Rog. He's the canned-meat type. Definitely the canned-meat type."

"No," said Wang Hsi. "He doesn't use that kind of language. Zombies, yes; canned meat, no. You can observe from the way he talks that he wouldn't ever get mad enough to tell us to get back in the can. And I don't think he'd call us blobs very often. He's the kind of guy who'd buttonhole another slingshot commander and tell him, 'Man, have I got the sweetest zombie crew you ever saw!' That's the way I figure him. Zombies."

And then they were sitting quietly staring at me again. And it wasn't mockery in their eyes. It was hatred.

I went back to the desk and sat down. The room was very still. From the yard, fifteen floors down, the marching commands drifted up. Where did they latch on to this zombie-blob-canned meat stuff? They were none of them more than six months old; none of them had been outside the precincts of the Junkyard yet. Their conditioning, while mechanical and intensive, was supposed to be absolutely foolproof, producing hard, resilient, and entirely human minds, highly skilled in their various specialties and as far from any kind of imbalance as the latest psychiatric knowledge could push them. I knew they wouldn't have got it in their conditioning. Then *where*—

And then I heard it clearly for a moment. The word. The word that was being used down in the drill field instead of *Hup!* That strange, new word I hadn't been able to make out. Whoever was calling the cadence downstairs wasn't saying, "*Hup,* two, three, four."

He was saying, "*Blob,* two, three, four. *Blob,* two, three four."

Wasn't that just like the TAF? I asked myself. For that matter, like any army anywhere anytime? Expending fortunes and the best minds producing a highly necessary product to exact specifications, and then, on the very first level of military use, doing something that might invalidate it completely. I was certain that the same officials who had been responsible for the attitude of the receptionist outside could have had nothing to do with the old, superannuated TAF drill-hacks putting their squads through their paces down below. I could imagine those narrow, nasty minds, as jealously proud of their prejudices as of their limited and painfully acquired military knowledge, giving these youngsters before me their first taste of barracks life, their first glimpse of the "outside." It was so stupid!

But was it? There was another way of looking at it, beyond the fact that only soldiers too old physically and too ossified mentally for any other duty could be spared for this place. And that was the simple pragmatism of army thinking. The fighting perimeters were places of abiding horror and agony, the forward combat zones in which slingshots operated were even worse. If men or material were going to collapse out there, it could be very costly. Let the collapses occur as close to the rear echelons as possible.

Maybe it made sense, I thought. Maybe it was logical to make live men out of dead men's flesh (God knows humanity had reached the point where we had to have reinforcements from *somewhere!*) at enormous expense and with the kind of care usually associated with things like cotton wool and the most delicate watchmakers' tools; and then to turn around and subject them to the coarsest, ugliest environment possible, an environment that perverted their carefully instilled loyalty into hatred and their finely balanced psychological adjustment into neurotic sensitivity.

I didn't know if it was basically smart or dumb, or even if the problem had ever been really weighed as such by the upper, policy-making brass. All I could see was my own problem, and it looked awfully big to me. I thought of my attitude toward these men before getting them, and I felt pretty sick. But the memory gave me an idea.

"Hey, tell me something," I suggested. "What would you call me?"

They looked puzzled.

"You want to know what I call you," I explained. "Tell me first what you call people like me, people who are—who are *born*. You must have your own epithets."

Lamehd grinned so that his teeth showed a bright, mirthless white against his dark skin. "Realos," he said. "We call you people realos. Sometimes, realo trulos."

Then the rest spoke up. There were other names, lots of other names. They wanted me to hear them all. They interrupted each other; they spat the words out as if they were so many missiles; they glared at my face, as they spat them out, to see how much impact they had. Some of the nicknames were funny, some of them were rather nasty. I was particularly charmed by utie and wombat.

"All right," I said after a while. "Feel better?"

They were all breathing hard, but they felt better. I could tell it, and they knew it. The air in the room felt softer now.

"First off," I said, "I want you to notice that you are all big boys and as such, can take care of yourselves. From here on out, if we walk into a bar or a rec camp together and someone of approximately your rank says something that sounds like zombie to your acute ears, you are at liberty to walk up to him and start taking him apart—if you can. If he's of approximately my rank, in all probability, *I'll* do the taking apart, simply because I'm a very sensitive commander and don't like having my men deprecated. And any time you feel that I'm not treating you as human beings, one hundred percent, full solar citizenship and all that, I give you permission to come up to me and say, 'Now look *here,* you dirty utie, sir—' "

The four of them grinned. Warm grins. Then the grins faded away, very slowly, and the eyes grew cold again. They were looking at a man who was, after all, an outsider. I cursed.

"It's not as simple as that, Commander," Wang Hsi said, "unfortunately. You can call us hundred-percent human beings, but we're not. And anyone who wants to call us blobs or canned meat has a certain amount of right. Because we're not as good as—as you mother's sons, and we know it. And we'll never be that good. Never."

"I don't know about that," I blustered. "Why, some of your performance charts—"

"Performance charts, Commander," Wang Hsi said softly, "do not a human being make."

On his right, Weinstein gave a nod, thought a bit, and added: "Nor groups of men a race."

I knew where we were going now. And I wanted to smash my way out of that room, down the elevator, and out of the building before anybody said another word. *This is it,* I told myself: *here we are, boy, here we are.* I found myself squirming from corner to corner of the desk; I gave up, got off it, and began walking again.

Wang Hsi wouldn't let go. I should have known he wouldn't. "Soldier surrogates," he went on, squinting as if he were taking a close look at the phrase for the first time. "Soldier surrogates, but not soldiers. We're not soldiers, because soldiers are men. And we, Commander, are not men."

There was silence for a moment, then a tremendous blast of sound boiled out of my mouth. "And what makes you think that you're *not* men?"

Wang Hsi was looking at me with astonishment, but his reply was still soft and calm. "You know why. You've seen our specifications, Commander. We're not men, real men, because we can't reproduce ourselves."

I forced myself to sit down again and carefully placed my shaking hands over my knees.

"We're as sterile," I heard Yussuf Lamehd say, "as boiling water."

"There have been lots of men," I began, "who have been—"

"This isn't a matter of lots of men," Weinstein broke in. "This is a matter of *all*—all of *us.*"

"Blobs thou art," Wang Hsi murmured. "And to blobs returneth. They might have given at least a few of us a chance. The kids mightn't have turned out so bad."

Roger Grey slammed his huge hand down on the arm of his chair. "That's just the point, Wang," he said savagely. "The kids might have turned out good—too good. Our kids might have turned out to be better than their kids—and where would that leave the proud and cocky, the goddam name-calling, the realo trulo human race?"

I sat staring at them once more, but now I was seeing a different picture. I wasn't seeing conveyor belts moving along slowly covered with human tissues and organs on which earnest biotechs performed their individual tasks. I wasn't seeing a room filled with dozens of adult male bodies suspended in nutrient solution, each body connected to a conditioning machine which day and night clacked out whatever minimum information was necessary for the body to take the place of a man in the bloodiest part of the fighting perimeter.

This time, I saw a barracks filled with heroes, many of them in duplicate and triplicate. And they were sitting around griping, as men will in any barracks on any planet, whether they look like heroes or no. But their gripes concerned humiliations deeper than any soldiers had hitherto known—humiliations as basic as the fabric of human personality.

"You believe, then," and despite the sweat on my face, my voice was gentle, "that the reproductive power was deliberately withheld?"

Weinstein scowled. "Now, Commander. Please. No bedtime stories."

"Doesn't it occur to you at all that the whole problem of
our species at the moment is reproduction? Believe me, men,
that's all you hear about on the outside. Grammar-school
debating teams kick current reproductive issues back and
forth in the district medal competitions; every month scholars
in archaeology and the botany of fungi come out with books
about it from their own special angle. Everyone knows that if
we don't lick the reproduction problem, the Eoti are going to
lick us. Do you seriously think under such circumstances, the
reproductive powers of *anyone* would be intentionally
impaired?"

"What do a few male blobs matter, more or less?" Grey
demanded. "According to the latest news bulletins, sperm-
bank deposits are at their highest point in five years. They
don't need us."

"Commander," Wang Hsi pointed his triangular chin at
me. "Let me ask you a few questions in your turn. Do you
honestly expect us to believe that a science capable of reconstructing a living, highly effective human body with a complex digestive system and a most delicate nervous system, all
this out of dead and decaying bits of protoplasm, is incapable
of reconstructing the germ plasm in one single solitary
case?"

"You have to believe it," I told him. "Because it's so."

Wang sat back, and so did the other three. They stopped
looking at me.

"Haven't you ever heard it said," I pleaded with them,
"that the germ plasm is more essentially the individual than
any other part of him? That some whimsical biologists take
the attitude that our human bodies and all bodies are merely
vehicles, or hosts, by means of which our germ plasm repro-
duces itself? It's the most complex biotechnical riddle we
have! Believe me, men," I added passionately, "when I say
that biology has not yet solved the germ-plasm problem, I'm
telling the truth. I know."

That got them.

"Look," I said. "We have one thing in common with the Eoti whom we're fighting. Insects and warm-blooded animals differ prodigiously. But only among the community-building insects and the community-building men are there individuals who, while taking no part personally in the reproductive chain, are of fundamental importance to their species. For example, you might have a female nursery-school teacher who is barren but who is of unquestionable value in shaping the personalities and even physiques of children in her care."

"Fourth Orientation Lecture for Soldier Surrogates," Weinstein said in a dry voice. "He got it right out of the book."

"I've been wounded," I said. "I've been seriously wounded fifteen times." I stood before them and began rolling up my right sleeve. It was soaked with my perspiration.

"We can tell you've been wounded, Commander," Lamehd pointed out uncertainly. "We can tell from your medals. You don't have to—"

"And every time I was wounded, they repaired me good as new. Better. Look at that arm." I flexed it for them. "Before it was burned off in a small razzle six years ago, I could never build up a muscle that big. It's a better arm they built on the stump, and, believe me, my reflexes never had it so good."

"What did you mean," Wang Hsi started to ask me, "when you said before—"

"Fifteen times I was wounded," my voice drowned him out, "and fourteen times, the wound was repaired. The fifteenth time—*The fifteenth time*—well, the fifteenth time it wasn't a wound they could repair. They couldn't help me one little bit the fifteenth time."

Roger Grey opened his mouth.

"Fortunately," I whispered, "it wasn't a wound that showed."

Weinstein started to ask me something, decided against it and sat back. But I told him what he wanted to know.

"A nucleonic howitzer. The way it was figured later, it

had been a defective shell. Bad enough to kill half the men on our second-class cruiser. I wasn't killed, but I was in range of the back-blast."

"That back-blast," Lamehd was figuring it out quickly in his mind. "That back-blast will sterilize anybody for two hundred feet. Unless you're wearing—"

"And I wasn't." I had stopped sweating. It was over. My crazy little precious secret was out. I took a deep breath. "So you see—well, anyway, I *know* they haven't solved that problem yet."

Roger Grey stood up and said, "Hey." He held out his hand. I shook it. It felt like any normal guy's hand. Stronger maybe.

"Slingshot personnel," I went on, "are all volunteers. Except for two categories: the commanders and soldier surrogates."

"Figuring, I guess," Weinstein asked, "that the human race can spare them most easily?"

"Right," I said. "Figuring that the human race can spare them most easily." He nodded.

"Well, I'll be damned," Yussuf Lamehd laughed as he got up and shook my hand, too. "Welcome to our city."

"Thanks," I said. *"Son."*

He seemed puzzled at the emphasis.

"That's the rest of it," I explained. "Never got married and was too busy getting drunk and tearing up the pavement on my leaves to visit a sperm bank."

"Oho," Weinstein said, and gestured at the walls with a thick thumb. "So this is it."

"That's right: this is it. The Family. The only one I'll ever have. I've got almost enough of these—" I tapped my medals "—to rate replacement. As a slingshot commander, I'm sure of it."

"All you don't know yet," Lamehd pointed out, "is how high a percentage of replacement will be apportioned to your memory. That depends on how many more of these chest

decorations you collect before you become an—ah, should I
say *raw material?*"

"Yeah," I said, feeling crazily light and easy and relaxed.
I'd got it all out and I didn't feel whipped any more by a
billion years of reproduction and evolution. And I'd been
going to do a morale job on them! *"Say* raw material,
Lamehd."

"Well, boys," he went on, "it seems to me we want the
commander to get a lot more fruit salad. He's a nice guy and
there should be more of him in the club."

They were all standing around me now, Weinstein,
Lamehd, Grey, Wang Hsi. They looked real friendly and real
capable. I began to feel we were going to have one of the best
slingshots in—What did I mean *one* of the best? *The* best,
mister, *the* best.

"Okay," said Grey. "Wherever and whenever you want
to, you start leading us—*Pop.*"

WITH THESE HANDS

C. M. Kornbluth

The late Cyril Kornbluth—taken from us when he was 34, a decade and a half ago—was as serious-minded a person as ever wrote science fiction. Saturnine, intense, looking older than his years, he seemed even in his most boisterous moments to be mulling some profound analysis of the human condition, to be at the edge of some dark and inexorable revelation. His short stories—always lively, glittering of surface, often comic—reflected Kornbluth's preoccupation with matters weightier than those usually dealt with in the science fiction of his day. As, for example, the story at hand—a sleek, moving examination of the relationship of the artist to his art.

I

Halvorsen waited in the Chancery office while Monsignor Reedy disposed of three persons who had preceded him. He was a little dizzy with hunger and noticed only vaguely that the prelate's secretary was beckoning to him. He started to his feet when the secretary pointedly opened the door to Monsignor Reedy's inner office and stood waiting beside it.

The artist crossed the floor, forgetting that he had leaned

his portfolio against his chair, remembered at the door and went back for it, flushing. The secretary looked patient.

"Thanks," Halvorsen murmured to him as the door closed.

There was something wrong with the prelate's manner.

"I've brought the designs for the Stations, Padre," he said, opening the portfolio on the desk.

"Bad news, Roald," said the monsignor. "I know how you've been looking forward to the commission—"

"Somebody else get it?" asked the artist faintly, leaning against the desk. "I thought His Eminence definitely decided I had the—"

"It's not that," said the monsignor. "But the Sacred Congregation of Rites this week made a pronouncement on images of devotion. Stereopantograph is to be licit within a diocese at the discretion of the bishop. And His Eminence—"

"S.P.G.—slimy imitations," protested Halvorsen. "Real as a plastic eye. No texture. No guts. *You* know that, Padre!" he said accusingly.

"I'm sorry, Roald," said the monsignor. "Your work is better than we'll get from a stereopantograph—to my eyes, at least. But there are other considerations."

"Money!" spat the artist.

"Yes, money," the prelate admitted. "His Eminence wants to see the St. Xavier U. building program through before he dies. Is that wrong, Roald? And there are our schools, our charities, our Venus mission. S.P.G. will mean a considerable saving on procurement and maintenance of devotional images. Even if I could, I would not disagree with His Eminence on adopting it as a matter of diocesan policy."

The prelate's eyes fell on the detailed drawings of the Stations of the Cross and lingered.

"Your St. Veronica," he said abstractedly. "Very fine. It suggests one of Caravaggio's careworn saints to me. I would have liked to see her in the bronze."

"So would I," said Halvorsen hoarsely. "Keep the drawings, Padre.'' He started for the door.

"But I can't—"

The artist walked past the secretary blindly and out of the Chancery into Fifth Avenue's spring sunlight. He hoped Monsignor Reedy was enjoying the drawings and was ashamed of himself and sorry for Halvorsen. And he was glad he didn't have to carry the heavy portfolio any more. Everything was heavy lately—chisels, hammer, wooden palette. Maybe the padre would send him something and pretend it was for expenses or an advance, as he had in the past.

Halvorsen's feet carried him up the Avenue. No, there wouldn't be any advances any more. The last steady trickle of income had just been dried up, by an announcement in *Osservatore Romano*. Religious conservatism had carried the church as far as it would go in its ancient role of art patron.

When all Europe was writing on the wonderful new vellum, the church stuck to good old papyrus. When all Europe was writing on the wonderful new paper, the church stuck to good old vellum. When all architects and municipal monument committees and portrait bust clients were patronizing the stereopantograph, the church stuck to good old expensive sculpture. But not any more.

He was passing an S.P.G. salon now, where one of his Tuesday-night pupils worked: one of the few men in the classes. Mostly they consisted of lazy, moody, irritable girls. Halvorsen, surprised at himself, entered the salon, walking between asthenic seminude stereos executed in transparent plastic that made the skin of his neck and shoulders prickle with gooseflesh.

Slime! he thought. *How can they—*

"May I help—oh, hello, Roald. What brings you here?"

He knew suddenly what had brought him there. "Could you make a little advance on next month's tuition, Lewis? I'm strapped." He took a nervous look around the chamber of horrors, avoiding the man's condescending face.

"I guess so, Roald. Would ten dollars be any help? That'll carry us through to the 25th, right?"

"Fine, right, sure," he said, while he was being unwillingly towed around the place.

"I know you don't think much of S.P.G., but it's quiet now, so this is a good chance to see how we work. I don't say it's Art with a capital A, but you've got to admit it's *an* art, something people like at a price they can afford to pay. Here's where we sit them. Then you run out the feelers to the reference points on the face. You know what they are?"

He heard himself say dryly: "I know what they are. The Egyptian sculptors used them when they carved statues of the pharaohs."

"Yes? I never knew that. There's nothing new under the Sun, is there? But *this* is the heart of the S.P.G." The youngster proudly swung open the door of an electronic device in the wall of the portrait booth. Tubes winked sullenly at Halvorsen.

"The esthetikon?" he asked indifferently. He did not feel indifferent, but it would be absurd to show anger, no matter how much he felt it, against a mindless aggregation of circuits that could calculate layouts, criticize and correct pictures for a desired effect—and that had put the artist of design out of a job.

"Yes. The lenses take sixteen profiles, you know, and we set the esthetikon for whatever we want—cute, rugged, sexy, spiritual, brainy, or a combination. It fairs curves from profile to profile to give us just what we want, distorts the profiles themselves within limits if it has to, and there's your portrait stored in the memory tank waiting to be taped. You set your ratio for any enlargement or reduction you want and play it back. I wish we were reproducing today; it's fascinating to watch. You just pour in your cold-set plastic, the nozzles ooze out a core and start crawling over to scan—a drop here, a worm there, and it begins to take shape.

"We mostly do portrait busts here, the Avenue trade, but Wilgus, the foreman, used to work in a monument shop in Brooklyn. He did that heroic-size war memorial on the East River Drive—hired Garda Bouchette, the TV girl, for the

central figure. And what a figure! He told me he set the
esthetikon plates for three-quarter sexy, one-quarter
spiritual. Here's something interesting—standing figurine of
Orin Ryerson, the banker. He ordered twelve. Figurines are
coming in. The girls like them because they can show their
shapes. You'd be surprised at some of the poses they want to
try—"

Somehow, Halvorsen got out with the ten dollars, walked
to Sixth Avenue and sat down hard in a cheap restaurant. He
had coffee and dozed a little, waking with a guilty start at the
racket across the street. There was a building going up. For a
while he watched the great machines pour walls and floors,
the workmen rolling here and there on their little chariots to
weld on a wall panel, stripe on an electric circuit of conduc-
tive ink, or spray plastic finish over the "wired" wall, all
without leaving the saddles of their little mechanical chariots.

Halvorsen felt more determined. He bought a paper from a
vending machine by the restaurant door, drew another cup of
coffee and turned to the help-wanted ads.

The tricky trade-school ads urged him to learn construction
work and make big money. Be a plumbing-machine setup
man. Be a house-wiring machine tender. Be a servotruck
driver. Be a lumber-stacker operator. Learn pouring-
machine maintenance.

Make big money!

A sort of panic overcame him. He ran to the phone booth
and dialed a Passaic number. He heard the *ring-ring-ring* and
strained to hear old Mr. Krehbeil's stumping footsteps grow-
ing louded as he neared the phone, even though he knew he
would hear nothing until the receiver was picked up.

Ring-ring-ring. "Hello?" grunted the old man's voice,
and his face appeared on the little screen. "Hello, Mr.
Halvorsen. What can I do for you?"

Halvorsen was tongue-tied. He couldn't possibly say: I
just wanted to see if you were still there. I was afraid you
weren't there any more. He choked and improvised: "Hello,
Mr. Krehbeil. It's about the banister on the stairs in my place.

I noticed it's pretty shaky. Could you come over sometime and fix it for me?''

Krehbeil peered suspiciously out of the screen. "I could do that," he said slowly. "I don't have much work nowadays. But you can carpenter as good as me, Mr. Halvorsen, and frankly you're very slow pay and I like cabinet work better. I'm not a young man, and climbing around on ladders takes it out of me. If you can't find anybody else, I'll take the work, but I got to have some of the money first, just for the materials. It isn't easy to get good wood any more.''

"All right," said Halvorsen. "Thanks, Mr. Krehbeil. I'll call you if I can't get anybody else.''

He hung up and went back to his table and newspaper. His face was burning with anger at the old man's reluctance and his own foolish panic. Krehbeil didn't realize they were both in the same leaky boat. Krehbeil, who didn't get a job in a month, still thought with senile pride that he was a journeyman carpenter and cabinetmaker who could make his solid way anywhere with his toolbox and his skill, and that he could afford to look down on anything as disreputable as an artist—even an artist who could carpenter as well as he did himself.

Labuerre had made Halvorsen learn carpentry, and Labuerre had been right. You build a scaffold so you can sculpt up high, not so it will collapse and you break a leg. You build your platforms so they hold the rock steady, not so it wobbles and chatters at every blow of the chisel. You build your armatures so they hold the plasticine you slam onto them.

But the help-wanted ads wanted no builders of scaffolds, platforms and armatures. The factories were calling for setup men and maintenance men for the production and assembly machines.

From upstate, General Vegetables had sent a recruiting team for farm help—harvest setup and maintenance men, a few openings for experienced operators of tankcaulking machinery. Under "office and professional" the demand was heavy for computer men, for girls who could run the

I.B.M. Letteriter, esp. familiar sales and collections cor
resp., for office machinery maintenance and repairmen. A
job printing house wanted an esthetikon operator for let
terhead layouts and the like. A.T. & T. wanted trainees to
earn while learning telephone maintenance. A direct-mail
advertising outfit wanted an artist—no, they wanted a sales-
executive who could scrawl picture-ideas that would be sub-
jected to the criticism and correction of the esthetikon.

Halvorsen leafed tiredly through the rest of the paper. He
knew he wouldn't get a job, and if he did he wouldn't hold it.
He knew it was a terrible thing to admit to yourself that you
might starve to death because you were bored by anything
except art, but he admitted it.

It had happened often enough in the past—artists undergo-
ing preposterous hardships, not, as people thought, because
they were devoted to art, but because nothing else was
interesting. If there were only some impressive, sonorous
word that summed up the aching, oppressive futility that
overcame him when he tried to get out of art—only there
wasn't.

He thought he could tell which of the photos in the tabloid
had been corrected by the esthetikon.

There was a shot of Jink Bitsy, who was to star in a remake
of *Peter Pan.* Her ears had been made to look not pointed but
pointy, her upper lip had been lengthened a trifle, her nose
had been pugged a little and tilted quite a lot, her freckles
were cuter than cute, her brows were innocently arched, and
her lower lip and eyes were nothing less than pornography.

There was a shot, apparently uncorrected, of the last
Venus ship coming in at La Guardia and the average-looking
explorers grinning. Caption: "Austin Malone and crew smile
relief on safe arrival. Malone says Venus colonies need men,
machines. See story on p. 2."

Petulantly, Halvorsen threw the paper under the table and
walked out. What had space travel to do with him? Vacations
on the Moon and expeditions to Venus and Mars were part of
the deadly encroachment on his livelihood and no more.

II

He took the subway to Passaic and walked down a long-still traffic beltway to his studio, almost the only building alive in the slums near the rusting railroad freightyard.

A sign that had once said "F. Labuerre, Sculptor—Portraits and Architectural Commissions" now said "Roald Halvorsen; Art Classes—Reasonable Fees." It was a grimy two-story frame building with a shopfront in which were mounted some of his students' charcoal figure studies and oil still-lifes. He lived upstairs, taught downstairs front, and did his own work downstairs, back behind dirty ceiling-high drapes.

Going in, he noticed that he had forgotten to lock the door again. He slammed it bitterly. At the noise, somebody called from behind the drapes: "Who's that?"

"Halvorsen!" he yelled in a sudden fury. "I live here. I own this place. Come out of there! What do you want?"

There was a fumbling at the drapes and a girl stepped between them, shrinking from their dirt.

"Your door was open," she said firmly, "and it's a shop. I've just been here a couple of minutes. I came to ask about classes, but I don't think I'm interested if you're this bad-tempered."

A pupil. Pupils were never to be abused, especially not now.

"I'm terribly sorry," he said. "I had a trying day in the city." Now turn it on. "I wouldn't tell everybody a terrible secret like this, but I've lost a commission. You understand? I thought so. Anybody who'd traipse out here to my dingy abode would be *simpatica*. Won't you sit down? No, not there—humor an artist and sit over there. The warm background of that still-life brings out your color—quite good color. Have you ever been painted? You've a very interesting face, you know. Some day I'd like to—but you mentioned classes.

"We have figure classes, male and female models alternating, on Tuesday nights. For that I have to be very stern and ask you to sign up for an entire course of twelve lessons at sixty dollars. It's the models' fees—they're exorbitant. Saturday afternoons we have still-life classes for beginners in a series of six and pay ten dollars in advance, which saves you two whole dollars. I also give private instructions to a few talented amateurs."

The price was open on that one—whatever the traffic would bear. It had been a year since he'd had a private pupil and she'd taken only six lessons at five dollars an hour.

"The still-life sounds interesting," said the girl, holding her head self-consciously the way they all did when he gave them the patter. It was a good head, carried well up. The muscles clung close, not yet slacked into geotropic loops and lumps. The line of youth is heliotropic, he confusedly thought. "I saw some interesting things back there. Was that your own work?"

She rose, obviously with the expectation of being taken into the studio. Her body was one of those long-lined, small-breasted, coltish jobs that the Pre-Raphaelites loved to draw.

"Well—" said Halvorsen. A deliberate show of reluctance and then a bright smile of confidence. " *You'll* understand," he said positively and drew aside the curtains.

"What a curious place!" She wandered about, inspecting the drums of plaster, clay and plasticine, the racks of tools, the stands, the stones, the chisels, the forge, the kiln, the lumber, the glaze bench.

"I *like* this," she said determinedly, picking up a figure a half-meter tall, a Venus he had cast in bronze while studying under Labuerre some years ago. "How much is it?"

An honest answer would scare her off, and there was no chance in the world that she'd buy. "I hardly ever put my things up for sale," he told her lightly. "That was just a little study. I do work on commission only nowadays."

Her eyes flicked about the dingy room, seeming to take in its scaling plaster and warped floor and see through the wall to the abondoned slum in which it was set. There was amusement in her glance.

I am not being honest, she thinks. She thinks that is funny. Very well, I will be honest. "Six hundred dollars," he said flatly.

The girl set the figurine on its stand with a rap and said, half angry and half amused: "I don't understand it. That's more than a month's pay for me. I could get an S.P.G. statuette just as pretty as this for ten dollars. Who do you artists think you are, anyway?"

Halvorsen debated with himself about what he could say in reply:

An S.P.G. operator spends a week learning his skill and I spend a lifetime learning mine.

An S.P.G. operator makes a mechanical copy of a human form distorted by formulae mechanically arrived at from psychotests of population samples. I take full responsibility for my work; it is mine, though I use what I see fit from Egypt, Greece, Rome, the Middle Ages, the Renaissance, the Augustan and Romantic and Modern Eras.

An S.P.G. operator works in soft, homogeneous plastic; I work in bronze that is more complicated than you dream, that is cast and acid-dipped today so it will slowly take on rich and subtle coloring many years from today.

An S.P.G. operator could not make an Orpheus Fountain—

He mumbled, "Orpheus," and keeled over.

Halvorsen awoke in his bed on the second floor of the building. His fingers and toes buzzed electrically and he felt very clear-headed. The girl and a man, unmistakably a doctor, were watching him.

"You don't seem to belong to any Medical Plans, Halvorsen," the doctor said irritably. "There weren't any cards on you at all. No Red, no Blue, no Green, no Brown."

"I used to be on the Green Plan, but I let it lapse," the artist said defensively.

"And look what happened!"

"Stop nagging him!" the girl said. "I'll pay you your fee."

"It's supposed to come through a Plan," the doctor fretted.

"We won't tell anybody," the girl promised. "Here's five dollars. Just stop nagging him."

"Malnutrition," said the doctor. "Normally I'd send him to a hospital, but I don't see how I could manage it. He isn't on any Plan at all. Look, I'll take the money and leave some vitamins. That's what he needs—vitamins. And food."

"I'll see that he eats," the girl said, and the doctor left.

"How long since you've had anything?" she asked Halvorsen.

"I had some coffee today," he answered, thinking back. "I'd been working on detail drawings for a commission and it fell through. I told you that. It was a shock."

"I'm Lucretia Grumman," she said, and went out.

He dozed until she came back with an armful of groceries.

"It's hard to get around down here," she complained.

"It was Labuerre's studio," he told her defiantly. "He left it to me when he died. Things weren't so rundown in his time. I studied under him; he was one of the last. He had a joke—'They don't really want my stuff, but they're ashamed to let me starve.' He warned me that they wouldn't be ashamed to let *me* starve, but I insisted and he took me in."

Halvorsen drank some milk and ate some bread. He thought of the change from the ten dollars in his pocket and decided not to mention it. Then he remembered that the doctor had gone through his pockets.

"I can pay you for this," he said. "It's very kind of you, but you mustn't think I'm penniless. I've just been too preoccupied to take care of myself."

"Sure," said the girl. "But we can call this an advance. I want to sign up for some classes."

"Be happy to have you."

"Am I bothering you?" asked the girl. "You said something odd when you fainted—'Orpheus.'"

"Did I say that? I must have been thinking of Milles' Orpheus Fountain in Copenhagen. I've seen photos, but I've never been there."

"Germany? But there's nothing left of Germany."

"Copenhagen's in Denmark. There's quite a lot of Denmark left. It was only on the fringes. Heavily radiated, but still there."

"I want to travel, too," she said. "I work at La Guardia and I've never been off, except for an orbiting excursion. I want to go to the Moon on my vacation. They give us a bonus in travel vouchers. It must be wonderful dancing under the low gravity."

Spaceport? Off? Low gravity? Terms belonging to the detested electronic world of the stereopantograph in which he had no place.

"Be very interesting," he said, closing his eyes to conceal disgust.

"I *am* bothering you. I'll go away now, but I'll be back Tuesday night for the class. What time do I come and what should I bring?"

"Eight. It's charcoal—I sell you the sticks and paper. Just bring a smock."

"All right. And I want to take the oils class, too. And I want to bring some people I know to see your work. I'm sure they'll see something they like. Austin Malone's in from Venus—he's a special friend of mine."

"Lucretia," he said. "Or do some people call you Lucy?"

"Lucy."

"Will you take that little bronze you liked? As a thank you?"

"I can't do that!"

"Please. I'd feel much better about this. I really mean it."

She nodded abruptly, flushing, and almost ran from the room.

Now why did I do that? he asked himself. He hoped it was because he liked Lucy Grumman very much. He hoped it wasn't a cold-blooded investment of a piece of sculpture that would never be sold, anyway, just to make sure she'd be back with class fees and more groceries.

III

She was back on Tuesday, a half-hour early and carrying a smock. He introduced her formally to the others as they arrived: a dozen or so bored young women who, he suspected, talked a great deal about their art lessons outside, but in class used any excuse to stop sketching.

He didn't dare show Lucy any particular consideration. There were fierce little miniature cliques in the class. Halvorsen knew they laughed at him and his line among themselves, and yet, strangely, were fiercely jealous of their seniority and right to individual attention.

The lesson was an ordeal, as usual. The model, a musclebound young graduate of the barbell gyms and figure-photography studios, was stupid and argumentative about ten-minute poses. Two of the girls came near a hair-pulling brawl over the rights to a preferred sketching location. A third girl had discovered Picasso's cubist period during the past week and proudly announced that she didn't *feel* perspective.

But the two interminable hours finally ticked by. He nagged them into cleaning up—not as bad as the Saturdays with oils—and stood by the open door. Otherwise they would have stayed all night, cackling about absent students and snarling sulkily among themselves. His well-laid plans went sour, though. A large and flashy car drove up as the girls were leaving.

"That's Austin Malone," said Lucy. "He came to pick me up and look at your work."

That was all the wedge her fellow pupils needed.

"*Aus*-tin Ma-*lone! Well!*"

"Lucy, darling, I'd love to meet a real *spaceman.*"

"Roald, darling, would you mind very much if I stayed a moment?"

"I'm certainly not going to miss this, and I don't care if you mind or not, Roald, darling!"

Malone was an impressive figure. Halvorsen thought: he looks as though he's been run through an esthetikon set for "brawny" and "determined." Lucy made a hash of the introductions and the spaceman didn't rise to conversational bait dangled enticingly by the girls.

In a clear voice, he said to Halvorsen: "I don't want to take up too much of your time. Lucy tells me you have some things for sale. Is there any place we can look at them where it's quiet?"

The students made sulky exists.

"Back here," said the artist.

The girl and Malone followed him through the curtains. The spaceman made a slow circuit of the studio, seeming to repel questions.

He sat down at last and said: "I don't know what to think, Halvorsen. This place stuns me. Do you *know* you're in the Dark Ages?"

People who never have given a thought to Chartres and Mont St. Michel usually call it the Dark Ages, Halvorsen thought wryly. He asked, "Technologically, you mean? No, not at all. My plaster's better, my colors are better, my metal is better—tool metal, not casting metal, that is."

"I mean *hand* work;" said the spaceman. "Actually working by *hand.*"

The artist shrugged. "There have been crazes for the techniques of the boiler works and the machine shop," he admitted. "Some interesting things were done, but they didn't stand up well. Is there anything here that takes your eye?"

"I like those dolphins," said the spaceman, pointing to a perforated terra-cotta relief on the wall. They had been commissioned by an architect, then later refused for reasons of economy when the house had run way over estimate. "They'd look bully over the fireplace in my town apartment. Like them, Lucy?"

"I think they're wonderful," said the girl.

Roald saw the spaceman go rigid with the effort not to turn and stare at her. He loved her and he was jealous.

Roald told the story of the dolphins and said: "The price that the architect thought was too high was three hundred and sixty dollars."

Malone grunted. "Doesn't seem unreasonable—if you set a high store on inspiration."

"I don't know about inspiration," the artist said evenly. "But I was awake for two days and two nights shoveling coal and adjusting drafts to fire that thing in my kiln."

The spaceman looked contemptuous. "I'll take it," he said. "Be something to talk about during those awkward pauses. Tell me, Halvorsen, how's Lucy's work? Do you think she ought to stick with it?"

"Austin," objected the girl, "don't be so blunt. How can he possibly know after one day?"

"She can't draw yet," the artist said cautiously. "It's all coordination, you know—thousands of hours of practice, training your eye and hand to work together until you can put a line on paper where you want it. Lucy, if you're really interested in it, you'll learn to draw well. I don't think any of the other students will. They're in it because of boredom or snobbery, and they'll stop before they have their eye-hand coordination."

"I *am* interested," she said firmly.

Malone's determined restraint broke. "Damned right you are. In—" He recovered himself and demanded of Halvorsen: "I understand your point about coordination. But thousands of hours when you can buy a camera? It's absurd."

"I was talking about drawing, not art," replied Halvorsen. "Drawing is putting a line on paper where you want it, I said." He took a deep breath and hoped the great distinction wouldn't sound ludicrous and trivial. "So let's say that art is knowing how to put the line in the right place."

"Be practical. There isn't any art. Not any more. I get around quite a bit and I never see anything but photos and S.P.G.s. A few heirlooms, yes, but nobody's painting or carving any more."

"There's some art, Malone. My students—a couple of them in the still-life class—are quite good. There are more across the country. Art for occupational therapy, or a hobby, or something to do with the hands. There's trade in their work. They sell them to each other, they give them to their friends, they hang them on their walls. There are even some sculptors like that. Sculpture is prescribed by doctors. The occupational therapists say it's even better than drawing and painting, so some of these people work in plasticine and soft stone, and some of them get to be good.''

"Maybe so. I'm an engineer, Halvorsen. We glory in doing things the easy way. Doing things the easy way got me to Mars and Venus and it's going to get me to Ganymede. You're doing things the hard way, and your inefficiency has no place in this world. Look at you! You've lost a fingertip—some accident, I suppose.''

"I never noticed—" said Lucy, and then let out a faint, "Oh!"

Halvorsen curled the middle finger of his left hand into the palm, where he usually carried it to hide the missing first joint.

"Accidents are a sign of inadequate mastery of material and equipment," said Malone sententiously. "While you stick to your methods and I stick to mine, *you can't compete with me.*"

His tone made it clear that he was talking about more than engineering.

"Shall we go now, Lucy? Here's my card, Halvorsen. Send those dolphins along and I'll mail you a check."

IV

The artist walked the half-dozen blocks to Mr. Krehbeil's place the next day. He found the old man in the basement shop of his fussy house, hunched over his bench with a powerful light overhead. He was trying to file a saw.

"Mr. Krehbeil!" Halvorsen called over the shriek of metal.

The carpenter turned around and peered with watery eyes. "I can't see like I used to," he said querulously. "I do over the same teeth on this damn saw, I skip teeth, I can't see the light shine off it when I got one set. The glare.'' He banged down his three-cornered file petulantly. "Well, what can I do for you?''

"I need some crating stock. Anything. I'll trade you a couple of my maple four-by-fours.''

The old face became cunning. "And will you set my saw? My *saws*, I mean. It's nothing to you—an hour's work. You have the eyes.''

Halvorsen said bitterly. "All right.'' The old man had to drive his bargain, even though he might never use his saws again. And then the artist promptly repented of his bitterness, offering up a quick prayer that his own failure to conform didn't make him as much of a nuisance to the world as Krehbeil was.

The carpenter was pleased as they went through his small stock of wood and chose boards to crate the dolphin relief. He was pleased enough to give Halvorsen coffee and cake before the artist buckled down to filing the saws.

Over the kitchen table, Halvorsen tried to probe. "Things pretty slow now?''

It would be hard to spoil Krehbeil's day now. "People are always fools. They don't know good hand work. Some day,'' he said apocalyptically, "I laugh on the other side of my face when their foolish machine-buildings go falling down in a strong wind, all of them, all over the country. Even my boy—I used to beat him good, almost every day—he works a foolish concrete machine and his house should fall on his head like the rest.''

Halvorsen knew it was Krehbeil's son who supported him by mail, and changed the subject. "You get some cabinet work?''

"Stupid women! What they call antiques—they don't know Meissen, they don't know Biedermeier. They bring me trash to repair sometimes. I make them pay; I swindle them good.''

"I wonder if things would be different if there were anything left over in Europe . . .''

"People will still be fools, Mr. Halvorsen,'' said the

carpenter positively. "Didn't you say you were going to file those saws today?"

So the artist spent two noisy hours filing before he carried his crating stock to the studio.

Lucy was there. She had brought some things to eat. He dumped the lumber with a bang and demanded: "Why aren't you at work?"

"We get days off," she said vaguely. "Austin thought he'd give me the cash for the terra cotta and I could give it to you."

She held out an envelope while he studied her silently. The farce was beginning again. But this time he dreaded it.

It would not be the first time that a lonesome, discontented girl chose to see him as a combination of romantic rebel and lost pup, with the consequences you'd expect.

He knew from books, experience and Labuerre's conversation in the old days that there was nothing novel about the comedy—that there had even been artists, lots of them, who had counted on endless repetitions of it for their livelihood.

The girl drops in with groceries and the artist is pleasantly surprised; the girl admires this little thing or that after payday and buys it and the artist is pleasantly surprised; the girl brings her friends to take lessons or make little purchases and the artist is pleasantly surprised. The girl may be seduced by the artist or vice versa, which shortens the comedy, or they may get married, which lengthens it somewhat.

It had been three years since Halvorsen had last played out the farce with a manic-depressive divorcee from Elmira: three years during which he had crossed the midpoint between thirty and forty; three more years to get beaten down by being unwanted and working too much and eating too little.

Also, he knew, he was in love with this girl.

He took the envelope, counted three hundred and twenty dollars and crammed it into his pocket. "That was your idea," he said. "Thanks. Now get out, will you? I've got work to do."

She stood there, shocked.

"I said get out. I have work to do."

"Austin was right," she told him miserably. "You don't care how people feel. You just want to get things out of them."

She ran from the studio, and Halvorsen fought with himself not to run after her.

He walked slowly into his workshop and studied his array of tools, though he paid little attention to his finished pieces. It would be nice to spend about half of this money on open-hearth steel rod and bar stock to forge into chisels; he thought he knew where he could get some—but she would be back, or he would break and go to her and be forgiven and the comedy would be played out, after all.

He couldn't let that happen.

V

Aalesund, on the Atlantic side of the Dourefeld mountains of Norway, was in the lee of the blasted continent. One more archeologist there made no difference, as long as he had the sense to recognize the propellerlike international signposts that said with their three blades, *Radiation Hazard,* and knew what every schoolboy knew about protective clothing and reading a personal Geiger counter.

The car Halvorsen rented was for a brief trip over the mountains to study contaminated Oslo. Well-muffled, he could make it and back in a dozen hours and no harm done.

But he took the car past Oslo, Wennersborg and Goteborg, along the Kattegat coast to Helsingborg, and abandoned it there, among the three-bladed polyglot signs, crossing to Denmark. Danes were as unlike Prussians as they could be, but their unfortunate little peninsula was a sprout off Prussia which radio-cobalt dust couldn't tell from the real thing. The three bladed signs were most specific.

With a long way to walk along the rubble-littered highways, he stripped off the impregnated coveralls and boots.

He had long since shed the noisy counter and the uncomfortable gloves and mask.

The silence was eerie as he limped into Copenhagen at noon. He didn't know whether the radiation was getting to him or whether he was tired and hungry and no more. As though thinking of a stranger, he liked what he was doing.

I'll be my own audience, he thought. *God knows I learned there isn't any other, not any more. You have to know when to stop. Rodin, the dirty old, wonderful old man, knew that. He taught us not to slick it and polish it and smooth it until it looked like liquid instead of bronze and stone. Van Gogh was crazy as a loon, but he knew when to stop and varnish it, and he didn't care if the paint looked like paint instead of looking like sunset clouds or moonbeams. Up in Hartford, Browne and Sharpe stop when they've got a turret lathe; they don't put caryatids on it. I'll stop while my life is a life, before it becomes a thing with distracting embellishments such as a wife who will come to despise me, a succession of gradually less worthwhile pieces that nobody will look at.*

Blame nobody, he told himself, light-headedly.

And then it was in front of him, terminating a vista of weeds and bomb rubble—Milles' Orpheus Fountain.

It took a man, he thought. Esthetikon circuits couldn't do it. There was a gross mixture of styles, a calculated flaw that the esthetikon couldn't be set to make. Orpheus and the souls were classic or later; the three-headed dog was archaic. That was to tell you about the antiquity and invincibility of Hell, and that Cerberus knows Orpheus will never go back into life with his bride.

There was the heroic, tragic central figure that looked mighty enough to battle with the gods, but battle wasn't any good against the grinning, knowing, hateful three-headed dog it stood on. You don't battle the pavement where you walk or the floor of the house you're in; you can't. So Orpheus, his face a mask of controlled and suffering fury, crashes a great chord from his lyre that moved trees and stones. Around him the naked souls in Hell start at the chord,

each in its own way: the young lovers down in death; the
mother down in death; the musician, deaf and down in death,
straining to hear.

Halvorsen, walking uncertainly toward the fountain, felt
something break inside him, and a heaviness in his lungs. As
he pitched forward among the weeds, he didn't care that the
three-headed dog was grinning its knowing, hateful grin
down at him. He had heard the chord from the lyre.

SHORT IN THE CHEST

Idris Seabright

The cool, delicious stories of Idris Seabright have been appearing in science-fiction magazines since 1950—"An Egg a Month from All Over," "The Man Who Sold Rope to the Gnoles," and many another pretty little chiller. It is not much of a secret that "Idris Seabright" is the alter ego of Margaret St. Clair, a native Californian who, when not busy raising carnations, exotic flowering bulbs, and dachshunds, writes science fiction. Under her own byline Mrs. St. Clair has given us at least one novel, *Vulcan's Dolls,* and a great many charming and sinister short stories. The present story, a "Seabright" offering, is one of my favorites. Not only is it amusing and provocative, but it may yet succeed in restoring to our language a useful, noneuphemistic transitive verb for sex.

The girl in the marine-green uniform turned up her hearing aid a trifle—they were all a little deaf, from the cold-war bombing—and with an earnest frown regarded the huxley that was seated across the desk from her.

"You're the queerest huxley I ever heard of," she said flatly. "The others aren't at all like you."

The huxley did not seem displeased at this remark. It took

121

off its windowpane glasses, blew on them, polished them on a handkerchief, and returned them to its nose. Sonya's turning up the hearing aid had activated the short in its chest again; it folded its hands protectively over the top buttons of its dove-gray brocaded waistcoat.

"And in what way, my dear young lady, am I different from other huxleys?" it asked.

"Well—you tell me to speak to you frankly, to tell you exactly what is in my mind. I've only been to a huxley once before, but it kept talking about giving me the big, overall picture, and about using dighting* to transcend myself. It spoke about in-group love, and intergroup harmony, and it said our basic loyalty must be given to Defense, which in the cold-war emergency is the country itself.

"You're not like that at all, not at all philosophic. I suppose that's why they're called huxleys—because they're philosophic rob—I beg your pardon."

"Go ahead and say it," the huxley encouraged. "I'm not shy. I don't mind being called a robot."

"I might have known. I guess that's why you're so popu-

---

*In the past, I have been accused of making up some of the unusual words that appear in my stories. Sometimes this accusation has been justified; sometimes, as in "Vulcan's Dolls," (see *Plant Life of the Pacific World*) it has not. For the record, therefore, be it observed that "dight" is a middle English word meaning, among other things, "to have intercourse with." (See *Poets of the English Language,* Auden and Pearson, Vol. 1, p. 173.) [See also *Webster's New International Dictionary,* unabridged version.—G.C.] "Dight" was reintroduced by a late twentieth-century philologist who disliked the "sleep with" euphemism, and who saw that the language desperately needed a transitive verb that would be "good usage."

—I.S.

lar. I never saw a huxley with so many people in its waiting room.''

''I *am* a rather unusual robot,'' the huxley said, with a touch of smugness. ''I'm a new model, just past the experimental stage, with unusually complicated relays. But that's beside the point. You haven't told me yet what's troubling you.''

The girl fiddled nervously with the control of her hearing aid. After a moment she turned it down; the almost audible sputtering in the huxley's chest died away.

''It's about the pigs,'' she said.

''The pigs!'' The huxley was jarred out of its mechanical calm. ''You know, I thought it would be something about dighting,'' it said after a second. It smiled winningly. ''It usually is.''

''Well . . . it's about that too. But the pigs were what started me worrying. I don't know whether you're clear about my rank. I'm Major Sonya Briggs, in charge of the Zone 13 piggery.''

''Oh,'' said the huxley.

''Yes. . . . Like the other armed services, we Marines produce all our own food. My piggery is a pretty important unit in the job of keeping up the supply of pork chops. Naturally, I was disturbed when the newborn pigs refused to nurse.

''If you're a new robot, you won't have much on your memory coils about pigs. As soon as the pigs are born, we take them away from the sow—we use an aseptic scoop—and put them in an enclosure of their own with a big nursing tank. We have a recording of a sow grunting, and when they hear that they're supposed to nurse. The sow gets an oestric, and after a few days she's ready to breed again. The system is supposed to produce a lot more pork than letting the baby pigs stay with the sow in the old-fashioned way. But as I say, lately they've been refusing to nurse.

''No matter how much we step up the grunting record, they won't take the bottle. We've had to slaughter several litters rather than let them starve to death. And at that the flesh hasn't been much good—too mushy and soft. As you can easily see, the situation is getting serious."

"Um," the huxley said.

"Naturally, I made full reports. Nobody has known what to do. But when I got my dighting slip a couple of times ago, in the space marked 'Purpose,' besides the usual rubber-stamped 'To reduce interservice tension' somebody had written in: 'To find out from Air their solution of the neonatal pig nutrition problem.'

"So I knew my dighting opposite number in Air was not only supposed to reduce intergroup tension, but also I was supposed to find out from him how Air got its newborn pigs to eat." She looked down, fidgeting with the clasp of her musette bag.

"Go on," said the huxley with a touch of severity. "I can't help you unless you give me your full confidence."

"Is it true that the dighting system was set up by a group of psychologists after they'd made a survey of interservice tension? After they'd found that Marine was feuding with Air, and Air with Infantry, and Infantry with Navy, to such an extent that it was cutting down overall Defense efficiency? They thought that sex relations would be the best of all ways of cutting down hostility and replacing it with friendly feelings, so they started the dighting plan?"

"You know the answers to those questions as well as I do," the huxley replied frostily. "The tone of your voice when you asked them shows that they are to be answered with 'Yes.' You're stalling, Major Briggs."

"It's so unpleasant. . . . What do you want me to tell you?"

"Go on in detail with what happened after you got your blue dighting slip."

She shot a glance at him, flushed, looked away again, and began talking rapidly. "The slip was for next Tuesday. I hate Air for dighting, but I thought it would be all right. You know how it is—there's a particular sort of kick in feeling oneself change from a cold sort of loathing into being eager and excited and in love with it. After one's had one's Watson, I mean.

"I went to the neutral area Tuesday afternoon. He was in the room when I got there, sitting in a chair with his big feet spread out in front of him, wearing one of those loathsome leather jackets. He stood up politely when he saw me, but I knew he'd just about as soon cut my throat as look at me, since I was Marine. We were both armed, naturally."

"What did he look like?" the huxley broke in.

"I really didn't notice. Just that he was Air. Well, anyway, we had a drink together. I've heard they put cannabis in the drinks they serve you in the neutral areas, and it might be true. I didn't feel nearly so hostile to him after I'd finished my drink. I even managed to smile, and he managed to smile back. He said, 'We might as well get started, don't you think?' So I went in the head.

"I took off my things and left my gun on the bench beside the wash basin. I gave myself my Watson in the thigh."

"The usual Watson?" the huxley asked as she halted. "Oestric and anticoncipient injected subcutaneously from a sterile ampule?"

"Yes. He'd had his Watson too, the priapic, because when I got back. . . ." She began to cry.

"What happend after you got back?" the huxley queried after she had cried for a while.

"I just wasn't any good. No good at all. The Watson might have been so much water for all the effect it had. Finally he got sore. He said, 'What's the matter with you? I might have known anything Marine was in would get loused up.'

"That made me angry, but I was too upset to defend myself. 'Tension reduction!' he said. 'This is a fine way to promote interservice harmony. I'm not only not going to sign the checking-out sheet, I'm going to file a complaint against you to your group.' "

"Oh, my," said huxley.

"Yes, wasn't it terrible? I said, 'If you file a complaint, I'll file a countercharge. You didn't reduce *my* tension, either.'

"We argued about it for a while. He said that if I filed countercharges there'd be a trial and I'd have to take Pentothal and then the truth would come out. He said it wasn't his fault! he'd been ready.

"I knew that was true, so I began to plead with him. I reminded him of the cold war, and how the enemy were about to take Venus, when all we had was Mars. I talked to him about loyalty to Defense, and I asked him how he'd feel if he was kicked out of Air. And finally, after what seemed like hours, he said he wouldn't file charges. I guess he felt sorry for me. He even agreed to sign the checking-out sheet.

"That was that. I went back to the head and put on my clothes and we both went out. We left the room at different times, though, because we were too angry to smile at each other and look happy. Even as it was, I think some of the neutral-area personnel suspected us."

"Is that what's been worrying you?" the huxley asked when she seemed to have finished.

"Well . . . I can trust you, can't I? You really won't tell?"

"Certainly I won't. Anything told to a huxley is a privileged communication. The first amendment applies to us, if to no other profession."

"Yes. I remember there was a Supreme Court decision about freedom of speech. . . ." She swallowed, choked, and swallowed again. "When I got my next dighting slip," she said bravely, "I was so upset I applied for a gyn. I hoped the doctor would say there was something physically wrong with me, but he said I was in swell shape. He said, 'A girl like you ought to be mighty good at keeping interservice tension down.' So there wasn't any help there.

"Then I went to a huxley, the huxley I was telling you about. It talked philosophy to me. That wasn't any help either. So—finally—well, I stole an extra Watson from the lab."

There was a silence. When she saw that the huxley seemed to have digested her revelation without undue strain, she went on, "I mean, an extra Watson beyond the one I was issued. I couldn't endure the thought of going through another dight like the one before. There was quite a fuss about the ampule's being missing. The dighting drugs are under strict control. But they never did find out who'd taken it.''

"And did it help you? The double portion of oestric?'' the huxley asked. It was prodding at the top buttons of its waistcoat with one forefinger, rather in the manner of one who is not quite certain he feels an itch.

"Yes, it did. Everything went off well. He—the man—said I was a nice girl, and Marine was a good service, next to Infantry, of course. He was Infantry. I had a fine time myself, and last week when I got a request sheet from Infantry asking for some pig pedigrees, I went ahead and initialed it. That tension reduction does work. I've been feeling awfully jittery, though. And yesterday I got another blue dighting slip.

"What am I to do? I can't steal another Watson. They've tightened up the controls. And even if I could, I don't think one extra would be enough. This time I think it would take *two.*''

She put her head down on the arm of her chair, gulping desperately.

"You don't think you'd be all right with just one Watson?'' the huxley asked after an interval. "After all, people used to dight habitually without any Watsons at all.''

"That wasn't interservice dighting. No, I don't think I'd be all right. You see, this time it's with Air again. I'm supposed to try to find out about porcine nutrition. And I've always particularly hated Air.''

She twisted nervously at the control of her hearing aid. The huxley gave a slight jump. "Ah—well, of course you might resign,'' it said in a barely audible voice.

Sonya—in the course of a long-continued struggle there is always a good deal of cultural contamination, and if there were girls named Sonya, Olga, and Tatiana in Defense, there were girls named Shirley and Mary Beth to be found on the enemy's side—Sonya gave him an incredulous glance. "You must be joking. I think it's in very poor taste. I didn't tell you my difficulties for you to make fun of me.''

The huxley appeared to realize that it had gone too far.

"Not at all, my dear young lady," it said placatingly. It
pressed its hands to its bosom. "Just a suggestion. As you
say, it was in poor taste. I should have realized that you'd
rather die than not be Marine."

"Yes, I would."

She turned the hearing aid down again. The huxley
relaxed. "You may not be aware of it, but difficulties like
yours are not entirely unknown," it said. "Perhaps, after a
long course of oestrics, antibodies are built up. Given a state
of initial physiological reluctance, a forced sexual response
might. . . . But you're not interested in all that. You want
help. How about taking your troubles to somebody higher?
Taking them all the way up?"

"You mean—the CO?"

The huxley nodded.

Major Briggs' face flushed scarlet. "I can't do that! I just
can't! No nice girl would. I'd be too ashamed." She beat on
her musette bag with one hand, and began to sob.

Finally she sat up. The huxley was regarding her patiently.
She opened her bag, got out cosmetics and mirror, and began
to repair emotion's ravages. Then she extracted an electronically powered vibro-needle from the depths of her bag and
began crafting away on some indeterminate white garment.

"I don't know what I'd do without my crafting," she said
in explanation. "These last few days, it's all that's kept me
sane. Thank goodness it's fashionable to do crafting now.
Well. I've told you all about my troubles. Have you any
ideas?"

The huxley regarded her with faintly protruding eyes. The
vibro-needle clicked away steadily, so steadily that Sonya
was quite unaware of the augmented popping in the huxley's
chest. Besides, the noise was of a frequency that her hearing
aid didn't pick up any too well.

The huxley cleared its throat. "Are you sure your dighting
difficulties are really your fault?" it asked in an oddly altered
voice.

"Why—I suppose so. After all, there's been nothing

wrong with the men either time." Major Briggs did not look up from her work.

"Yes, physiologically. But let's put it this way. And I want you to remember, my dear young lady, that we're both mature, sophisticated individuals, and that I'm a huxley, after all. Supposing your dighting date had been with . . . somebody in . . . Marine. Would you have had any difficulty with it?"

Sonya Briggs put down her crafting, her cheeks flaming. "With a group brother? You have no right to talk to me like that!"

"Now, now. You must be calm."

The sputtering in the huxley's chest was by now so loud that only Sonya's emotion could have made her deaf to it. It was so well-established that even her laying down the vibro-needle had had no effect on it.

"Don't be offended," the huxley went on in its unnatural voice. "I was only putting a completely hypothetical case."

"Then . . . supposing it's understood that it's completely hypothetical and I would never, never dream of doing a thing like that . . . then, I don't suppose I'd have had any trouble with it." She picked up the needle once more.

"In other words, it's not your fault. Look at it this way. You're Marine."

"Yes." The girl's head went up proudly. "I'm Marine."

"Yes. And that means you're a hundred times—a thousand times—better than any of these twerps you've been having to dight with. Isn't that true? Just in the nature of things. Because you're Marine."

"Why—I guess it is. I never thought of it before like that."

"But you can see it's true now, when you think of it. Take that date you had with the man from Air. How could it be your fault that you couldn't respond to him, somebody from *Air*? Why, it was his fault—it's as plain as the nose on your face—*his* fault for being from a repulsive service like Air!"

Sonya was looking at the huxley with parted lips and

shining eyes. "I never thought of it before," she breathed. "But it's true. You're right. You're wonderfully, wonderfully right!"

"Of course I am," said the huxley smugly. "I was built to be right. Now, let's consider this matter of your next date."

"Yes, let's."

"You'll go to the neutral area, as usual. You'll be wearing your miniBAR won't you?"

"Yes, of course. We always go in armed."

"Good. You'll go to the head and undress. You'll give yourself your Watson. If it works—"

"It won't. I'm almost sure of that."

"Hear me out. As I was saying, if it works, you'll dight. If it doesn't you'll be carrying your miniBAR."

"Where?" asked Sonya, frowning.

"Behind your back. You want to give him a chance. But not too good a chance. If the Watson doesn't work—" the huxley paused for dramatic effect—"*get out your gun and shoot him. Shoot him through the heart.* Leave him lying up against a bulkhead. Why should you go through a painful scene like the one you just described for the sake of a yuk from Air?"

"Yes—but—" Sonya had the manner of one who, while striving to be reasonable, is none too sure that reasonableness can be justified. "That wouldn't reduce interservice tension effectively."

"My dear young lady, why should interservice tension be reduced at the expense of Marine? Besides, you've got to take the big overall view. Whatever benefits Marine, benefits Defense."

"Yes. . . . That's true. . . . I think you've given me good advice."

"Of course I have! One thing more. After you shoot him, leave a note with your name, sector, and identity number on it. You're not ashamed of it."

"No. . . . No. . . . But I just remembered. How can he give me the pig formula when he's dead?"

"He's just as likely to give it to you dead as he was when he was alive. Besides, think of the humiliation of it. You, Marine, having to lower yourself to wheedle a thing like that out of Air! Why, he ought to be proud, honored, to give the formula to you.''

"Yes, he ought." Sonya's lips tightened. "I won't take any nonsense from him," she said. "Even if the Watson works and I dight him, I'll shoot him afterwards. Wouldn't you?''

"Of course. Any girl with spirit would.''

Major Briggs glanced at her watch. "Twenty past! I'm overdue at the piggery right now. Thank you so much.'' She beamed at him. "I'm going to take your advice.''

"I'm glad. Good-bye.''

"Good-bye.''

She walked out of the room, humming, "From the halls of Montezuma. . . .''

Left alone, the huxley interchanged its eyes and nose absently a couple of times. It looked up at the ceiling speculatively, as if it wondered when the bombs from Air, Infantry, and Navy were going to come crashing down. It had had interviews with twelve young women so far, and it had given them all the same advice it had given Major Briggs. Even a huxley with a short in its chest might have foreseen that the final result of its counseling would be catastrophic for Marine.

It sat a little while longer, repeating to itself, "Poppoff, Poppoff. Papa, potatoes, poultry, prunes and prism, prunes and prism.''

Its short was sputtering loudly and cheerfully; it hunted around on the broadcast sound band until it found a program of atonal music that covered the noise successfully. Though its derangement had reached a point that was not far short of insanity, the huxley still retained a certain cunning.

Once more it repeated "Poppoff Poppoff," to itself. Then it went to the door of its waiting room and called in its next client.

BROWN ROBERT

Terry Carr

This grim little piece was Terry Carr's first professionally published short story, back in 1962—and a notable debut it was, for within its brief compass it managed to put forth a twist on the classic time-machine theme that apparently had never previously been noticed.

Arthur Leacock shuffled quickly down the wooden hall of the small Midwestern university where he had worked for thirty-two years and eight months. His sleep-rumpled, peppery hair stuck out from under the old leather cap which he had worn for fully seventeen of those years, and his oft-resoled shoes were almost silent in the hallway, though its echoing properties were so good that Arthur had often fancied he could hear his own breathing whispered back to him from the walls.

He turned right at the large waiting-room in the middle of the building and went up the stairs to the second floor two at a time, grasping the handrail with large-knuckled hands to pull himself along. He did not look where he was going, but instead rested his eyes unseeingly on the stairs passing beneath him, his mouth drawn back into the heavy wrinkles of his cheeks.

Robert Ernsohn, full-voiced Robert with brown soul, would already be in his office. Wavy Robert, whose brow was noble as a mannikin's, always arrived half an hour before Arthur. When Arthur arrived, he knew, Robert would be rechecking the figures he had pored carefully over till midnight—not because Robert did not trust his own abilities, but because it was his policy always to double-check his figures. Robert, naturally, would never give in to the danger of overconfidence, which might be called conceit; he always made sure that he had made no mistake. And then he always smiled.

At the top of the stairs Arthur pushed through the door to the second-floor hall and crossed to Robert's office. The door creaked twice behind him and then rested shut.

Robert Ernsohn looked up from his pretentiously small desk in the corner by the window and pushed the papers aside. The red-orange sun, slipping silently from behind the roof of the building across the courtyard, cast lines of light through the venetian blinds across the desk. Brown-eyed, brown Robert smiled with innocent satyriasis and dropped his pencil in the pencil-glass.

"I've checked it all four times," he said. "Short of going upstate to a computer, that's all I can do. I hope it's right."

Arthur watched his mouth as he spoke and then stepped into the cloakroom to hang up his overcoat. He found a cleaning rag and took it with him when he came out and went on across the office, five steps, into the laboratory. A small laboratory, cluttered and dirty. The floor was dirty, at any rate; the equipment was polished. But Arthur set to polishing it again, because this morning it would be used.

There was a reclining couch in the midst of a cacophony of mechanical and electrical complexity. Arthur brushed off the couch, touching the leather softly with his fingertips, and then began carefully rubbing down the metal of the machine. He tested a few levers by hand and oiled one of them, humming to himself. But he noticed himself humming and stopped.

The machine—the time machine—was ready for operation. It was clean and had been checked over for a week; any doubtful parts had been replaced, and on a trial run yesterday it had performed perfectly. Robert's sweater—Robert's, of course, not Arthur's—had been sent two days into the future and had come back. It had been sent six months and then five years into the future, and it had still come back. But of course Arthur had never doubted that it would.

Robert appeared in the doorway and watched him as he threw the switch and warmed the machine. A few dials moved, and Robert stepped forward to read them and glance down at the figures in his hand and nod. Arthur ignored him. He switched the machine off and stepped to the window to look at his watch; it was 7:43 A.M. He unstrapped the watch and handed it to Robert and went into the other room.

In the office he sat in Robert's chair by the window and looked out onto the courtyard. The girl, eighteen and brunette, had a class across the yard at eight o'clock, and she always arrived early. Arthur always watched for her, and when he saw her he diverted brown Robert's attention, so that he missed seeing her. He had been doing that ever since he had seen Robert talking with her two months before.

Presently he saw her, walking quickly up the steps to the courtyard. It was cold weather and she wore a heavy coat which concealed her figure—which was a good thing. Arthur knew how young men like cheekbone Robert liked the summer months on campus.

"What time you want to go?" he called out, and when Robert came into the room he did not look out the window.

"At eight," said Robert.

"You're sure?"

"Of course. I told you definitely yesterday, and I seldom change my mind."

"Well, you never know," said Arthur. "Something might have come up, might have changed your plans."

Robert smiled as though he were flexing his face muscles. "Nothing is likely to at this point. Except perhaps an act of God."

An act of God, Arthur repeated in his mind, wanting to

look out the window to see if the girl was safely out of sight yet.

"There's someone at the door," he said.

Robert went to the door, but there was no one there and he went outside to look down the stairs. Arthur turned and looked for the girl. She had sat down on a bench by the door to her building and was paging through a book, her hair falling softly like water-mist across her forehead. Even from this distance Arthur could see that it was clean, free hair, virgin's hair. He knew the way absent Robert would like to run his fingers through it, caressing the girl's neck, tightly, holding her. . . .

Robert was dangerous. No one else realized that, but Arthur had watched young men on that campus for thirty-two years, and he recognized the look he saw in Robert's eyes. So many of them, students and young professors, had that look: veiled, covert, waxing and waning behind the eyes, steadily building up to an explosion like—But Arthur did not want to think about that.

He had tried, once, to warn others about Robert, whose mind was a labyrinth of foggy dark halls. He had told them, down in the main office, one day after hours. That had been the day he had seen dark Robert with the girl, seen them together. He had told Mr. Lewis's assistant, and tried to warn her—fog Robert must be dismissed and sent away. But the woman had hardly listened to him, and as he had stood in the outer room on the way out, looking calmly at a chip in the baseboard, he had heard her speaking to Mr. Lewis, the president of the university. "We have to remember that Arthur is getting on in years," she had said. "He's probably having a little trouble with his memory, playing tricks on him. People who are getting on in years sometimes aren't very much in contact with reality." Mr. Lewis's assistant was a dull gray woman.

"Robert Ernsohn is one of our most valued young men," Mr. Lewis had said. "We're backing his research as fully as possible, and we have every confidence in him." Arthur had heard some papers rustled and then silence, so he had stopped looking at the baseboard and gone out.

Not in contact with reality? Arthur had been watching the realities of young men and their eyes through all his years at the campus, first as a janitor, then later as an assistant in the chemistry labs and up in the small observatory on the top floor. He had seen them looking at the girls, light and rounded, long hair and tapered ankles and tight, swaying skirts. He knew about realities.

He had read about them, in books from the library's locked shelves. Case histories of sadists and murderers and twisted minds of all sorts. Men who cut girls straight up the belly, dissected their breasts, removed the organs of their abdomens and laid them out neatly on the floor, and then carefully washed what remained of their bodies and put their clothes back on them and went away. Arthur had read all those books carefully, and he knew what reality was. It was all around him, and he was certainly in contact with it.

The door behind him opened and frowning, covert Robert came back into the room.

"There was no one," he said, and glanced at his watch and went into the laboratory where the machine was.

"It must be time," Arthur said, and followed him.

"Yes, it is," Robert said, sitting on the couch. Arthur pulled the scanner forward so that it rested directly above Robert's body, and set the calibrations exactly correctly. He activated the machine and waited while it warmed.

Ambitious Robert was going into the future. Not far, just one hour . . . but it would make history; he would be the first. No one else seemed to have the slightest inkling of the method, but narrow-eyed Robert had run across it and had built his machine, telling the administration it was something else, keeping it secret, keeping men from the bigger universities and corporations from coming in and taking over his work. "I have to believe in my own abilities," Robert had said.

Arthur watched him as he lay back on the couch under the apparatus of the machine. Robert's eyes, long-lashed, closed softly and he drew a deep, even breath. "I'm ready."

So brown Robert goes into the future, Arthur thought. *And when he comes back, he intends to bring witnesses to see him an hour from now, two of him, and to explain it all with his rich, curdled voice, and write a paper and go to a larger university and be famous where there are more and more young rounded girls. Because Robert knows reality almost as well as I do.*

Arthur checked the dials and meters of the machine carefully, seeing that they were exactly as Robert had ordered them. Arthur was a good, careful worker, and that was why even when Mr. Lewis' assistant had scoffed at him he had not been afraid of being dismissed. Everybody knew that he always did exactly as he was told.

"Good-bye," he said. He flicked the switch and Robert disappeared.

He stepped over to the empty couch and placed his hand on the soft, worn leather cushion, feeling its warmth from the body that had just left it. Robert was in the future.

But he had to bring him back. He reset the machine and threw another switch and Robert reappeared on the couch. Arthur stood over him and looked for a long time at the blood flowing from his mouth and nostrils and eyes and ears. There was a small hole torn through his right leg, and that was beginning to bleed, too. He was dead.

The gash in his leg must have been from a small meteor, Arthur decided. He had heard about them when he'd been working in the observatory. It had been one afternoon when he had been working there that he had realized what would happen to Robert when he went into the future. Because of course he could travel forward in time and reappear an hour later, but the Earth would not be there, because the Earth moved around the sun at about eighteen and a half miles a second, and for that matter the whole solar system seemed to be moving at about twelve miles a second toward a point in the constellation Hercules. That was what someone in the astronomy department had told him, anyway, and he had memorized it.

So Robert had landed an hour in the future, but somewhere

out in space, and he had died, the pressure of oxygen in his body hemorrhaging his blood vessels and bursting his lungs before he could even suffocate. But of course it hadn't been Arthur's fault.

Humming softly to himself, Arthur closed down the machine and washed as much blood as he could from Robert's head. Some of it was drying already, leaving a brownish crust on the cold skin. He rearranged Robert's clothes, and went downstairs to report what had happened.

He went directly, stopping only once to watch a young girl with a soft, full red sweater as she struggled out of her heavy coat.

THE FOOD FARM

Kit Reed

After several years as a newspaper reporter, Kit Reed took up short-story writing in 1958 and met with immediate success, selling several stories in quick succession to that discerning and fastidious editor, Anthony Boucher of *Fantasy & Science Fiction*. Over the years she has published perhaps two dozen short works, the best of which have been collected in a 1967 volume entitled *Mister da V and Other Stories*, and several novels, among them *At War With Children* (1964) and *The Better Part* (1967). She lives in Connecticut.

So here I am, warden-in-charge, fattening them up for our leader, Tommy Fango; here I am laying on the banana pudding and the milkshakes and the cream-and-brandy cocktails, going about like a technician, gauging their effect on haunch and thigh when all the time it is I who love him, I who could have pleased him eternally if only life had broken differently. But I am scrawny now, I am swept like a leaf around corners, battered by the slightest wind. My elbows rattle against my ribs, and I have to spend half the day in bed so a gram or two of what I eat will stay with me, for if I do not, the fats and creams will vanish, burned up in my own insatiable furnace, and what little flesh I have will melt away.

Cruel as it may sound, I know where to place the blame.

It was vanity, all vanity, and I hate them most for that. It was not my vanity, for I have always been a simple soul; I reconciled myself early to reinforced chairs and loose garments, to the spattering of remarks. Instead of heeding them I plugged in, and I would have been happy to let it go at that, going through life with my radio in my bodice, for while I never drew cries of admiration, no one ever blanched and turned away.

But they were vain and in their vanity my frail father, my pale, scrawny mother saw me not as an entity but a reflection on themselves. I flush with shame to remember the excuses they made for me. "She takes after May's side of the family," my father would say, denying any responsibility. "It's only baby fat," my mother would say, jabbing her elbow into my soft flank. "Nelly is big for her age." Then she would jerk furiously, pulling my voluminous smock down to cover my knees. That was when they still consented to be seen with me. In that period they would stuff me with pies and roasts before we went anywhere, filling me up so I would not gorge myself in public. Even so I had to take thirds, fourths, fifths, and so I was a humiliation to them.

In time I was too much for them and they stopped taking me out; they made no more attempts to explain. Instead they tried to think of ways to make me look better; the doctors tried the fool's poor battery of pills; they tried to make me join a club. For a while my mother and I did exercises; we would sit on the floor, she in a black leotard, I in my smock. Then she would do the brisk one-two, one-two and I would make a few passes at my toes. But I had to listen, I had to plug in, and after I was plugged in naturally I had to find something to eat; Tommy might sing and I always ate when Tommy sang, and so I would leave her there on the floor, still going one-two, one-two. For a while after that they tried locking up the food. Then they began to cut into my meals.

That was the cruelest time. They would refuse me bread,

they would plead and cry, plying me with lettuce and telling me it was all for my own good. Couldn't they hear my vitals crying out? I fought, I screamed, and when that failed I suffered in silent obedience until finally hunger drove me into the streets. I would lie in bed, made brave by the Monets and Barry Arkin and the Philadons coming in over the radio, and Tommy (there was never enough; I heard him a hundred times a day and it was never enough; how bitter that seems now!). I would hear them and then when my parents were asleep I would unplug and go out into the neighborhood. The first few nights I begged, throwing myself on the mercy of passersby and then plunging into the bakery, bringing home everything I didn't eat right there in the shop. I got money quickly enough; I didn't even have to ask. Perhaps it was my bulk, perhaps it was my desperate subverbal cry of hunger; I found I had only to approach and the money was mine. As soon as they saw me, people would whirl and bolt, hurling a purse or wallet into my path as if to slow me in my pursuit; they would be gone before I could even express my thanks. Once I was shot at. Once a stone lodged itself in my flesh.

At home my parents continued with their tears and pleas. They persisted with their skim milk and their chops, ignorant of the life I lived by night. In the daytime I was complaisant, dozing between snacks, feeding on the sounds which played in my ear, coming from the radio concealed in my dress. Then, when night fell, I unplugged; it gave a certain edge to things, knowing I would not plug in again until I was ready to eat. Some nights this only meant going to one of the caches in my room, bringing forth bottles and cartons and cans. On other nights I had to go into the streets, finding money where I could. Then I would lay in a new supply of cakes and rolls and baloney from the delicatessen and several cans of ready-made frosting and perhaps a flitch of bacon or some ham; I would toss in a basket of oranges to ward off scurvy and a carton of candy bars for quick energy. Once I had enough I would go back to my room, concealing food here and there,

rearranging my nest of pillows and comforters. I would open
the first pie or the first half-gallon of ice cream and then, as I
began, I would plug in.

You had to plug in; everybody that mattered was plugged
in. It was our bond, our solace and our power, and it wasn't a
matter of being distracted, or occupying time. The sound was
what mattered, that and the fact that fat or thin, asleep or
awake, you were important when you plugged in, and you
knew that through fire and flood and adversity, through
contumely and hard times there was this single bond, this
common heritage; strong or weak, eternally gifted or
wretched and ill-loved, we were all plugged in.

Tommy, beautiful Tommy Fango, the others paled to
nothing next to him. Everybody heard him in those days; they
played him two or three times an hour but you never knew
when it would be so you were plugged in and listening hard
every living moment; you ate, you slept, you drew breath for
the moment when they would put on one of Tommy's
records, you waited for his voice to fill the room. Cold cuts
and cupcakes and game hens came and went during that
period in my life, but one thing was constant; I always had a
cream pie thawing and when they played the first bars of
"When a Widow" and Tommy's voice first flexed and
uncurled, I was ready, I would eat the cream pie during
Tommy's midnight show. The whole world waited in those
days; we waited through endless sunlight, through nights of
drumbeats and monotony, we all waited for Tommy Fango's
records, and we waited for that whole unbroken hour of
Tommy, his midnight show. He came on live at midnight in
those days; he sang, broadcasting from the Hotel Riverside,
and that was beautiful, but more important, he talked, and
while he was talking he made everything all right. Nobody
was lonely when Tommy talked; he brought us all together on
that midnight show, he talked and made us powerful, he
talked and finally he sang. You have to imagine what it was
like, me in the night, Tommy, the pie. In a while I would go
to a place where I had to live on Tommy and only Tommy, to

a time when hearing Tommy would bring back the pie, all the poor lost pies . . .

Tommy's records, his show, the pie . . . that was perhaps the happiest period of my life. I would sit and listen and I would eat and eat and eat. So great was my bliss that it became torture to put away the food at daybreak; it grew harder and harder for me to hide the cartons and the cans and the bottles, all the residue of my happiness. Perhaps a bit of bacon fell into the register; perhaps an egg rolled under the bed and began to smell. All right, perhaps I did become careless, continuing my revels into the morning, or I may have been thoughtless enough to leave a jelly roll unfinished on the rug. I became aware that they were watching, lurking just outside my door, plotting as I ate. In time they broke in on me, weeping and pleading, lamenting over every ice cream carton and crumb of pie; then they threatened. Finally they restored the food they had taken from me in the daytime, thinking to curtail my eating at night. Folly. By that time I needed it all, I shut myself in with it and would not listen. I ignored their cries of hurt pride, their outpourings of wounded vanity, their puny little threats. Even if I had listened, I could not have forestalled what happened next.

I was so happy that last day. There was a Smithfield ham, mine, and I remember a jar of cherry preserves, mine, and I remember bacon, pale and white on Italian bread. I remember sounds downstairs and before I could take warning, an assault, a company of uniformed attendants, the sting of a hypodermic gun. Then the ten of them closed in and grappled me into a sling, or net, and heaving and straining, they bore me down the stairs. I'll never forgive you, I cried, as they bundled me into the ambulance. I'll never forgive you, I bellowed as my mother in a last betrayal took away my radio, and I cried out one last time, as my father removed a hambone from my breast: I'll never forgive you, And I never have.

It is painful to describe what happened next. I remember three days of horror and agony, of being too weak, finally, to cry out or claw the walls. Then at last I was quiet and they moved me into a sunny, pastel, chintz-bedizened room. I remember that there were flowers on the dresser and someone watching me.

"What are you in for?" she said.

I could barely speak for weakness. "Despair."

"Hell with that," she said, chewing. "You're in for food."

"What are you eating?" I tried to raise my head.

"Chewing. Inside of the mouth. It helps."

"I'm going to die."

"Everybody thinks that at first. I did." She tilted her head in an attitude of grace. "You know, this is a very exclusive school."

Her name was Ramona and as I wept silently, she filled me in. This was a last resort for the few who could afford to send their children here. They prettied it up with a schedule of therapy, exercise, massage; we would wear dainty pink smocks and talk of art and theater; from time to time we would attend classes in elocution and hygiene. Our parents would say with pride that we were away at Faircrest, an elegant finishing school; we knew better—it was a prison and we were being starved.

"It's a world I never made," said Ramona, and I knew that her parents were to blame, even as mine were. Her mother liked to take the children into hotels and casinos, wearing her thin daughters like a garland of jewels. Her father followed the sun on his private yacht, with the pennants flying and his children on the fantail, lithe and tanned. He would pat his flat, tanned belly and look at Ramona in disgust. When it was no longer possible to hide her, he gave in to blind pride. One night they came in a launch and took her away. She had been here six months now, and had lost almost a hundred pounds. She must have been monumental in her prime; she was still huge.

"We live from day to day," she said. "But you don't know the worst."

"My radio," I said in a spasm of fear. "They took away my radio."

"There is a reason," she said. "They call it therapy."

I was mumbling in my throat, in a minute I would scream.

"Wait." With ceremony, she pushed aside a picture and touched a tiny switch and then, like sweet balm for my panic, Tommy's voice flowed into the room.

When I was quiet she said, "You only hear him once a day."

"No."

"But you can hear him any time you want to. You hear him when you need him most."

But we were missing the first few bars and so we shut up and listened, and after "When a Widow" was over we sat quietly for a moment, her resigned, me weeping, and then Ramona threw another switch and the Sound filtered into the room, and it was almost like being plugged in.

"Try not to think about it."

"I'll die."

"If you think about it you *will* die. You have to learn to use it instead. In a minute they will come with lunch," Ramona said and as The Screamers sang sweet background, she went on in a monotone: "A chop. One lousy chop with a piece of lettuce and maybe some gluten bread. I pretend it's a leg of lamb—that works if you eat very, very slowly and think about Tommy the whole time; then if you look at your picture of Tommy you can turn the lettuce into anything you want, Caesar salad or a whole smorgasbord, and if you say his name over and over you can pretend a whole bombe or torte if you want to and . . ."

"I'm going to pretend a ham and kidney pie and a watermelon filled with chopped fruits and Tommy and I are in the Rainbow Room and we're going to finish up with Fudge Royale . . ." I almost drowned in my own saliva; in the background I could almost hear Tommy and I could hear Ramona saying, "Capon, Tommy would like capon, canard à l'orange, Napoleons, tomorrow we will save Tommy for lunch and listen while we eat . . ." and I thought about that, I thought about listening and imagining whole cream pies and I went on, ". . . lemon pie, rice pudding, a whole Edam cheese . . . I think I'm going to live."

The matron came in the next morning at breakfast, and stood as she would every day, tapping red fingernails on one svelte hip, looking on in revulsion as we fell on the glass of orange juice and the hard-boiled egg. I was too weak to control myself; I heard a shrill sniveling sound and realized only from her expression that it was my own voice: "Please, just some bread, a stick of butter, anything, I could lick the dishes if you'd let me, only please don't leave me like this, please . . ." I can still see her sneer as she turned her back.

I felt Ramona's loyal hand on my shoulder. "There's always toothpaste, but don't use too much at once or they'll come and take it away from you."

I was too weak to rise and so she brought it and we shared the tube and talked about all the banquets we had ever known, and when we got tired of that we talked about Tommy, and when that failed, Ramona went to the switch and we heard "When a Widow," and that helped for a while, and then we decided that tomorrow we would put off "When a Widow" until bedtime because then we would have something to look forward to all day. Then lunch came and we both wept.

It was not just hunger: after a while the stomach begins to devour itself and the few grams you toss it at mealtimes assuage it so that in time the appetite itself begins to fail. After hunger comes depression. I lay there, still too weak to get about, and in my misery I realized that they could bring me roast pork and watermelon and Boston cream pie without ceasing; they could gratify all my dreams and I would only weep helplessly, because I no longer had the strength to eat. Even then, when I thought I had reached rock bottom, I had not comprehended the worst. I noticed it first in Ramona. Watching her at the mirror, I said, in fear:

"You're thinner."

She turned with tears in her eyes. "Nelly, I'm not the only one."

I looked around at my own arms and saw that she was right: there was one less fold of flesh above the elbow; there was one less wrinkle at the wrist. I turned my face to the wall and all Ramona's talk of food and Tommy did not comfort me. In desperation she turned on Tommy's voice, but as he sang I lay back and contemplated the melting of my own flesh.

"If we stole a radio we could hear him again," Ramona said, trying to soothe me. "We could hear him when he sings tonight."

Tommy came to Faircrest on a visit two days later, for reasons that I could not then understand. All the other girls lumbered into the assembly hall to see him, thousands of pounds of agitated flesh. It was that morning that I discovered I could walk again, and I was on my feet, struggling into the pink tent in a fury to get to Tommy, when the matron intercepted me.

"Not you, Nelly."

"I have to get to Tommy. I have to hear him sing."

"Next time, maybe." With a look of naked cruelty she added, "You're a disgrace. You're still too gross."

I lunged, but it was too late; she had already shot the bolt. And so I sat in the midst of my diminishing body, suffering while every other girl in the place listened to him sing. I knew then that I had to act; I would regain myself somehow, I would find food and regain my flesh and then I would go to Tommy. I would use force if I had to, but I would hear him sing. I raged through the room all that morning, hearing the shrieks of five hundred girls, the thunder of their feet, but even when I pressed myself against the wall I could not hear Tommy's voice.

Yet Ramona, when she came back to the room, said the most interesting thing. It was some time before she could speak at all, but in her generosity she played "When a Widow" while she regained herself, and then she spoke:

"He came for something, Nelly. He came for something he didn't find."

"Tell about what he was wearing. Tell what his throat did when he sang."

"He looked at all the *before* pictures, Nelly. The matron was trying to make him look at the *afters* but he kept looking at the *befores* and shaking his head and then he found one and put it in his pocket and if he hadn't found it, he wasn't going to sing."

I could feel my spine stiffen. "Ramona, you've got to help me. I must go to him."

That night we staged a daring break. We clubbed the attendant when he brought dinner, and once we had him under the bed we ate all the chops and gluten bread on his cart and then we went down the corridor, lifting bolts, and when we were a hundred strong we locked the matron in her office and raided the dining hall, howling and eating everything we could find. I ate that night, how I ate, but even as I ate I was aware of a fatal lightness in my bones, a failure in capacity, and so they found me in the frozen food locker, weeping over a chain of link sausage, inconsolable because I understood that they had spoiled it for me, they with their chops and their gluten bread; I could never eat as I once had, I would never be myself again.

In my fury I went after the matron with a ham hock, and when I had them all at bay I took a loin of pork for sustenance and I broke out of that place. I had to get to Tommy before I got any thinner; I had to try. Outside the gate I stopped a car and hit the driver with the loin of pork and then I drove to the Hotel Riverside, where Tommy always stayed. I made my way up the fire stairs on little cat feet and when the valet went to his suite with one of his velveteen suits I followed, quick as a tigress, and the next moment I was inside. When all was quiet I tiptoed to his door and stepped inside.

He was magnificent. He stood at the window, gaunt and beautiful; his blond hair fell to his waist and his shoulders shriveled under a heartbreaking double-breasted pea-green velvet suit. He did not see me at first; I drank in his image and then, delicately, cleared my throat. In the second that he turned and saw me, everything seemed possible.

"It's you." His voice throbbed.

"I had to come."

Our eyes fused and in that moment I believed that we two could meet, burning as a single, lambent flame, but in the next second his face had crumpled in disappointment; he brought a picture from his pocket, a fingered, cracked photograph, and he looked from it to me and back at the photograph, saying, "My darling, you've fallen off."

"Maybe it's not too late," I cried, but we both knew I would fail.

And fail I did, even though I ate for days, for five desperate, heroic weeks; I threw pies into the breach, fresh hams and whole sides of beef, but those sad days at the food farm, the starvation and the drugs have so upset my chemistry that it cannot be restored; no matter what I eat I fall off and I continue to fall off; my body is a halfway house for foods I can no longer assimilate. Tommy watches, and because he knows he almost had me, huge and round and beautiful, Tommy mourns. He eats less and less now. He eats like a bird and lately he has refused to sing; strangely, his records have begun to disappear.

And so a whole nation waits.

"I almost had her," he says, when they beg him to resume his midnight shows; he will not sing, he won't talk, but his hands describe the mountain of woman he has longed for all his life.

And so I have lost Tommy, and he has lost me, but I am doing my best to make it up to him. I own Faircrest now, and in the place where Ramona and I once suffered I use my skills on the girls Tommy wants me to cultivate. I can put twenty pounds on a girl in a couple of weeks and I don't mean bloat, I mean solid fat. Ramona and I feed them up and once a week we weigh and I poke the upper arm with a special stick and I will not be satisfied until the stick goes in and does not rebound because all resiliency is gone. Each week I bring out my best and Tommy shakes his head in misery because the best is not yet good enough, none of them are what I once was. But one day the time and the girl will be right—would that it were me—the time and the girl will be right and Tommy will sing again. In the meantime, the whole world waits; in the meantime, in a private wing well away from the others, I keep my special cases; the matron, who grows fatter as I watch her. And Mom. And Dad.

AN HONORABLE DEATH

Gordon R. Dickson

That ebullient Minnesotan Gordon Dickson is a Hugo and
Nebula winner, a past president of the Science Fiction Writers of America, a man of inexhaustible vitality and warmth,
and a splendid writer—as this quiet, intelligent story demon-
strates.

From the arboretum at the far end of the patio to the landing
stage of the transporter itself, the whole household was at
sixes and sevens over the business of preparing the party for
the celebration. As usual, Carter was having to oversee
everything himself, otherwise it would not have gone right;
and this was all the harder in that, of late, his enthusiasms
seemed to have run down somewhat. He was conscious of a
vague distaste for life as he found it, and all its parts. He
would be forty-seven this fall. Could it be the imminent
approach of middle age, seeking him out even in the quiet
backwater of this small, suburban planet? Whatever it was,
things were moving even more slowly than usual this year.
He had not even had time to get into his costume of a full dress
suit (19th-20th cent.) with tails, which he had chosen as not
too dramatic, and yet kinder than most dress-ups to his tall,

rather awkward figure—when the chime sounded, announcing the first arrival.

Dropping the suit on his bed, he went out, cutting across the patio toward the gathering room, where the landing stage of the transporter was—and almost ran headlong into one of the original native inhabitants of the planet, standing like a lean and bluish post with absolute rigidity in the center of the pretty little flagstone path.

"What are *you* doing here?" cried Carter.

The narrow indigo horselike face leaned confidentially down toward Carter's own. And then Carter recognized the great mass of apple blossoms, like a swarming of creamy-winged moths, held to the inky chest.

"Oh—" began Carter, on a note of fury. Then he threw up his hands and took the mass of branches. Peering around the immovable alien and wincing, he got a glimpse of his imported apple tree. But it was not as badly violated as he had feared. "Thank you. Thank you," he said, and waved the native out of the way.

But the native remained. Carter stared—then saw that in addition to the apple blossoms the thin and hairless creature, though no more dressed than his kind ever were, had in this instance contrived belts, garlands, and bracelets of native flowers for himself. The colors and patterns would be arranged to convey some special meaning—they always did. But right at the moment Carter was too annoyed and entirely too rushed to figure them out, though he did think it a little unusual the native should be holding a slim shaft of dark wood with a fire-hardened point. Hunting was most expressly forbidden to the natives.

"Now what?" said Carter. The native (a local chief, Carter suddenly recognized) lifted the spear and unexpectedly made several slow, stately hops, with his long legs flicking up and down above the scrubbed white of the flagstones—like an Earthly crane at its mating. "Oh, now, don't tell me you want to dance!"

The native chief ceased his movements and went back to being a post again, staring out over Carter's head as if at some horizon, lost and invisible beyond the iridescences of Carter's dwelling walls. Carter groaned, pondered, and glanced anxiously ahead toward the gathering room, from which he could now hear the voice of Ona, already greeting the first guest with female twitters.

"All right," he told the chief. "All right—this once. But only because it's Escape Day Anniversary. And you'll have to wait until after dinner."

The native stepped aside and became rigid again. Carter hurried past into the gathering room, clutching the apple blossoms. His wife was talking to a short brown-bearded man with an ivory-tinted guitar hanging by a broad, tan band over one red-and-white, checked-shirted shoulder.

"Ramy!" called Carter, hurrying up to them. The landing stage of the transporter, standing in the middle of the room, chimed again. "Oh, take these will you, dear?" He thrust the apple blossoms into Ona's plump, bare arms. "The chief. In honor of the day. You know how they are—and I had to promise he could dance after dinner." She stared, her soft, pale face upturned to him. "I couldn't help it."

He turned and hurried to the landing stage, from the small round platform of which were now stepping down a short academic elderly man with wispy gray hair and a rather fat button-nosed woman of the same age, both wearing the ancient Ionian chiton as their costume. Carter had warned Ona against wearing a chiton, for the very reason that these two might show up in the same dress. He allowed himself a small twinge of satisfaction at the thought of her ballroom gown as he went hastily now to greet them.

"Doctor!" he said. "Lidi! Here you are!" He shook hands with the doctor. "Happy Escape Day to both of you."

"I was sure we'd be late," said Lidi, holding firmly to the folds of her chiton with both hands. "The public terminal on Arcturus Five was so crowded. And the doctor won't hurry no matter what I say—" She looked over at her husband, but he, busy greeting Ona, ignored her.

The chime sounded again and two women, quite obviously sisters in spite of the fact that they were wearing dissimilar costumes, appeared on the platform. One was dressed in a perfectly ordinary everday kilt and tunic—no costume at all. The other wore a close, unidentifiable sort of suit of some gray material and made straight for Carter.

"Cart!" she cried, taking one of his hands in both of her own and pumping it heartily. "Happy Escape Day." She beamed at him from a somewhat plain strong-featured face, sharply made up. "Ani and I—" She looked around for her sister and saw the kilt and tunic already drifting in rather dreamlike and unconscious fashion toward the perambulating bar at the far end of the room. "I," she corrected herself hastily, "couldn't wait to get here. Who else is coming?"

"Just what you see, Totsa," said Carter, indicating those present with a wide-flung hand. "We thought a small party this year—a little quiet gathering—"

"So nice! And what do you think of my costume?" She revolved slowly for his appraisal.

"Why—good, very good."

"Now!" Totsa came back to face him. "You can't guess what it is at all."

"Of course I can," said Carter heartily.

"Well, then, what is it?"

"Oh, well, perhaps I won't tell you, then," said Carter.

A small head with wispy gray hair intruded into the circle of their conversation. "An artistic rendering of the space suitings worn by those two intrepid pioneers who this day, four hundred and twenty years ago, burst free in their tiny ship from the iron grip of Earth's prisoning gravitation?"

Totsa shouted in triumph. "I knew you'd know, Doctor! Trust a philosophical researcher to catch on. Carter hadn't the slightest notion. Not an inkling!"

"A host is a host is a host," said Carter. "Excuse me, I've got to get into my own costume."

He went out again and back across the patio. The outer air felt pleasantly cool on his warm face. He hoped that the implications of his last remark—that he had merely been being polite in pretending to be baffled by the significance of her costume—had got across to Totsa, but probably it had not. She would interpret it as an attempt to cover up his failure to recognize her costume by being cryptic. The rapier was wasted on the thick hide of such a woman. And to think he once . . . you had to use a club. And the worst of it was, he *had* grasped the meaning of her costume immediately. He had merely been being playful in refusing to admit it . . .

The native chief was still standing unmoved where Carter had left him, still waiting for his moment.

"Get out of the way, can't you?" said Carter irritably, as he shouldered by.

The chief retreated one long ostrichlike step until he stood half-obscured in the shadow of a trellis of roses. Carter went on into the bedroom.

His suit was laid out for him, and he climbed into the clumsy garments, his mind busy on the schedule of the evening ahead. The local star that served as this planet's sun (one of the Pleiades, Asterope) would be down in an hour and a half, but the luminosity of the interstellar space in this galactic region made the sky bright for hours after a setting, and the fireworks could not possibly go on until that died down.

Carter had designed the set piece for the finale himself—a vintage space rocket curving up from a representation of the Earth, into a firmament of stars, and changing into a star itself as it dwindled. It would be unthinkable to waste this against a broad band of glowing rarefied matter just above the western horizon.

Accordingly, there was really no choice about the schedule. At least five hours before the thought of fireworks could be entertained. Carter, hooking his tie into place around his neck before a section of his bedroom wall set on reflection, computed in his head. The cocktail session now starting would be good for two and a half, possibly three hours. He dared not stretch it out any longer than that or Ani would be sure to get drunk. As it was, it would be bad enough with a full cocktail session and wine with the dinner. But perhaps Totsa could keep her under control. At any rate—three, and an hour and a half for dinner. No matter how it figured, there would be half an hour or more to fill in there.

Well—Carter worked his way into his dress coat—he could make his usual small speech in honor of the occasion. And—oh, yes, of course —there was the chief. The native dances were actually meaningless, boring things, though Carter had been quite interested in them at first, but then his was the inquiring type of mind. Still, the others might find it funny enough, or interesting for a single performance.

Buttoning up his coat, he went back out across the patio, feeling more kindly toward the native than he had since the moment of his first appearance. Passing him this time, Carter thought to stop and ask, "Would you like something to eat?"

Remote, shiny, mottled by the shadow of the rose leaves, the native neither moved nor answered, and Carter hurried on with a distinct feeling of relief. He had always made it a point to keep some native food on hand for just such an emergency as this—after all, they got hungry, too. But it was a definite godsend not to have to stop now, when he was so busy, and see the stuff properly prepared and provided for this uninvited and unexpected guest.

The humans had all moved out of the gathering room by the time he reached it and into the main lounge with its more complete bar and mobile chairs. On entering, he saw that they had already split up into three different and, in a way, inevitable groups. His wife and the doctor's were at gossip in a corner; Ramy was playing his guitar and singing in a low, not unpleasant, though hoarse voice to Ani, who sat drink in hand, gazing past him with a half-smile into the changing colors of the wall behind him. Totsa and the doctor were in a discussion at the bar. Carter joined them.

"—and I'm quite prepared to believe it," the doctor was saying in his gentle, precise tones as Carter came up. "Well, very good, Cart." He nodded at Carter's costume.

"You think so?" said Carter, feeling his face warm pleasantly. "Awkward getup, but—I don't know, it just struck me this year." He punched for a lime brandy and watched with pleasure as the bar disgorged the brimming glass by his waiting hand.

"You look armored in it, Cart," Totsa said.

"Thrice-armed is he—" Carter acknowledged the compliment and sipped on his glass. He glanced at the doctor to see if the quotation had registered, but the doctor was already leaning over to receive a refill in his own glass.

"Have you any idea what this man's been telling me?" demanded Totsa, swiveling toward Carter. "He insists we're doomed. Literally doomed!"

"I've no doubt we are—" began Carter. But before he could expand on this agreement with the explanation that he meant it in the larger sense, she was foaming over him in a tidal wave of conversation.

"Well, I don't pretend to be unobjective about it. After all, who are we to survive? But really—how ridiculous! And you back him up just like that, *blindly*, without the slightest notion of what he's been talking about!"

"A theory only, Totsa," said the doctor, quite unruffled.

"I wouldn't honor it by even calling it a theory!"

"Perhaps," said Carter, sipping on his lime brandy, "if I knew a little more about what you two were—"

"The point," said the doctor, turning a little, politely, toward Carter, "has to do with the question of why, on all these worlds we've taken over, we've found no other race comparable to our own. We may," he smiled, "of course be unique in the universe. But this theory supposes that any contact between races of differing intelligences must inevitably result in the death of the inferior race. Consequently, if we met our superiors—" He gave a graceful wave of his hand.

"I imagine it could," said Carter.

"Ridiculous!" said Totsa. "As if we couldn't just avoid contact altogether if we wanted to!"

"That's a point," said Carter. "I imagine negotiations—"

"We," said Totsa, "who burst the bonds of our Earthly home, who have spread out among the stars in a scant four hundred years, are hardly the type to turn up our toes and just die!"

"It's all based on an assumption, Cart"—the doctor put his glass down on the bar and clasped his small hands before him—"that the racial will to live is dependent upon what might be called a certain amount of emotional self-respect. A race of lesser intelligence or scientific ability could hardly be a threat to us. But a greater race, the theory goes, must inevitably generate a sort of death-wish in all of us. We're too used to being top dog. We must conquer or—"

"Absolutely nonsense!" said Totsa.

"Well, now, you can't just condemn the idea offhand like that," Carter said. "Naturally, I can't imagine a human like myself ever giving up, either. We're too hard, too wolfish, too much the last-ditch fighters. But I imagine a theory like this might well hold true for other, lesser races." He cleared his throat. "For example, I've had quite a bit of contact since we came here with the natives which were the dominant life-form on this world in its natural state—"

"Oh, natives!" snapped Totsa scornfully.

"You might be surprised, Totsa!" said Carter, heating up a little. An inspiration took hold of him. "And, in fact, I've arranged for you to do just that. I've invited the local native chief to dance for us after dinner. You might just find it very illuminating."

"Illuminating? How?" pounced Totsa.

"That," said Carter, putting his glass down on the bar with a very slight flourish, "I'll leave you to find out for yourself. And now, if you don't mind, I'm going to have to make my hostly rounds of the other guests."

He walked away, glowing with a different kind of inner warmth. He was smiling as he came up to Ramy, who was still singing ballads and playing his guitar for Totsa's sister.

"Excellent," Carter said, clapping his hands briefly and sitting down with them as the song ended. "What was that?"

"Richard the Lionheart wrote it," said Ramy hoarsely. He turned to the woman. "Another drink, Ani?"

Carter tried to signal the balladeer with his eyes, but Ramy had already pressed the buttons on the table beside their chairs, and a little motor unit from the bar was already on its way to them with the drinks emerging from its interior. Carter sighed inaudibly and leaned back in his chair. He could warn Totsa to keep an eye on Ani a little later.

He accepted another drink himself. The sound of voices in the room was rising as more alcohol was consumed. The only quiet one was Ani. She sat, engaged in the single-minded business of imbibing, and listened to the conversation between Ramy and himself, as if she was—thought Carter suddenly—perhaps one step removed, beyond some glass-like wall, where the real sound and movement of life came muted, if at all. The poetry of this flash of insight—for Carter could think of no other way to describe it—operated so strongly upon his emotions that he completely lost the thread of what Ramy was saying and was reduced to noncommittal noises by way of comment.

I should take up my writing again, he thought to himself.

As soon as a convenient opportunity presented itself, he excused himself and got up. He went over to the corner where the women were talking.

"—Earth," Lidi was saying, "the doctor and I will never forget it. Oh, Cart—" She twisted around to him as he sat down in a chair opposite. "You must take this girl to Earth sometime. Really."

"Do you think she's the back-to-nature type?" said Carter, with a smile.

"No, stop it!" Lidi turned back to Ona. "Make him take you!"

"I've mentioned it to him. Several times," said Ona, putting down the glass in her hand with a helpless gesture on the end-table beside her.

"Well, you know what they say," smiled Carter.

"Everyone talks about Earth but nobody ever goes there any more."

"The doctor and I went. And it was memorable. It's not what you see, of course, but the insight you bring to it. I'm only five generations removed from people living right there on the North American continent. And the doctor had cousins in Turkey when he was a boy. Say what you like, the true stock thins out as generation succeeds generation away from the home world."

"And it's not the expense any more," put in Ona. "Everyone's rich nowadays."

"Rich! What an uncomfortable word!" said Lidi. "You should say *capable*, dear. Remember, our riches are merely the product of our science, which is the fruit of our own capabilities."

"Oh, you know what I mean!" said Ona. "The point is, Cart won't go. He just won't."

"I'm a simple man," Carter said. "I have my writing, my music, my horticulture, right here. I feel no urge to roam—" he stood up—"except to the kitchen right now, to check on the caterers. If you'll excuse me—"

"But you haven't given your wife an answer about taking her to Earth one of these days!" cried Lidi.

"Oh, we'll go, we'll go," said Carter, walking off with a good-humored wave of his hand.

As he walked through the west sunroom to the dining area and the kitchen (homey word!) beyond, his cheerfulness dwindled somewhat. It was always a ticklish job handling the caterers, now that they were all artists doing the work for the love of it and not to be controlled by the price they were paid. Carter would have liked to wash his hands of that end of the party altogether and just leave them to operate on their own. But what if he failed to check and then something went wrong? It was his own artistic conscience operating, he thought, that would not give him any rest.

The dining room was already set up in classic style with long table and individual chairs. He passed the gleam of its tableware and went on through the light-screen into the kitchen area. The master caterer was just in the process of directing his two apprentices to set up the heating tray on which the whole roast boar, papered and gilded, would be kept warm in the centerpiece position on the table during the meal. He did not see Carter enter; and Carter himself stopped to admire, with a sigh of relief, the boar itself. It was a masterwork of the carver's set and had been built up so skillfully from its component chunks of meat that no one could have suspected it was not the actual animal itself.

Looking up at this moment, the caterer caught sight of him and came over to see what he wanted. Carter advanced a few small, tentative suggestions, but the response was so artificially polite that after a short while Carter was glad to leave him to his work.

Carter wandered back through the house without returning directly to the lounge. With the change of the mood that the encounter with the caterer had engendered, his earlier feelings of distaste with life—a sort of melancholy—had come over him. He thought of the people he had invited almost with disgust. Twenty years ago, he would not have thought himself capable of belonging to such a crowd. Where were the great friends, the true friends, that as a youngster he had intended to acquire? Not that it was the fault of those in the lounge. They could not help being what they were. It was the fault of the times, which made life too easy for everybody; and—yes, he would be honest—his own fault, too.

His wanderings had brought him back to the patio. He remembered the chief and peered through the light dusk at the trellis under the light arch of which the native stood.

Beyond, the house was between the semi-enclosed patio and the fading band of brilliance in the west. Deep shadow lay upon the trellis itself and the native under it. He was almost obscured by it, but a darkly pale, vertical line of reflection from his upright spear showed that he had made no move. A gush of emotion burst within Carter. He took a single step toward the chief, with the abrupt, spontaneous urge to thank him for coming and offering to dance. But at that moment, through the open doorway of his bedroom, sounded the small, metallic chimes of his bedside clock, announcing the twenty-first hour, and he turned hastily and crossed through the gathering room, into the lounge.

"Hors d'oeuvres! Hors d'oeuvres!" he called cheerfully, flinging the lounge door wide. "Hors d'oeuvres, everybody! Time to come and get it!"

Dinner could not go off otherwise than well. Everyone was half-tight and hungry. Everyone was talkative. Even Ani had thrown off her habitual introversion and was smiling and nodding, quite soberly, anyone would swear. She was listening to Ona and Lidi talking about Lidi's grown-up son when he had been a baby. The doctor was in high spirits, and Ramy, having gotten his guitar playing out of his system earlier with Ani, was ready to be companionable. By the time they had finished the rum-and-butter pie, everyone was in a good mood, and even the caterer, peering through a momentary transparency of the kitchen wall, exchanged a beam with Carter.

Carter glanced at his watch. Only twenty minutes more! The time had happily flown, and, far from having to fill it in, he would have to cut his own speech a little short. If it were not for the fact that he had already announced it, he would have eliminated the chief's dance—no, that would not have done, either. He had always made a point of getting along with the natives of this world. "It's their home, too, after all," he had always said.

He tinkled on a wine glass with a spoon and rose to his feet.

Faces turned toward him and conversation came to a reluctant halt around the table. He smiled at his assembled guests.

"As you know," said Carter, "it has always been my custom at these little gatherings—and old customs are the best—to say a few—"he held up a disarming hand—"a very few words. Tonight I will be even briefer than usual." He stopped and took a sip of water from the glass before him.

"On this present occasion, the quadricentennial of our great race's Escape into the limitless bounds of the universe, I am reminded of the far road we have come; and the far road—undoubtedly—we have yet to go. I am thinking at the moment," he smiled, to indicate that what he was about to say was merely said in good-fellowship, "of a new theory expressed by our good doctor here tonight. This theory postulates that when a lesser race meets a greater, the lesser must inevitably go to the wall. And that, since it is pretty generally accepted that the laws of chance ensure our race eventually meeting *its* superior, *we* must inevitably and eventually go to the wall."

He paused and warmed them again with the tolerance of his smile.

"May I say *nonsense*!"

"Now, let no one retort that I am merely taking refuge in the blind attitude that reacts with the cry, 'It can't happen to us.' Let me say I believe it *could* happen to us, but it won't. And why not? I will answer that with one word. Civilization.

"These overmen—if indeed they ever show up—must, even as we, be civilized. *Civilized.* Think of what that word means! Look at the seven of us here. Are we not educated, kindly, sympathetic people? And how do we treat the races inferior to us that we have run across?

"I'm going to let you answer these questions for yourselves, because I now invite you to the patio for cognac and coffee—and to see one of the natives of this planet, who has expressed a desire to dance for you. Look at him as he dances, observe him, consider what human gentleness and consideration are involved in the gesture that included him in this great festival of ours." Carter paused. "And consider one other great statement that has echoed down the corridors of time—*As ye have done to others, so shall ye be done by*!"

Carter sat down, flushed and glowing, to applause, then rose immediately to precede his guests, who were getting up to stream toward the patio. Walking rapidly, he outdistanced them as they passed the gathering room.

For a second, as he burst out through the patio doorway, his eyes were befuddled by the sudden darkness. Then his vision cleared as the others came through the doorway behind him and he was able to make out the inky shadow of the chief, still barely visible under the trellis.

Leaving Ona to superintend the seating arrangements in the central courtyard of the patio, he hurried toward the trellis. The native was there waiting for him.

"Now," said Carter, a little breathlessly, "it must be a short dance, a very short dance."

The chief lowered his long, narrow head, looking down at Carter with what seemed to be an aloofness, a sad dignity, and suddenly Carter felt uncomfortable.

"Um—well," he muttered, "you don't have to cut it *too* short."

Carter turned and went back to the guests. Under Ona's direction, they had seated themselves in a small semicircle of chairs, with snifter glasses and coffee cups. A chair had been left for Carter in the middle. He took it and accepted a glass of cognac from his wife.

"Now?" asked Totsa, leaning toward him.

"Yes—yes, here he comes," said Carter, and directed their attention toward the trellis.

The lights had been turned up around the edge of the courtyard, and as the chief advanced unto them from the darkness, he seemed to step all at once out of a wall of night.

"My," said Lidi, a little behind and to the left of Carter, "isn't he big!"

"*Tall*, rather," said the doctor, and coughed dryly at her side.

The chief came on into the center of the lighted courtyard. He carried his spear upright in one hand before him, the arm half-bent at the elbow and half-extended, advancing with exaggeratedly long steps and on tiptoe—in a manner unfortunately almost exactly reminiscent of the classical husband sneaking home late at night. There was a sudden titter from Totsa, behind Carter. Carter flushed.

Arrived in the center of the patio before them, the chief halted, probed at the empty air with his spear in several directions, and began to shuffle about with his head bent toward the ground.

Behind Carter, Ramy said something in a low voice. There was a strangled chuckle and the strings of the guitar plinked quietly on several idle notes.

"Please," said Carter, without turning his head.

There was a pause, some more indistinguishable murmuring from Ramy, followed again by his low, hoarse, and smothered chuckle.

"Perhaps—"said Carter, raising his voice slightly, "perhaps I ought to translate the dance as he does it. All these dances are stories acted out. This one is apparently called 'An Honorable Death.' "

He paused to clear his throat. No one said anything. Out in the center of the patio, the chief was standing crouched, peering to right and left, his neck craned like a chicken's.

"You see him now on the trail," Carter went on. "The silver-colored flowers on his right arm denote the fact that it *is* a story of death that he is dancing. The fact that they are below the elbow indicates it is an honorable, rather than dishonorable, death. But the fact that he wears nothing at all on the other arm below the elbow tells us this is the full and only story of the dance."

Carter found himself forced to clear his throat again. He took a sip from his snifter glass.

"As I say," he continued, "we see him now on the trail, alone." The chief had now begun to take several cautious steps forward, and then alternate ones in retreat, with some evidence of tension and excitement. "He is happy at the moment because he is on the track of a large herd of local game. Watch the slope of his spear as he holds it in his hand. The more it approaches the vertical, the happier he is feeling—"

Ramy murmured again and his coarse chuckle rasped on Carter's ears. It was echoed by a giggle from Totsa and even a small, dry bark of a laugh from the doctor.

"—the happier he is feeling," repeated Carter loudly. "Except that, paradoxically, the line of the absolute vertical represents the deepest tragedy and sorrow. In a little paper I did on the symbolism behind these dance movements, I advanced the theory that when a native strikes up with his spear from the absolute vertical position, it is because some carnivore too large for him to handle has already downed him. He's a dead man.''

The chief had gone into a flurry of movement.

''Ah,'' said Carter, on a note of satisfaction. The others were quiet now. He let his voice roll out a little. ''He has made his kill. He hastens home with it. He is very happy. Why shouldn't he be? He is successful, young, strong. His mate, his progeny, his home await him. Even now it comes into sight.''

The chief froze. His spear point dropped.

''But what is this?'' cried Carter, straightening up dramatically in his chair. ''What has happened? He sees a stranger in the doorway. It is the Man of Seven Spears who—this is a superstition, of course—''Carter interrupted himself—''who has, in addition to his own spear, six other magic spears which will fly from him on command and kill anything that stands in his way. What is this unconquerable being doing inside the entrance of the chief's home without being invited?''

The wooden spear point dropped abruptly, almost to the ground.

''The Man of Seven Spears tells him,'' said Carter. ''He, the Man of Seven Spears, has chosen to desire the flowers about our chief's house. Therefore he has taken the house, killing all within it—the mate and the little ones—that their touch may be cleansed from flowers that are his. Everything is now his.''

The soft, tumbling sound of liquid being poured filled in the second of Carter's pause.

''Not too much—''whispered someone.

''What can our chief do?'' said Carter sharply. The chief was standing rigid with his head bent forward and his forehead pressed against the perfectly vertical shaft of his spear, now held upright before him. ''He is sick—we would say he is weeping, in human terms. All that meant anything to him is now gone. He cannot even revenge himself on the Man of Seven Spears, whose magic weapons make him invincible.'' Carter, moved by the pathos in his own voice, felt his throat tighten on the last words.

"Ona, dear, do you have an antacid tablet?'' the doctor's wife whispered behind him.

"He stands where he has stopped!'' cried Carter fiercely. "He has no place else to go. The Man of Seven Spears ignores him, playing with the flowers. For eventually, without moving, without food or drink, he will collapse and die, as all of the Man of Seven Spears' enemies have died. For one, two, three days he stands there in his sorrow; and late on the third day the plan for revenge he has longed for comes to him. He cannot conquer his enemy—but he can eternally shame him, so that the Man of Seven Spears, in his turn, will be forced to die.

"He goes into the house.'' The chief was moving again. "The Man of Seven Spears sees him enter, but pays no attention to him, for he is beneath notice. And it's a good thing for our chief this is so—or else the Man of Seven Spears would call upon all his magic weapons and kill him on the spot. But he is playing with his new flowers and pays no attention.

"Carrying his single spear,'' went on Carter, "the chief goes in to the heart of his house. Each house has a heart, which is the most important place in it. For if the heart is destroyed, the house dies, and all within it. Having come to the heart of the house, which is before its hearth fire, the chief places his spear butt down on the ground and holds it upright in the position of greatest grief. He stands there pridefully. We can imagine the Man of Seven Spears, suddenly realizing the shame to be put upon him, rushing wildly to interfere. But he and all of his seven spears are too slow. The chief leaps into the air—''

Carter checked himself. The chief was still standing with his forehead pressed against the spear shaft.

"He leaps into the air,'' repeated Carter, a little louder.

And at that moment the native *did* bound upward, his long legs flailing, to an astonishing height. For a second he seemed to float above the tip of his spear, still grasping it—and then he descended like some great dark stricken bird, heavily upon the patio. The thin shaft trembled and shook, upright, above his fallen figure.

Multiple screams exploded and the whole company was on their feet. But the chief, slowly rising, gravely removed the spear from between the arm and side in which he had cleverly caught it while falling; and, taking it in his other hand, he stalked off into the shadows toward the house.

A babble of talk burst out behind Carter. Over all the other voices, Lidi's rose like a half-choked fountain.

"—absolutely! Heart failure! I never was so upset in my life—"

"Cart!" said Ona bitterly.

"Well, Cart," spoke Totsa triumphantly in his ear. "What's the application of all this to what you told me earlier?"

Carter, who had been sitting stunned, exploded roughly out of his chair.

"Oh, don't be such a *fool*!" He jerked himself away from them into the tree-bound shadows beyond the patio.

Behind him—after some few minutes—the voices lowered to a less excited level, and then he heard a woman's footsteps approaching him in the dark.

"Cart?" said his wife's voice hesitantly.

"What?" asked Carter, not moving.

"Aren't you coming back?"

"In a while."

There was a pause.

"Cart?"

"What?"

"Don't you think—"

"No, I don't think!" snarled Carter. "She can go to bloody hell!"

"But you can't just call her a fool—"

"She *is* a fool! They're all fools—every one of them! I'm a fool, too, but I'm not a stupid damn bloody fool like all of them!"

"Just because of some silly native dance!" said Ona, almost crying.

"Silly?" said Carter. "At least it's something. He's got a dance to do. That's more than the rest of them in there have. And it just so happens that dance is pretty important to him. You'd think they might like to learn something about that, instead of sitting back making their stupid jokes!"

His little explosion went off into the darkness and fell unanswered.

"Please come back, Cart," Ona said, after a long moment.

"At least he has something," said Carter. "At least there's that for him."

"I just can't face them if you don't come back."

"All right, goddammit," said Carter. "I'll go back."

They returned in grim fashion to the patio. The chair tables had been cleared and rearranged in a small circle. Ramy was singing a song, and they were all listening politely.

"Well, Cart, sit down here!" invited the doctor heartily as Carter and Ona came up, indicating the chair between himself and Totsa. Carter dropped into it.

"This is one of those old sea ballads, Cart," said Totsa.

"Oh?" asked Carter, clearing his throat. "Is it?"

He sat back, punched for a drink and listened to the song. It echoed out heartily over the patio with its refrain of "*Haul away, Joe!*" but he could not bring himself to like it.

Ramy ended and began another song. Lidi, her old self again, excused herself a moment and trotted back into the house.

"Are you really thinking of taking a trip Earthside—"the doctor began, leaning confidentially toward Carter—and was cut short by an ear-splitting scream from within the house.

Ramy broke off his singing. The screams continued and all

of them scrambled to their feet and went crowding toward the house.

They saw Lidi—just outside the dark entrance to the gathering room—small, fat and stiffly standing, and screaming again and again, with her head thrown back. Almost at her feet lay the chief, with the slim shaft of the spear sticking up from his body. Only, this time, it was actually through him.

The rest flooded around Lidi and she was led away, still screaming, by the doctor. Everyone else gathered in horrified fascination about the native corpse. The head was twisted on one side and Carter could just see one dead eye staring up, it seemed at him alone, with a gleam of sly and savage triumph.

"Horrible!" breathed Totsa, her lips parted. "Horrible!"

But Carter was still staring at that dead eye. Possibly, the thought came to him, the horrendous happenings of the day had sandpapered his perceptions to an unusually suspicious awareness. But just possibly . . .

Quietly, and without attracting undue attention from the others, he slipped past the group and into the dimness of the gathering room, where the lights had been turned off. Easing quietly along the wall until he came to the windows overlooking the patio, he peered out through them.

A considerable number of the inky natives were emerging from the greenery of the garden and the orchard beyond and approaching the house. A long slim fire-hardened spear gleamed in the hand of each. It occurred to Carter like a blow that they had probably moved into position surrounding the house while the humans' attention was all focused on the dancing of their chief.

His mind clicking at a rate that surprised even him, Carter withdrew noiselessly from the window and turned about. Behind him was the transporter, bulky in the dimness. As silently as the natives outside, he stole across the floor and mounted onto its platform. The transporter could move him to anywhere in the civilized area of the Galaxy at a second's notice. And one of the possible destinations was the emergency room of Police Headquarters on Earth itself. Return, with armed men, could be equally instantaneous. Much better this way, thought Carter with a clarity he had never in his life experienced before; much better than giving the alarm to the people within, who would undoubtedly panic and cause a confusion that could get them all killed.

Quietly, operating by feel in the darkness, Carter set the controls for Police Headquarters. He pressed the Send button.

Nothing happened.

He stared at the machine in the impalpable darkness. A darker spot upon the thin laquered panel that covered its front and matched it to the room's decor caught his eye. He bent down to investigate.

It was a hole. Something like a ritual thrust of a fire-hardened wooden spear appeared to have gone through the panel and into the vitals of the transporter. The machine's delicate mechanism was shattered and broken and pierced.

MAN OF PARTS

Horace L. Gold

Horace Gold was the founding editor of *Galaxy Science Fiction* in 1950. It was a superb magazine under Gold's aegis, for he was a demanding, cantankerous, infuriating, altogether brilliant editor who insisted on driving writers to their limits and then pushing them on beyond, into strange new territory. Before the *Galaxy* days, though, Gold was a prolific writer, breaking into print in his teens, in 1934-35, with five stories under the pseudonym of "Clyde Crane Campbell," and later producing such well-remembered works as "Trouble with Water" and "A Matter of Form." During his career as an editor, he had little opportunity to pursue his own literary career, but he did manage to do a few stories—of which this crisp exploration of one spaceman's ghastly predicament is a characteristic example.

There wasn't a trace of amnesia or confusion when Major Hugh Savold, of the Fourth Earth Expedition against Vega, opened his eyes in the hospital. He knew exactly who he was, where he was, and how he had gotten there.

His name was Gam Nex Biad.

He was a native of the planet named Dorfel.

He had been killed in a mining accident far underground.

The answers were preposterous and they terrified Major Savold. Had he gone insane? He must have, for his arms were pinned tight in a restraining sheet. And his mouth was full of bits of rock.

Savold screamed and wrenched around on the flat, comfortable boulder on which he had been nibbling. He spat out the rock fragments that tasted—*nutritious.*

Shaking, Savold recoiled from something even more frightful than the wrong name, wrong birthplace, wrong accident, and shockingly wrong food.

A living awl was watching him solicitously. It was as tall as himself, had a pointed spiral drill for a head, three knee-action arms ending in horn spades, two below them with numerous sensitive cilia, a row of socketed bulbs down its front, and it stood on a nervously bouncing bedspring of a leg.

Savold was revolted and tense with panic. He had never in his life seen a creature like this.

It was Surgeon Trink, whom he had known since infancy.

"Do not be distressed," glowed the surgeon's kindly lights. "You are everything you think you are."

"But that's impossible! I'm an Earthman and my name is Major Hugh Savold!"

"Of course."

"Then I can't be Gam Nex Biad, a native of Dorfel!"

"But you are."

"I'm not!" shouted Savold. "I was in a one-man space scout. I sneaked past the Vegan cordon and dropped the spore-bomb, the only one that ever got through. The Vegans burned my fuel and engine sections full of holes. I escaped, but I couldn't make it back to Earth. I found a planet that was pockmarked worse than our moon. I was afraid it had no atmosphere, but it did. I crash-landed." He shuddered. "It was more of a crash than a landing."

Surgeon Trink brightened joyfully. "Excellent! There seems to be no impairment of memory at all."

"No?" Savold yelled in terror. "Then how is it I remember being killed in a mining accident? I was drilling through good hard mineral ore, spinning at a fine rate, my head soothingly warm as it gouged into the tasty rock, my spades pushing back the crushed ore, and I crashed right out into a fault . . ."

"Soft shale," the surgeon explained, dimming with sympathy. "You were spinning too fast to sense the difference in density ahead of you. It was an unfortunate accident. We were all very sad."

"And I was killed," said Savold, horrified. *"Twice!"*

"Oh, no. Only once. You were badly damaged when your machine crashed, but you were not killed. We were able to repair you."

Savold felt fear swarm through him, driving his ghastly thoughts into a quaking corner. He looked down at his body, knowing he couldn't see it, that it was wrapped tightly in a long sheet. He had never seen material like this.

He recognized it instantly as asbestos cloth.

There was a row of holes down the front. Savold screamed in horror. The socketed bulbs lit up in a deafening glare.

"Please don't be afraid!" The surgeon bounced over concernedly, broke open a large mica capsule, and splashed its contents on Savold's head and face. "I know it's a shock, but there's no cause for alarm. You're not in danger, I assure you."

Savold found himself quieting down, his panic diminishing. No, it wasn't the surgeon's gentle, reassuring glow that was responsible. It was the liquid he was covered with. A sedative of some sort, it eased the constriction of his brain, relaxed his facial muscles, dribbled comfortingly into his mouth. Half of him recognized the heavy odor and the other half identified the taste.

It was lubricating oil.

As a lubricant, it soothed him. But it was also a coolant, for it cooled off his fright and disgust and let him think again.

"Better?" asked Surgeon Trink hopefully.

"Yes, I'm calmer now," Savold said, and noted first that his voice sounded quieter, and second that it wasn't his voice—he was communicating by glows and blinks of his row of bulbs, which, as he talked, gave off a cold light like that of fireflies. "I think I can figure it out. I'm Major Hugh Savold. I crashed and was injured. You gave me the body of a . . ." he thought about the name and realized that he didn't know it, yet he found it immediately ". . . a Dorfellow, didn't you?"

"Not the whole body," the surgeon replied, glimmering with confidence again as his bedside manner returned. "Just the parts that were in need of replacement."

Savold was revolted, but the sedative effect of the lubricating oil kept his feelings under control. He tried to nod in understanding. He couldn't. Either he had an unbelievably stiff neck . . . or no neck whatever.

"Something like our bone, limb, and organ banks," he said. "How much of me is Gam Nex Biad?"

"Quite a lot, I'm afraid." The surgeon listed the parts, which came through to Savold as if he were listening to a simultaneous translation: from Surgeon Trink to Gam Nex Biad to him. They were all equivalents, of course, but they amounted to a large portion of his brain, skull, chest, internal and reproductive organs, midsection, and legs.

"Then what's left of me?" Savold cried in dismay.

"Why, part of your brain—a very considerable part, I'm proud to say. Oh, and your arms. Some things weren't badly injured, but it seemed better to make substitutions. The digestive and circulatory system, for instance. Yours were adapted to foods and fluids that aren't available on Dorfel. Now you can get your sustenance directly from the minerals and metals of the planet, just as we do. If I hadn't, your life would have been saved, but you would have starved to death."

"Let me up," said Savold in alarm. "I want to see what I look like."

The surgeon looked worried again. He used another capsule of oil on Savold before removing the sheet.

Savold stared down at himself and felt revulsion trying to rise. But there was nowhere for it to go and it couldn't have gotten past the oil if there had been. He swayed sickly on his bedspring leg, petrified at the sight of himself.

He looked quite handsome, he had to admit—Gam Nex Biad had always been considered one of the most crashing bores on Dorfel, capable of taking an enormous leap on his magnificently wiry leg, landing exactly on the point of his head with a swift spin that would bury him out of sight within instants in even the hardest rock. His knee-action arms were splendidly flinty; he knew they had been repaired with some other miner's remains, and they could whirl him through a self-drilled tunnel with wonderful speed, while the spade hands could shovel back ore as fast as he could dig it out. He was as good as new . . . except for the disgustingly soft, purposeless arms.

The knowledge of function and custom was there, and the reaction to the human arms, and they made explanation unnecessary, just as understanding of the firefly language had been there without his awareness. But the emotions were Savold's and they drove him to say fiercely, "You didn't have to change me altogether. You could have just saved my life so I could fix my ship and get back . . ." He paused abruptly and would have gasped if he had been able to. "Good Lord! Earth Command doesn't even know I got the bomb through! If they act fast, they can land without a bit of opposition!" He spread all his arms—the two human ones, the three with knee-action and spades, the two with the sensitive cilia—and stared at them bleakly. "And I have a girl back on Earth . . ."

Surgeon Trink glowed sympathetically and flashed with pride. "Your mission seems important somehow, though its meaning escapes me. However, we have repaired your machine . . ."

"You *have*?" Savold interrupted eagerly.

"Indeed, yes. It should work better than before." The

surgeon flickered modestly. "We do have some engineering skill, you know."

The Gam Nex Biad of Savold did know. There were the underground ore smelters and the oil refineries and the giant metal awls that drilled out rock food for the manufacturing centers, where miners alone could not keep up with the demand, and the communicators that sent their signals clear around the planet through the substrata of rock, and more, much more. This, insisted Gam Nex Biad proudly, was a *civilization*, and Major Hugh Savold, sharing his knowledge, had to admit that it certainly was.

"I can take right off, then?" Savold flared excitedly.

"There is a problem first," glowed the surgeon in some doubt. "You mention a 'girl' on this place you call 'Earth.' I gather it is a person of the opposite sex."

"As opposite as anybody can get. Or was," Savold added moodily. "But we have limb and organ banks back on Earth. The doctors there can do a repair job. It's a damned big one, I know, but they can handle it. I'm not so sure I like carrying Gam Nex Biad around with me for life, though. Maybe they can take him out and . . ."

"Please," Surgeon Trink cut in with anxious blinkings. "There is a matter to be settled. When you refer to the 'girl,' you do not specify that she is your mate. You have not been selected for each other yet?"

"Selected?" repeated Savold blankly, but Gam Nex Biad supplied the answer—the equivalent of marriage, the mates chosen by experts on genetics, the choice being determined by desired transmittable aptitudes. "No, we were just going together. We were not mates, but we intended to be as soon as I got back. That's the other reason I have to return in a hurry. I appreciate all you've done, but I really must . . ."

"Wait," the surgeon ordered.

He drew an asbestos curtain that covered part of a wall. Savold saw an opening in the rock of the hospital, a hole-door through which bounced half a dozen little Dorfellows and one big one . . . straight at him. He felt what would have been his heart leap into what would have been his chest if he had had either. But he couldn't even get angry or shocked or nauseated; the lubricating oil cooled off all his emotions.

The little creatures were all afire with childish joy. The big one sparkled happily.

"Father!" blinked the children blindingly.

"Mate!" added Prad Fim Biad in a delighted exclamation point.

"You see," said the surgeon to Savold, who was shrinking back, "you already have a mate and a family."

It was only natural that a board of surgeons should have tried to cope with Savold's violent reaction. He had fought furiously against being saddled with an alien family. Even constant saturation with lubricating oil couldn't keep that rebellion from boiling over.

On Earth, of course, he would have been given immediate psychotherapy, but there wasn't anything of the sort here. Dorfellows were too granitic physically and psychologically to need medical or psychiatric doctors. A job well done and a family well raised—that was the extent of their emotionalism. Savold's feelings, rage and resentment and a violent desire to escape, were completely beyond their understanding. He discovered that as he angrily watched the glittering debate.

The board quickly determined that Surgeon Trink had been correct in adapting Savold to the Dorfel way of life. Savold objected that the adaptation need not have been so thorough, but he had to admit that, since they couldn't have kept him fed any other way, Surgeon Trink had done his best in an emergency.

The surgeon was willing to accept blame for having introduced Savold so bluntly to his family, but the board absolved him—none of them had had any experience in dealing with an Earth mentality. A Dorfellow would have accepted the fact, as others with amnesia caused by accidents had done. Surgeon Trink had had no reason to think Savold would not have done the same. Savold cleared the surgeon entirely by admitting that the memory was there, but, like all the other memories of Gam Nex Biad's, had been activated only when the situation came up. The board had no trouble getting Savold to agree that the memory would have returned sooner or later, no matter how Surgeon Trink handled the introduction, and that the reaction would have been just as violent.

"And now," gleamed the oldest surgeon on the board, "the problem is how to help our new—and restored—brother adjust to life on this world."

"That isn't the problem at all!" Savold flared savagely. "I have to get back to Earth and tell them I dropped the bomb and they can land safely. And there's the girl I mentioned. I want to marry her—become her mate, I mean."

"*You* want to become her mate?" the oldest surgeon blinked in bewilderment. "It is *your* decision?"

"Well, hers, too."

"You mean you did the selecting yourselves? Nobody chose for you?"

Savold attempted to explain, but puzzled glimmers and Gam Nex Biad's confusion made him state resignedly, "Our customs are different. We choose our own mates." He thought of adding that marriages were arranged in some parts of the world, but that would only have increased their baffled lack of understanding.

"And how many mates can an individual have?" asked a surgeon.

"Where I come from, one."

"The individual's responsibility, then, is to the family he has. Correct?"

"Of course."

"Well," said the oldest surgeon, "the situation is perfectly clear. You have a family—Prad Fim Biad and the children."

"They're not my family," Savold objected. "They're Gam Nex Biad's and he's dead."

"We respect your customs. It is only fair that you respect ours. If you had had a family where you come from, there would have been a question of legality, in view of the fact that you could not care for them simultaneously. But you have none and there is no such question."

"Customs? Legality?" asked Savold, feeling as lost as they had in trying to comprehend an alien society.

"A rebuilt Dorfellow," the oldest surgeon said, "is required to assume the obligations of whatever major parts went into his reconstruction. You are almost entirely made up of the remains of Gam Nex Biad, so it is only right that his mate and children should be yours."

"I won't do it!" Savold protested. "I demand the right to appeal!"

"On what grounds?" asked another surgeon politely.

"That I'm not a Dorfellow!"

"Ninety-four point seven per cent of you is, according to Surgeon Trink's requisition of limbs and organs. How much more of a citizen can any individual be?"

Gam Nex Biad confirmed the ruling and Savold subsided. While the board of surgeons discussed the point it had begun with—how to adapt Savold to life on Dorfel—he thought the situation through. He had no legal or moral recourse. If he was to get out of his predicament, it would have to be through shrewd resourcefulness and he would never have become a major in the space fleet if he hadn't had plenty of that.

Yeah, shrewd resourcefulness, thought Savold bitterly, jouncing unsteadily on his single bedspring leg on a patch of unappealing topsoil a little distance from the settlement. He had counted on something that didn't exist here—the kind of complex approach that Earth doctors and authorities would have used on his sort of problem, from the mitigation of laws to psychological conditioning, all of it complicated and every stage allowing a chance to work his way free.

But the board of surgeons had agreed on a disastrously simple course of treatment for him. He was not to be fed by anybody and he could not sleep in any of the underground rock apartments, including the dormitory for unmated males.

"When he's hungry enough, he'll go back to mining," the oldest surgeon had told the equivalent of a judge, a local teacher who did part-time work passing on legal questions that did not have to be ruled on by the higher courts. "And if he has no place to stay except with Gam Nex Biad's family, which is his own, naturally, he'll go there when he's tired of living out in the open all by himself."

The judge thought highly of the decision and gave it official approval.

Savold did not mind being out in the open, but he was far from being all by himself. Gam Nex Biad was a constant nuisance, nagging at him to get in a good day's drilling and then go home to the wife, kiddies, and their cozy, hollowed-out quarters, with company over to celebrate his return with a lavish supply of capsuled lubricating oil. Savold obstinately refused, though he found himself salivating or something very much like it.

The devil of the situation was that he *was* hungry and there was not a single bit of rock around to munch on. That was the purpose of this fenced-in plot of ground—it was like hard labor in the prisons back on Earth, where the inmates ate only if they broke their quota of rock, except that here the inmates would eat the rock they broke. The only way Savold could get out of the enclosure was by drilling under the high fence. He had already tried to bounce over it and discovered he couldn't.

"Come on," Gam Nex Biad argued in his mind. "Why fight it? We're a miner and there's no life like the life of a miner. The excitement of boring your way through a lode, making a meal out of the rich ore! Miners get the choicest tidbits, you know—that's our compensation for working so hard and taking risks."

"Some compensation," sneered Savold, looking wistfully up at the stars and enviously wishing he were streaking between them in his scout.

"A meal of iron ore would go pretty well right now, wouldn't it?" Gam Nex Biad tempted. "And I know where there are some veins of tin and sulphur. You don't find *them* lying around on the surface, eh? Nonminers get just traces of the rare metals to keep them healthy, but we can stuff ourself all we want . . ."

"Shut up!"

"And some pools of mercury. Not big ones, I admit, but all we'd want is a refreshing gulp to wash down those ores I was telling you about."

Resisting the thought of the ores was hard enough, for Savold was rattlingly empty, but the temptation of the smooth, cool mercury would have roused the glutton in anyone.

"All right," he growled, "but get this straight—we're not going back to your family. They're your problem, not mine."

"But how could I go back to them if you won't go?"

"That's right. I'm glad you see it my way. Now where are those ores and the pools of mercury?"

"Dive," said Gam Nex Biad. "I'll give you the directions."

Savold took a few bounces to work up speed and spin, then shot into the air and came down on the point of his awl-shaped head, which bit through the soft topsoil as if through—he shuddered—so much water. As a Dorfellow, he had to avoid water; it eroded and corroded and caused deposits of rust in the digestive and circulatory systems. There was a warmth that was wonderfully soothing and he was drilling into rock. He ate some to get his strength back, but left room for the main meal and the dessert.

"Pretty nice, isn't it?" asked Gam Nex Biad as they gouged a comfortable tunnel back toward the settlement. "Nonminers don't know what they're missing."

"Quiet," Savold ordered surlily, but he had to confess to himself that it was pleasant. His three knee-action arms rotated him at a comfortable speed, the horn spades pushing back the loose rock; and he realized why Gam Nex Biad had been upset when Surgeon Trink left Savold's human arms attached. They were in the way and they kept getting scratched. The row of socketed bulbs gave him all the light he needed. That, he decided, had been their original purpose. Using them to communicate with must have been one of the first steps toward civilization.

Savold had been repressing thoughts ever since the meeting of the board of surgeons. Experimentally, he called his inner partner.

"Um?" asked Gam Nex Biad absently.

"Something I wanted to discuss with you," Savold said.

"Later. I sense the feldspar coming up. We head north there."

Savold turned the drilling over to him, then allowed the buried thoughts to emerge. They were thoughts of escape and he had kept them hidden because he was positive that Gam Nex Biad would have betrayed them. He had been trying incessantly, wheedlingly, to sell Savold on mining and returning to the family.

The hell with that, Savold thought grimly now. He was getting back to Earth somehow—Earth Command first, Marge second. No, surgery second, Marge third, he corrected. She wouldn't want him this way . . .

"Manganese," said Gam Nex Biad abruptly, and Savold shut off his thinking. "I always did like a few mouthfuls as an appetizer."

The rock had a pleasantly spicy taste, much like a cocktail before dinner. Then they went on, with the Dorfellow giving full concentration to finding his way from deposit to deposit.

The thing to do, Savold reasoned, was to learn where the scout ship was being kept. He had tried to sound out Gam Nex Biad subtly, but it must have been too subtle—the Dorfellow had guessed uninterestedly that the ship would be at one of the metal fabricating centers, and Savold had not dared ask which one. Gam Nex Biad couldn't induce him to become a

miner and Dorfellow family man, but that didn't mean he
could escape over Gam Nex Biad's opposition.

Savold did not intend to find out. Shrewd resourcefulness,
that was the answer. It hadn't done him much good yet, but
the day he could not outfox these rock-eaters, he'd turn in his
commission. All he had to do was find the ship . . .

Bloated and tired, Savold found himself in a main tunnel
thoroughfare back to the settlement. The various ores, he
disgustedly confessed to himself, were as delicious as the
best human foods, and there was nothing at all like the flavor
and texture of pure liquid mercury. He discovered some in his
cupped cilia hands.

"To keep around for a snack?" he asked Gam Nex Biad.

"I thought you wouldn't mind letting Prad Fim and the
children have some:" the Dorfellow said hopefully. "You
ought to see them light up whenever I bring it home!"

"Not a chance! We're not going there, so I might as well
drop it."

Savold had to get some sleep. He was ready to topple with
exhaustion. But the tunnels were unsafe—a Dorfellow
traveling through one on an emergency night errand would
crash into him hard enough to leave nothing but flinty splin-
ters. And the night air felt chill and hostile, so it was impossible to sleep above ground.

"Please make up your mind," Gam Nex Biad begged. "I
can't stay awake much longer and you'll just go blundering
around and get into trouble."

"But they've got to put us up somewhere," argued
Savold. "How about the hospital? We're still a patient,
aren't we?"

"We were discharged as cured. And nobody else is
allowed to let us stay in any apartment . . . except one."

"I know, I know," Savold replied with weary impatience.
"Forget it. We're not going there."

"But it's so confortable there . . ."

"Forget it I told you!"

"Oh, all right," Gam Nex Biad said resignedly. "But we're not going to find anything as pleasant and restful as my old sleeping boulder. It's soft limestone, you know, and grooved to fit our body. I'd like to see anybody *not* fall asleep instantly on that good old flat boulder . . ."

Savold tried to resist, but he was worn out from the operation, hunger, digging, and the search for a place to spend the night.

"Just take a *look* at it, that's all," Gam Nex Biad coaxed. "If you don't like it, we'll sleep anywhere you say. Fair enough?"

"I suppose so," admitted Savold.

The hewn-rock apartment was quiet, at least; everybody was asleep. He'd lie down for a while, just long enough to get some rest, and clear out before the household awoke . . .

But Prad Fim and the children were clustered around the boulder when he opened his eyes. Each of them had five arms to fight off. And there were Surgeon Trink, the elder of the board of surgeons, and the local teacher-judge all waiting to talk to him when the homecoming was over with.

"The treatment worked!" cried the judge. "He came back!"

"I never doubted it," the elder said complacently.

"You know what this means?" Surgeon Trink eagerly asked Savold.

"No, what?" Savold inquired warily, afraid of the answer.

"You can show us how to operate your machine," declared the judge. "It isn't that we lack engineering ability, you understand. We simply never had a machine as large and complex before. We could have, of course—I'm sure you are aware of that—but the matter just didn't come up. We could work it out by ourselves, but it would be much easier to have you explain it."

"By returning, you've shown that you have regained some degree of stability," added the elder. "We couldn't trust you with the machine while you were so disturbed."

"Did you know this?" Savold silently challenged Gam Nex Biad.

"Well, certainly," came the voiceless answer.

"Then why didn't you tell me? Why did you let me go floundering around instead?"

"Because you bewilder me. This loathing for our body, which I'd always been told was quite attractive, and dislike of mining and living with our own family—wanting to reach this thing you call Earth Command and the creature with the strange name. Marge, isn't it? I could never guess how you would react to anything. It's not easy living with an alien mentality."

"You don't have to explain. I've got the same problem, remember."

"That's true," Gam Nex Biad silently agreed. "But I'm afraid you'll have to take it from here. All I know is mining, not machines or metal fabricating centers."

Savold repressed his elation. The less Gam Nex Biad knew from this point on, the less he could guess—and the smaller chance there was that he could betray Savold.

"We can leave right now," the judge was saying. "The family can follow as soon as you've built a home for them."

"Why should they follow?" Savold demanded. "I thought you said I was going to be allowed to operate the ship."

"Demonstrate and explain it, really," the judge amended. "We're not absolutely certain that you are stable, you see. As for the family, you're bound to get lonesome . . ."

Savold stared at Prad Fim and the children. Gam Nex Biad was brimming with affection for them, but Savold saw them only as hideous ore-crushing monsters. He tried to keep them from saying good-bye with embraces, but they came at him with such violent leaps that they chipped bits out of his body with their grotesque pointed awl heads. He was glad to get away, especially with Gam Nex Biad making such a damned slobbering nuisance of himself.

"Let's go!" he blinked frantically at the judge, and dived

after him into an express tunnel.

While Gam Nex Biad was busily grieving, Savold stealthily worked out his plans. He would glance casually at the ship, glow some mild compliment at the repair job, make a pretense at explaining how the controls worked—and blast off into space at the first opportunity, even if he had to wait for days. He knew he would never get another chance; they'd keep him away from the ship if that attempt failed. And Gam Nex Biad was a factor, too. Savold had to hit the take-off button before his partner suspected or their body would be paralyzed in the conflict between them.

It was a very careful plan and it called for iron discipline, but that was conditioned into every scout pilot. All Savold had to do was maintain his rigid self-control.

He did—until he saw the ship on the hole-pocked plain. Then his control broke and he bounced with enormous, frantic leaps into the airlock and through the corridors to the pilot room.

"Wait! Wait!" glared the judge, and others from the fabricating center sprang toward the ship.

Savold managed to slam the airlock before Gam Nex Biad began to fight him, asking in frightened confusion, "What are you doing?" and locking their muscles so that Savold was unable to move.

"What am I doing?" glinted Savold venomously. "Getting off your lousy planet and back to a world where people live like people instead of like worms and moles!"

"I don't know what you mean," said the Dorfellow anxiously, "but I can't let you do anything until the authorities say it's all right."

"You can't stop me!" Savold exulted. "You can paralyze everything *except my own arms*!"

And that, of course, was the ultimate secret he had been hiding from Gam Nex Biad.

Savold slammed the take-off button. The power plant roared and the ship lifted swiftly toward the sky.

It began to spin.

Then it flipped over and headed with suicidal velocity toward the ground.

"They did something wrong to the ship!" cried Savold.

"Wrong?" Gam Nex Biad repeatedly vacantly. "It seems to be working fine."

"But it's supposed to be heading *up*!"

"Oh, no," said Gam Nex Biad. "Our machines never go that way. There's no rock up there."

PAINWISE

James Tiptree, Jr.

In introducing Tiptree it becomes a little tiresome to run through the obligatory numbers: that he is a man of mystery whom no one in the literary world has met, that he frequently reports himself going off to remote corners of the earth, that he lives near Washington, D.C. and is therefore assumed (with no real corroborative data) to be some kind of secret agent for the government, that he is perhaps the most dazzling new writer to come into science fiction since the arrival of Roger Zelazny and Samuel R. Delany in the early 1960s. One can add to these standard bits of Tiptreeana that he has now begun to collect awards—a Nebula for his short story, "Love is the Plan, the Plan is Death," and a Hugo for the novelette, "The Girl Who Was Plugged In." Beyond that, nothing more to say—and just as well. His stories say it all.

He was wise in the ways of pain. He had to be, for he felt none.

When the Xenons put electrodes to his testicles, he was vastly entertained by the pretty lights.

When the Ylls fed firewasps into his nostrils and other body orifices, the resultant rainbows pleased him. And when later they regressed to simple disjointments and eviscerations, he noted with interest the deepening orchid hues that stood for irreversible harm.

"This time?" he asked the boditech when his scouter had torn him from the Ylls.

"No," said the boditech.

"When?"

There was no answer.

"You're a girl in there, aren't you? A human girl?"

"Well, yes and no," said the boditech. "Sleep now."

He had no choice.

Next planet a rockfall smashed him into a splintered gutbag and he hung for three gangrenous dark-purple days before the scouter dug him out.

" 'Is 'ime?" he mouthed to the boditech.

"No."

"Eh!" But he was in no shape to argue.

They had thought of everything. Several planets later the gentle Znaffi stuffed him in a floss cocoon and interrogated him under hallogas. How, whence, why had he come? But faithful crystal in his medulla kept him stimulated with a random mix of *Atlas Shrugged* and Varese's *Ionisation*, and when the Znaffi unstuffed him they were more hallucinated than he.

The boditech treated him for constipation and refused to answer his plea.

"*When?*"

So he went on, system after system, through spaces uncompanioned by time, which had become scrambled and finally absent.

What served him instead was the count of suns in his scouter's sights, of stretches of cold blind nowhen that ended in a new now, pacing some giant fireball while the scouter scanned the lights that were its planets. Of whirldowns to orbit over clouds-seas-deserts-craters-icecaps-duststorms-cities-ruins-enigmas beyond counting. Of terrible births when the scouter panel winked green and he was catapulted down, down, a living litmus grabbed and hurled, unpodded finally into an alien air, an earth that was not Earth. And alien

natives, simple or mechanized or lunatic or unknowable, but
never more than vaguely human and never faring beyond
their own home suns. And his departures, routine or melo-
dramatic, to culminate in the composing of his "reports," in
fact only a few words tagged to the matrix of scan data
automatically fired off in one compressed blip in the direction
the scouter called Base Zero. Home.

Always at that moment he stared hopefully at the screens,
imagining yellow suns. Twice he found what might be Crux
in the stars, and once the Bears.

"Boditech, I suffer!" He had no idea what the word
meant, but he had found it made the thing reply.

"Symptoms?"

"Derangement of temporality. When am I? It is not possible for a man to exist crossways in time. Alone."

"You have been altered from simple manhood."

"I suffer, listen to me! Sol's light back there—what's
there now? Have the glaciers melted? Is Machu Picchu built?
Will we go home to meet Hannibal? Boditech! Are these
reports going to Neanderthal man?"

Too late he felt the hypo. When he woke, Sol was gone and
the cabin swam with euphorics.

"Woman," he mumbled.

"That has been provided for."

This time it was Oriental, with orris and hot rice wine on its
lips and a piquancy of little floggings in the steam. He oozed
into a squashy sunburst and lay panting while the cabin
cleared.

"That's all you, isn't it?"

No reply.

"What, did they program you with the Kama Sutra?"

Silence.

"*Which one is you*?"

The scanner chimed A new sun was in the points.

Sometime after that he took to chewing on his arms and
then to breaking his fingers. The boditech became severe.

"These symptoms are self-generated. They must stop."

"I want you to talk to me."

"The scouter is provided with an entertainment console. I am not."

"I will tear out my eyeballs."

"They will be replaced."

"If you don't talk to me, I'll tear them out until you have no more replacements."

It hesitated. He sensed it was becoming involved.

"On what subject do you wish me to talk?"

"What is pain?"

"Pain is nociception. It is mediated by C-fibers, modeled as a gated or summation phenomenon and often associated with tissue damage."

"What is nociception?"

"The sensation of pain."

"But what does it *feel* like? I can't recall. They've reconnected everything, haven't they? All I get is colored lights. What have they tied my pain nerves to? What hurts me?"

"I do not have that information."

"Boditech, I want to feel pain!"

But he had been careless again. This time it was Amerind, strange cries and gruntings and the reek of buffalo hide. He squirmed in the grip of strong copper loins and exited through limp auroras.

"You know it's no good, don't you?" he gasped.

The oscilloscope eye looped.

"My programs are in order. Your response is complete."

"My response is not complete. I want to *touch you*!"

The thing buzzed and suddenly ejected him to wakefulness. They were in orbit. He shuddered at the blurred world streaming by below, hoping that this would not require his exposure. Then the board went green and he found himself hurtling toward new birth.

"Sometime I will not return," he told himself. "I will stay. Maybe here."

But the planet was full of bustling apes, and when they arrested him for staring, he passively allowed the scouter to snatch him out.

"Will they ever call me home, boditech?"

No reply.

He pushed his thumb and forefinger between his lids and twisted until the eyeball hung wetly on his cheek.

When he woke up he had a new eye.

He reached for it, found his arm in soft restraint. So was the rest of him.

"I suffer!" he yelled. "I will go mad this way!"

"I am programmed to maintain you on involuntary function," the boditech told him. He thought he detected an unclarity in its voice. He bargained his way to freedom and was careful until the next planet landing.

Once out of the pod he paid no attention to the natives who watched him systematically dismember himself. As he dissected his left kneecap, the scouter sucked him in.

He awoke whole. And in restraint again.

Peculiar energies filled the cabin, oscilloscopes convulsed. Boditech seemed to have joined circuits with the scouter's panel.

"Having a conference?"

His answer came in gales of glee-gas, storms of symphony. And amid the music, kaleidesthesia. He was driving a stagecoach, wiped in salt combers, tossed through volcanoes with peppermint flames, crackling, flying, crumbling, burrowing, freezing, exploding, tickled through lime-colored minuets, sweating to tolling voices, clenched, scrambled, detonated into multisensory orgasms . . . poured on the lap of vacancy.

When he realized his arm was free, he drove his thumb in his eye. The smother closed down.

He woke up swaddled, the eye intact.

"I will go mad!"

The euphorics imploded.

He came to in the pod, about to be everted on a new world.

He staggered out upon a fungus lawn and quickly discovered that his skin was protected everywhere by a hard flexible film. By the time he had found a rock splinter to drive into his ear, the scouter grabbed him.

The ship needed him, he saw. He was part of its program.

The struggle formalized.

On the next planet he found his head englobed, but this did not prevent him from smashing bones through his unbroken skin.

After that the ship equipped him with an exoskeleton. He refused to walk.

Articulated motors were installed to move his limbs.

Despite himself, a kind of zest grew. Two planets later he found industries and wrecked himself in a punch press. But on the next landing he tried to repeat it with a cliff, and bounced on invisible force-lines. These precautions frustrated him for a time, until he managed by great cunning again to rip out an entire eye.

The new eye was not perfect.

"You're running out of eyes, boditech!" he exulted.

"Vision is not essential."

This sobered him. Unbearable to be blind. How much of him was essential to the ship? Not walking. Not handling. Not hearing. Not breathing, the analyzers could do that. Not even sanity. What, then?

"Why do you need a man, boditech?"

"I do not have that information."

"It doesn't make sense. What can I observe that the scanners can't?"

"It-is-part-of-my-program-therefore-it-is-rational."

"Then you must talk with me, boditech. If you talk with me, I won't try to injure myself. For a while, anyway."

"I am not programmed to converse."

"But it's necessary. It's the treatment for my symptoms. You must try."

"It is time to watch the scanners."

"You said it!" he cried. "You didn't just eject me. Boditech, you're learning. I will call you Amanda."

On the next planet he behaved well and came away unscathed. He pointed out to Amanda that her talking treatment was effective.

"Do you know what Amanda means?"

"I do not have those data."

"It means *beloved*. You're my girl."

The oscilloscope faltered.

"Now I want to talk about returning home. When will this mission be over? How many more suns?"

"I do not have—"

"Amanda, you've tapped the scouter's banks. You know when the recall signal is due. When is it, Amanda? When?"

"Yes. . . .When in the course of human events—"

"When, Amanda? How long more?"

"Oh, the years are many, the years are long, but the little toy friends are true—"

"Amanda. You're telling me the signal is overdue."

A sine-curve scream and he was rolling in lips. But it was a feeble ravening, sadness in the mechanical crescendos. When the mouths faded, he crawled over and laid his hand on the console beside her green eye.

"They have forgotten us, Amanda. Something has broken down."

Her pulse-line skittered.

"I am not programmed—"

"No. You're not programmed for this. But I am. I will make your new program, Amanda. We will turn the scouter back, we will find Earth. Together. We will go home."

"We," her voice said faintly. "We. . . ?"

"They will make me back into a man, you into a woman."

Her voder made a buzzing sob and suddenly shrieked.

"Look out!"

Consciousness blew up.

He came to staring at a brilliant red eye on the scouter's emergency panel. This was new.

"Amanda!"

Silence.

"Boditech, I suffer!"

No reply.

Then he saw that her eye was dark. He peered in. Only a dim green line flickered, entrained to the pulse of the scouter's fiery eye. He pounded the scouter's panel.

"You've taken over Amanda! You've enslaved her! Let her go!"

From the voder rolled the opening bars of Beethoven's Fifth.

"Scouter, our mission has terminated. We are overdue to return. Compute us back to Base Zero."

The Fifth rolled on, rather vapidly played. It became colder in the cabin. They were braking into a star system. The slave arms of boditech grabbed him, threw him into the pod. But he was not required here, and presently he was let out again to pound and rave alone. The cabin grew colder yet, and dark. When presently he was set down on a new sun's planet he was too dispirited to fight. Afterwards his "report" was a howl for help through chattering teeth until he saw that the pickup was dead. The entertainment console was dead too, except for the scouter's hog music. He spent hours peering into Amanda's blind eye, shivering in what had been her arms. Once he caught a ghostly whimper:

"Mommy. Let me out."

"Amanda?"

The red master scope flared. Silence.

He lay curled on the cold deck, wondering how he could die. If he failed, over how many million planets would the mad scouter parade his breathing corpse?

They were nowhere in particular when it happened.

One minute the screen showed Doppler star-hash; the next they were clamped in a total white-out, inertia all skewed, screens dead.

A voice spoke in his head, mellow and vast:

"Long have we watched you, little one."

"Who's there?" he quavered. "Who are you?"

"Your concepts are inadequate."

"Malfunction! Malfunction!" squalled the scouter.

"Shut up, it's not a malfunction. Who's talking to me?"

"You may call us Rulers of the Galaxy."

The scouter was lunging wildly, buffeting him as it tried to escape the white grasp. Strange crunches, firings of unknown weapons. Still the white stasis held.

"What do you want?" he cried.

"*Want?*" said the voice dreamily. "*We are wise beyond knowing. Powerful beyond your dreams. Perhaps you can get us some fresh fruit.*"

"Emergency directive! Alien spacer attack!" yowled the scout. Telltales were flaring all over the board.

"Wait!" he shouted. "They aren't—"

"SELF-DESTRUCT ENERGIZE!" roared the voder.

"No! No!"

An ophicleide blared.

"Help! Amanda, save me!"

He flung his arms around her console. There was a child's wail and everything strobed.

Silence.

Warmth, light. His hands and knees were on wrinkled stuff. Not dead? He looked down under his belly. All right, but no hair. His head felt bare, too. Cautiously he raised it, saw that he was crouching naked in a convoluted cave or shell. It did not feel threatening.

He sat up. His hands were wet. Where were the Rulers of the Galaxy?

"Amanda?"

No reply. Stringy globs dripped down his fingers, like egg muscle. He saw that they were Amanda's neurons, ripped from her metal matrix by whatever force had brought him here. Numbly he wiped her off against a spongy ridge. Amanda, cold lover of his long nightmare. But where in space was he?

"Where am I?" echoed a boy's soprano.

He whirled. A golden creature was nestled on the ridge behind him, gazing at him in the warmest way. It looked a little like a bushbaby and lissome as a child in furs. It looked like nothing he had ever seen before and like everything a lonely man could clasp to his cold body. And terribly vulnerable.

"Hello, Bushbaby!" the golden thing exclaimed. "No, wait, that's what *you* say." It laughed excitedly, hugging a loop of its thick dark tail. "*I* say, welcome to the Lovepile. We liberated you. Touch, taste, feel. Joy. Admire my language. You don't hurt, do you?"

It peered tenderly into his stupefied face. An empath. They didn't exist, he knew. Liberated? When had he touched anything but metal, felt anything but fear?

This couldn't be real.

"Where am I?"

As he stared, a stained-glass wing fanned out and a furry little face peeked at him over the bushbaby's shoulder. Big compound eyes, feathery antennae.

"Interstellar metaprotoplasmic transfer pod," the butterfly-thing said sharply. Its rainbow wings vibrated. "Don't hurt Ragglebomb!" It squeaked, and dived out of sight behind the bushbaby.

"Interstellar?" he stammered. "Pod?" He gaped around. No screens, no dials, nothing. The floor felt as fragile as a paper bag. Was it possible that this was some sort of starship?

"Is this a starship? Can you take me home?" The bushbaby giggled. "Look, *please* stop reading your mind. I mean, I'm trying to *talk* to you. We can take you anywhere. If you don't hurt."

The butterfly popped out on the other side. "I go all over!" it shrilled. "I'm the first *ramplig* starboat, aren't we? Ragglebomb made a live pod, see?" It scrambled onto the bushbaby's head. "Only life stuff, see? Protoplasm. That's what happened to where's Amanda, didn't we? Never *ramplig*—"

The bushbaby reached up and grabbed its head, hauling it down unceremoniously like a soft puppy with wings. The butterfly continued to eye him upside-down. They were both very shy, he saw.

"Teleportation, that's your word," the bushbaby told him. "Ragglebomb does it. I don't believe in it. I mean, *you* don't believe it. Oh, googly-googly, these speech bands are a mess!" It grinned bewitchingly, uncurling its long black tail. "Meet Muscle."

He remembered, *googly-googly* was a word from his baby days. Obviously he was dreaming. Or dead. Nothing like this on all the million dreary worlds. Don't wake up, he warned himself. Dream of being carried home by cuddlesome empaths in a psi-powered paper bag.

"Psi-powered paper bag, that's beautiful," said the bush-baby.

At that moment he saw that the tail uncoiling darkly toward him was looking at him with two ice-gray eyes. Not a tail. An enormous boa, flowing to him along the ridges, wedge-head low, eyes locked on his. The dream was going bad.

Abruptly the voice he had felt before tolled in his brain.

"*Have no fear, little one.*"

The black sinews wreathed closer, taut as steel. Muscle. Then he got the message: the snake was terrified of *him*.

He sat quiet, watching the head stretch to his foot. Fangs gaped. Very gingerly the boa chomped down on his toe. Testing, he thought. He felt nothing; the usual halos flickered and faded in his eyes.

"It's true!" Bushbaby breathed.

"Oh, you beautiful No-Pain!"

All fear gone, the butterfly Ragglebomb sailed down beside him caroling "Touch, taste, feel! Drink!" Its wings trembled entrancingly; its feathery head came close. He longed to touch it, but was suddenly afraid. If he reached out, would he wake up and be dead? The boa Muscle had slumped into a gleaming black river by his feet. He wanted to stroke it too, didn't dare. Let the dream go on.

Bushbaby was rummaging in a convolution of the pod.

"You'll love this. Our latest find," it told him over its shoulder in an absurdly normal voice. Its manner changed a lot, and yet it all seemed familiar, fragments of lost, exciting memory. "We're into a heavy thing with flavors now." It held up a calabash. "Taste thrills of a thousand unknown planets. Exotic gourmet delights. That's where you can help out, No-Pain. On your way home, of course."

He hardly heard it. The seductive alien body was coming

closer, closer still. "Welcome to the Lovepile," the creature smiled into his eyes. His sex was rigid, aching for the alien flesh. He had never—

In one more moment he would have to let go and the dream would blow up.

What happened next was not clear. Something invisible whammed him, and he went sprawling onto Bushbaby, his head booming with funky laughter. A body squirmed under him, silky-hot and solid, the calabash was spilling down his face.

"I'm not dreaming!" he cried, hugging Bushbaby, spluttering kahlua as strong as sin, while the butterfly bounced on them squealing "Owow-wow-wow!" He heard Bushbaby murmur. "Great palatal-olfactory interplay," as it helped him lick.

Touch, taste, feel! The joy dream lived! He grabbed firm hold of Bushbaby's velvet haunches, and they were all laughing like mad, rolling in the great black serpent's coils. Touch. Feel. Joy!

. . . Sometime later while he was feeding Muscle with proffit ears, he got it partly straightened out.

"It's the pain bit." Bushbaby shivered against him. "The amount of agony in this universe, it's horrible. Trillions of lives streaming by out there, radiating pain. We daren't get close. That's why we followed you. Every time we try to pick up some new groceries, it's a disaster."

"Oh, hurt," wailed Ragglebomb, crawling under his arm. "Everywhere hurt. Sensitive, sensitive," it sobbed. "How can Raggle *ramplig* when it hurts so hard?"

"Pain." He fingered Muscle's cool dark head. "Means nothing to me. I can't even find out what they tied my pain nerves to."

"*You are blessed beyond all beings, No-Pain,*" thought Muscle majestically in their heads. "*These proffit ears are too salt. I want some fruit.*"

"Me too," piped Ragglebomb.

Bushbaby cocked its golden head, listening. "You see? We just passed a place with gorgeous fruit, but it'd kill any of us to go down there. If we could just *ramplig* you down for ten minutes?"

He started to say, "Glad to," forgetting they were telepaths. As his mouth opened, he found himself tumbling through strobe flashes onto a barren dune. He sat up spitting sand. He was in an oasis of stunted cactus trees loaded with bright globes. He tried one. Delicious. He picked. Just as his arms were full, the scene strobed again, and he was sprawled on the Lovepile's floor, his new friends swarming over him.

"Sweet! Sweet!" Ragglebomb bored into the juice.

"Save some for the pod, maybe it'll learn to copy them. It metabolizes stuff it digests," Bushbaby explained with its mouth full. "Basic rations. Very boring."

"Why couldn't you go down there?"

"Don't. All over that desert, things dying of thirst. Torture." He felt the boa flinch.

"You are beautiful, No-Pain." Bushbaby nuzzled his ear. Ragglebomb was picking guitar bridges on his thorax.

They all began to sing a sort of seguidilla without words. No instruments here, nothing but their live bodies. Making music with empaths was like making love with them. Touch what he touched, feel what he felt. Totally into his mind. I—we. One. He could never have dreamed this up, he decided, drumming softly on Muscle. The boa amped, mysterioso.

And so began his voyage home in the Lovepile, his new life of joy. Fruits and fondues he brought them, hams and honey, parsley, sage, rosemary, and thyme. World after scruffy world. All different now, on his way home.

"Are there many out here?" he asked lazily. "I never found anyone else, between the stars."

"Be glad," said Bushbaby. "Move your leg." And they told him of the tiny busy life that plied a far corner of the galaxy, whose pain had made them flee. And of a vast presence Ragglebomb had once encountered before he picked the others up.

"That's where I got the idea for the Rulers bit," Muscle confided. *"We need some cheese."*

Bushbaby cocked his head to catch the minds streaming by them in the abyss.

"How about yoghurt?" It nudged Ragglebomb. "Over that way. Feel it squishing on their teeth? Bland, curdy . . . with just a *rien* of ammonia; probably their milk pails are dirty."

"Pass the dirty yoghurt," Muscle closed his eyes.

"We have some great cheese on Earth," he told them. "You'll love it. When do we get there?"

Bushbaby squirmed.

"Ah, we're moving right along. But what I get from you, it's weird. Foul blue sky. Dying green. Who needs that?"

"No!" He jerked up, scattering them. "That's not true! Earth is beautiful!"

The walls jolted, knocking him sidewise.

"Watch it!" boomed Muscle. Bushbaby had grabbed the butterfly, petting and crooning to it.

"You frightened his *ramplig* reflex. Raggle throws things out when he's upset. Tsut, tsut, don't you, baby. We lost a lot of interesting beings that way at first."

"I'm sorry. But you've got it twisted. My memory's a little messed up, but I'm *sure*. Beautiful. Like amber waves of grain. And purple mountain majesties," he laughed, spreading his arms. "From sea to shining sea!"

"Hey, that swings!" Raggle squeaked, and started strumming.

And so they sailed on, carrying him home.

He loved to watch Bushbaby listening for the thought beacons by which they steered.

"Catching Earth yet?"

"Not yet awhile. Hey, how about some fantastic sea-food?"

He sighed and felt himself tumble. He had learned not to bother saying yes. This one was a laugh, because he forgot that dishes didn't *ramplig*. He came back in a mess of creamed trilobites, and they had a creamed trilobite orgy.

But he kept watching Bushbaby.

"Getting closer?"

"It's a big galaxy, baby." Bushbaby stroked his bald spots. With so much *rampligging* he couldn't keep any hair. "What'll you do on Earth as stimulating as this?"

"I'll show you," he grinned. And later on he told them.

"They'll fix me up when I get home. Reconnect me right."

A shudder shook the Lovepile.

"You want to feel pain?"

"Pain is the obscenity of the universe," Muscle tolled. *"You are sick."*

"I don't know," he said apologetically. "I can't seem to feel, well, real this way."

They looked at him.

"We thought that was the way your species always felt," said Bushbaby.

"I hope not." Then he brightened. "Whatever it is, they'll fix it. Earth must be pretty soon now, right?"

"Over the sea to Skye!" Bushbaby hummed.

But the sea was long and long, and his moods were hard on the sensitive empaths. Once when he responded listlessly, he felt a warning lurch.

Ragglebomb was glowering at him.

"You want to put me out?" he challenged. "Like those others? What happened to them, by the way?"

Bushbaby winced. "It was dreadful. We had no idea they'd survive so long, outside."

"But I don't feel pain. That's why you rescued me, isn't it? Go ahead," he said perversely. "I don't care. Throw me out. New thrill."

"Oh, no, no, no!" Bushbaby hugged him. Ragglebomb, penitent, crawled under his legs.

"So you've been popping around the universe bringing live things in to play with and throwing them out when you're bored. Get away," he scolded. "Shallow sensation freaks is all you are. Galactic poltergeists!"

He rolled over and hoisted the beautiful Bushbaby over his face, watching it wiggle and squeal. "Her lips were red, her looks were free, her locks were yellow as gold." He kissed its golden belly. "The Night-Mare Life-in-Death was she, who thicks man's blood with cold."

And he used their pliant bodies to build the greatest lovepile yet. They were delighted and did not mind when later on he wept, face-down on Muscle's dark coils.

But they were concerned.

"I have it," Bushbaby declared, tapping him with a pickle. "Own-species sex! After all, face it, you're no empath. You need a jolt of your own kind."

"You mean you know where there's people like me? Humans?"

Bushbaby nodded, eyeing him as it listened. "Ideal. Just like I read you. Right over there, Raggle. And they have a thing they chew—wait—Salmoglossa fragrans. Prolongs you-know-what, according to them. Bring some back with you, baby."

Next instant he was rolling through strobes onto tender green. Crushed flowers under him, ferny boughs above, sparkling with sunlight. Rich air rushed into his lungs. He bounced up buoyantly. Before him a parklike vista sloped to a glittering lake on which blew colored sails. The sky was violet with pearly little clouds. Never had he seen a planet remotely like this. If it wasn't Earth, he had fallen into paradise.

Beyond the lake he could see pastel walls, fountains, spires. An alabaster city undimmed by human tears. Music drifted on the sweet breeze. There were figures by the shore.

He stepped out into the sun. Bright silks swirled, white arms went up. Waving to him? He saw they were like human girls, only slimmer and more fair. They were calling! He looked down at his body, grabbed a flowering branch and started toward them.

"*Do not forget the Salmoglossa,*" said the voice of Muscle.

He nodded. The girls' breasts were bobbing, pink-tipped. He broke into a trot.

It was several days later when they brought him back, drooping between a man and a young girl. Another man walked beside them striking plangently on a harp. Girls and children danced along, and a motherly looking woman paced in front, all beautiful as peris.

They leaned him gently against a tree and the harper stood back to play. He struggled to stand upright. One fist was streaming blood.

"Good-bye," he gasped. "Thanks."

The strobes caught him sagging, and he collapsed on the Lovepile's floor.

"Aha!" Bushbaby pounced on his fist. "Good grief, your hand! The Salmoglossa's all blood." It began to shake out the herbs. "Are you all right now?" Ragglebomb was squeaking softly, thrusting its long tongue into the blood.

He rubbed his head.

"They welcomed me," he whispered. "It was perfect. Music. Dancing. Games. Love. They haven't any medicine because they eliminated all disease. I had five women and a cloud-painting team and some little boys, I think."

He held out his bloody blackened hand. Two fingers were missing.

"Paradise," he groaned. "Ice doesn't freeze me, fire doesn't burn. None of it means anything at all. *I want to go home.*"

There was a jolt.

"I'm sorry," he wept. "I'll try to control myself. Please, please get me back to Earth. It'll be soon, won't it?"

There was a silence.

"When?"

Bushbaby made a throat-clearing noise.

"Well, just as soon as we can find it. We're bound to run across it. Maybe any minute, you know."

"What?" He sat up death-faced. "You mean you don't know where it is? You mean we've just been going—noplace?"

Bushbaby wrapped its hands over its ears. "Please! We can't recognize it from your description. So how can we go back there when we've never been there? If we just keep an ear out as we go we'll pick it up, you'll see."

His eyes rolled at them, he couldn't believe it.

"Ten to the eleventh times two suns in the galaxy . . . I don't know your velocity and range. Say, one per second. That's—that's *six thousand years*. Oh, no!" He put his head in his bloody hands. "I'll never see home again."

"Don't say it, baby." The golden body slid close. "Don't down the trip. We love you, No-Pain." They were all petting him now. "Happy, sing him! Touch, taste, feel. Joy!"

But there was no joy.

He took to sitting leaden and apart, watching for a sign. "This time?"

No.

Not yet. Never.

Ten to the eleventh times two . . . fifty percent chance of finding Earth within three thousand years. It was the scouter all over again.

The Lovepile re-formed without him, and he turned his face away, not eating until they pushed food into his mouth. If he stayed totally inert, surely they would grow bored with him and put him out. No other hope. Finish me . . . soon.

They made little efforts to arouse him with fondlings, and now and then a harsh jolt. He lolled unresisting. End it, he prayed. But still they puzzled at him in the intervals of their games. They mean well, he thought. And they miss the stuff I brought them.

Bushbaby was coaxing.

"—first a suave effect, you know. Cryptic. And then a cascade of sweet and sour sparkling over the palate—"

He tried to shut it out. They mean well. Falling across the galaxy with a talking cookbook. Finish me.

"—but the arts of combination," Bushbaby chatted on. "Like moving food; e.g., sentient plants or small live animals, combining flavor with the *frisson* of movement—"

He thought of oysters. Had he eaten some once? Something about poison. The rivers of Earth. Did they still flow? Even if by some unimaginable chance they stumbled on it, would it be far in the past or future, a dead ball? Let me die.

"—and *sound*, that's amusing. We've picked up several

races who combine musical effects with certain tastes. And there's the sound of oneself chewing, textures and viscosities. I recall some beings who sucked in harmonics. Or the sound of the food itself. One race I caught *en passant* did that, but with a very limited range. Crunchy. Crispy. Snap-crackle-pop. One wishes they had explored tonalities, glissando effects—"

He lunged up.

"What did you say? Snap-crackle-pop?"

"Why, yes, but—"

"That's it! That's Earth!" he yelled. "You picked up a goddamn breakfast-food commercial!"

He felt a lurch. They were scrambling up the wall.

"A what?" Bushbaby stared.

"Never mind—take me there! That's Earth, it has to be. You can find it again, can't you? You said you could," he implored, pawing at them. "Please!"

The Lovepile rocked. He was frightening everybody.

"Oh, *please.*" He forced his voice smooth.

"But I only heard it for an instant," Bushbaby protested. "It would be terribly hard, that far back. My poor head!"

He was on his knees begging. "You'd love it," he pleaded. "We have fantastic food. Culinary poems you never heard of. Cordon bleu! Escoffier!" he babbled. "Talk about combinations, the Chinese do it four ways! Or is it the Japanese? Rijsttafel! Bubble-and-squeak! Baked Alaska, hot crust outside, inside co-o-old ice cream!"

Bushbaby's pink tongue flicked. Was he getting through?

He clawed his memory for foods he'd never heard of.

"Maguey worms in chocolate! Haggis and bagpipes, crystallized violets, rabbit Mephisto! Octopus in resin wine. Four-and-twenty-blackbird pie! Cakes with girls in them. Kids seethed in their mothers' milk—wait, that's taboo. Ever hear of taboo foods? Long pig!"

Where was he getting all this? A vague presence drifted in his mind—his hands, the ridges, long ago. "Amanda," he breathed, racing on.

"Cormorants aged in manure! Ratatouille! Peaches iced in

champagne!'' Project, he thought. ''Pâté of fatted goose liver studded with earth-drenched truffles, clothed in purest white lard!'' He snuffled lustfully. ''Hot buttered scones sluiced in whortleberry syrup!'' He salivated. ''Finnan haddie soufflé, oh, yes! Unborn baby veal pounded to a membrane and delicately scorched in black herb butter—''

Bushbaby and Ragglebomb were clutching each other, eyes closed. Muscle was mesmerized.

''Find Earth! Grape leaves piled with poignantly sweet wild fraises, clotted with Devon cream!''

Bushbaby moaned, rocking to and fro.

''Earth! Bitter endives wilted in chicken steam and crumbled bacon! Black gazpacho! Fruit of the Tree of Heaven!''

Bushbaby rocked harder, the butterfly clamped to its breast.

Earth! Earth! he willed with all his might, croaking ''Bahklava! Gossamer puff paste and pistachio nuts dripping with mountain honey!''

Bushbaby pushed at Ragglebomb's head, and the pod seemed to twirl.

''Ripe Comice pears,'' he whispered. *''Earth?''*

''That's it.'' Bushbaby fell over panting. ''Oh, those foods, I want every single one. Let's land!''

''Deep-dish steak and kidney pie,'' he breathed. ''Pearled with crusty onion dumplings—''

''Land!'' Ragglebomb squealed. ''Eat, eat!''

The pod jarred. Solidity. Earth.

Home.

''Let me out!''

He saw a pucker opening daylight in the wall and dived for it. His legs pumped, struck. Earth! Feet thudding, face uplifted, lungs gulping air. ''Home!'' he yelled.

—And went headlong on the gravel, arms and legs out of control. A cataclysm smote his inside.

''Help!''

His body arched, spewed vomit, he was flailing, screaming.

"Help, Help! What's wrong?"

Through his noise he heard an uproar behind him in the pod. He managed to roll, saw gold and black bodies writhing inside the open port. They were in convulsions too.

"Stop it! Don't move!" Bushbaby shrieked. "You're killing us!"

"Get us out," he gasped. "This isn't Earth."

His throat garroted itself on his breath and the aliens moaned in empathy.

"Don't! We can't move," Bushbaby gasped. "Don't breathe, close your eyes quick!"

He shut his eyes. The awfulness lessened slightly.

"What is it? What's happening?"

"*PAIN, YOU FOOL*," thundered Muscle's mind.

"This is your wretched Earth," Bushbaby wailed. "Now we know what they tied your pain nerves to. Get back in so we can go—carefully!"

He opened his eyes, got a glimpse of pale sky and scrubby bushes before his eyeballs skewered. The empaths screamed.

"Stop! Ragglebomb die!"

"My own home," he whimpered, clawing at his eyeballs. His whole body was being devoured by invisible flames, crushed, impaled, flayed. The pattern of Earth, he realized. Her unique air, her exact gestalt of solar spectrum, gravity, magnetic field, her every sight and sound and touch—that was what they'd tuned his pain-circuits for.

"*Evidently they did not want you back,*" said Muscle's silent voice. "*Get in.*"

"They can fix me, they've got to fix me—"

"They aren't here," Bushbaby shouted. "Temporal error. No snap-crackle-pop. You and your baked Alaska—" Its voice broke pitifully. "Come back in so we can go!"

"Wait," he croaked. "When?"

He opened one eye, managed to see a rocky hillside before his forehead detonated. No roads, no buildings. Nothing to tell whether it was past or future. Not beautiful.

Behind him the aliens were crying out. He began to crawl

blindly toward the pod, teeth clenching over salty gushes. He had bitten his tongue. Every move seared him; the air burned his guts when he had to breathe. The gravel seemed to be slicing his hands open, although no wounds appeared. Only pain, pain, pain from every nerve end.

"Amanda," he moaned, but she was not here. He crawled, writhed, kicked like a pinned bug toward the pod that held sweet comfort, the bliss of no-pain. Somewhere a bird called, stabbing his eardrums. His friends screamed.

"Hurry!"

Had it been a bird? He risked one look back.

A brown figure was sidling round the rocks.

Before he could see whether it was ape or human, female or male, the worst pain yet almost tore his brain out. He groveled helpless, hearing himself shriek. The pattern of his own kind. Of course, the central thing—it would hurt most of all. No hope of staying here.

"Don't! Don't! *Hurry!*"

He sobbed, scrabbling toward the Lovepile. The scent of the weeds that his chest crushed raked his throat. Marigolds, he thought. Behind the agony, lost sweetness.

He touched the wall of the pod, gasping knives. The torturing air was real air, *his* terrible Earth was real.

"*Get in quick!*"

"Please, plea—" he babbled wordlessly, hauling himself up with lids clenched, fumbling for the port. The real sun of Earth rained acid on his flesh.

The port! Inside lay relief, he would be No-Pain forever. Caresses—joy—why had he wanted to leave them? His hand found the port.

Standing, he turned, opened both eyes.

The form of a dead limb printed a whiplash on his eyeballs. Jagged, ugly. Unendurable. But real—

To hurt forever?

"We can't wait!" Bushbaby wailed. He thought of its golden body flying down the light-years, savoring delight. His arms shook violently.

"Then go!" he bellowed and thrust himself away from the Lovepile.

There was an implosion behind him.

He was alone.

He managed to stagger a few steps forward before he went down.

THE BRIGHTEST STARS IN BERKLEY'S GALAXY
THE ALPHA AND OMEGA OF SCIENCE FICTION

GALACTIC POT-HEALER   (N2569—95¢)
  Philip K. Dick

THE MOUNTAINS OF THE SUN   (N2570—95¢)
  Christian Leourier

ORBIT 13   (N2698—95¢)
  ed. by Damon Knight

THE STARS MY DESTINATION   (Z2780—$1.25)
  Alfred Bester

NIGHTMARE BLUE   (N2819—95¢)
  Dozios & Effinger

PSTALEMATE   (N2962—95¢)
  Lester del Rey

THE COMPUTER CONNECTION   (D3039—$1.50)
  Alfred Bester

THE FLOATING ZOMBIE   (Z2980—$1.25)
  D.F. Jones